RESTORING
HARMONY

RESTORING

HARMONY

JOËLLE ANTHONY

SCHOLASTIC INC.
New York Toronto London Auckland
Sydney Mexico City New Delhi Hong Kong

ISBN 978-0-545-40105-0

Copyright © 2010 by Joëlle Anthony.
Quotation on page 95 from *The Garden That You Are*, by Katherine Gordon, published by Sono Nis Press, Winlaw, BC. Haiku on page 142 accredited to Bob Deck. Lyrics on page 289 from "Everybody Wants a Good Life," written by Victor Mecyssne © 2000, published by Commercialfree Music. All rights reserved. Published by Scholastic Inc., 557 Broadway, New York, NY 10012, by arrangement with G. P. Putnam's Sons, a division of Penguin Young Readers Group, a member of Penguin Group (USA) Inc. SCHOLASTIC and associated logos are trademarks and/or registered trademarks of Scholastic Inc.

12 11 10 9 8 7 6 5 4 3 2 1   11 12 13 14 15 16/0

Printed in the U.S.A.   75

First Scholastic printing, September 2011

Design by Marikka Tamura
Text set in Kennerly

This book is dedicated to my two favorite storytellers,
whose books have enriched my life and
the lives of countless others.

Nevil Shute
1899–1960
and
John Rowe Townsend
1922–

RESTORING

HARMONY

1

July 10th—Oaks fall, but bending reeds brave the storm.
–English proverb

WHEN THE PLANE'S ENGINE TOOK ON A WHINING roar, my grip tightened on my fiddle case. We lifted and skimmed across the waves. All I could see through the window was a fine spray shooting out beside us. In one swift motion, the old floatplane was airborne. I squeezed my eyes shut.

If all the big governments hadn't seized the last of the oil ten years ago, I could've simply gotten into a car and driven from British Columbia to Oregon in twelve hours, like my parents used to do in the "good old days," before the Collapse.

Eight weeks ago, we'd received a letter from my grandpa that he'd written almost a month before saying Grandma had suffered a stroke. After the letter came, Mom had tried to reach him on CyberSpeak, but kept getting a message saying his account had been closed. Her letters to my grandparents had also gone unanswered.

The hospital where my grandfather had worked for over

thirty years was close to their house and so Mom was sure my grandmother had gone there. It had taken her three weeks of trying during the one hour a day they accepted CyberSpeak inquiries before she finally got a connection.

"I'm sorry," the nurse had said. "We don't have a Katharine Buckley."

"Did she go home?" Mom asked.

The family had all gathered around the computer together, watching the nurse on her video cam. The woman looked up at us, her heavy-framed glasses reflecting the bright hospital lights.

"You are *all* her immediate family, aren't you? I can't give this info out to anyone but the *immediate* family."

In spite of the seriousness of the situation, all of us except Mom cracked up laughing. My parents looked so much alike, with crazy, curly dark hair, big brown eyes, and the same wiry build that strangers had mistaken them for brother and sister a million times. And all four of us kids looked like carbon copies of them, just in different sizes.

"Yes, yes . . . I'm her daughter," Mom had said impatiently. "Brianna Buckley."

"Hang on," the nurse said.

The tapping of her fingers on the keyboard came across loud and clear at first, but then everything changed. The sound began to distort, and the nurse's face turned fuzzy.

"I'm sorry," she said. "Mrs. Buckley is d–"

And then we'd lost the connection and we couldn't get it back.

"Did she say deceased?" Mom yelled.

"I think she was saying discharged," Dad said.

Mom burst into tears. "No . . . she said *is*. You say *is* deceased or *was* discharged."

"Brianna," Dad said, putting his hands on her shoulders and trying to sound firm, "calm down. Think about the baby."

"I can't worry about the baby right now," she sobbed.

Mom was forty-two, and my six-year-old brother Jackie was supposed to be the last kid in the family, so even though my parents didn't admit it, it was pretty obvious that this baby had been a surprise. After the initial shock, we were all excited.

The problem was that Mom's blood pressure was sky-high and Dr. Robinson had told her to take it slow, but to her, slow meant making four batches of jam instead of six. Before the call to the hospital about her mother, she wouldn't even consider his advice. She'd ignored our pleas and kept doing all her regular chores. On one hand, we were sad about Grandma too, and hated to see Mom depressed, but it was also sort of a relief that she was finally spending time in bed, even if she was crying a lot. The whole family took turns trying to cheer her up, but she refused to be consoled.

"We never made up properly, Molly," Mom had cried into the fresh spinach soup I made for her. "My mother will never know that I was sorry!"

"What do you mean?" I'd asked, confused. "You've talked to Grandma on CyberSpeak every week for years."

"But not about anything important," she wailed. "We

haven't seen each other since 2028! Or maybe even 2027 . . . I can't remember, it's been so long."

My sister, Katie, brought Mom strawberry shortcake, but she pushed it away untouched. James, my older brother, who claimed he was her favorite (although none of the rest of us believed it), tried cheering her up in the evenings on Cyber-Speak. He was working in the Okanagan Valley on the mainland for the summer, and he told her silly stories about his days in the vineyards, but she didn't even crack a smile. Little Jackie even brought in a kitten from the barn to perch on her pregnant belly, but nothing helped.

Eventually Dad sent me on my bike for Dr. Robinson, but he couldn't give her a sedative because this was a risky pregnancy.

Dad, Katie, and I held a family conference in the barn and secretly agreed Mom was probably right and that Grandma had died. And if Grandma was gone, then Grandpa was all on his own. According to my mom, Grandpa had never washed a shirt or cooked a meal. She was sure that if she didn't go down and rescue him, he'd die of starvation. If it hadn't happened already.

Before the Collapse, Grandpa could've driven his car to restaurants and hired someone to do his laundry, but now with so many businesses closed, and everyone too careful with their money to employ a housekeeper, he'd probably have to fend for himself. Mom had convinced herself he was living in squalor without anything to eat.

To keep Mom from doing something crazy like going to Oregon herself, I had been elected to make the trip instead.

Katie flatly refused to go because she was planning the wedding of the century, but even if she'd wanted to, I doubt my dad would've trusted her. She'd either get distracted by the stores along the way and spend all her money on clothes, or she'd come running home at the first sign of hardship.

It had taken my dad a while to get the money together. The people on our tiny island barter for almost everything, and Dad had to export most of our early lettuce, leeks, and spinach to Vancouver Island to raise the cash. He'd gotten as much as he could, and I think that some of our friends had chipped in to help too, but I was still going to have to be very careful with my money.

The wind tossed the little plane from side to side, and I grabbed at the seat in front of me. The other nine passengers held on too, their hands tightly gripping the cracked leather seats, nervous laughter filling the cabin.

"Just a little turbulence," the pilot called from the cockpit. "Nothing to worry about!"

Easy for him to say. I had all kinds of things to worry about. Like would my aunt Poppy's American boyfriend be there to meet me when the plane landed? And if he wasn't, how much trouble would I be in?

Aunt Poppy had broken all kinds of laws sneaking me aboard this government flight from Victoria to Seattle, risking God knows what? Maybe even prison. I wasn't sure what they did to teenagers who broke international law, but I didn't want to find out.

Poppy worked for the Canadian government, and she flew to Seattle regularly for meetings with the Department of Agriculture. She hadn't been available to travel with me because of work, and you have to be eighteen to cross the border alone so she'd bribed a pilot she knew to ignore that my passport clearly showed I was only sixteen.

I was also dressed up like all the other passengers in business attire to help me pass for an adult. Poppy had provided me with a white silk blouse, knee-length navy skirt, and high heels. Not only did I feel totally ridiculous, but I also could barely walk in the stupid shoes.

As if the whole thing with my grandparents wasn't bad enough, right before I was supposed to leave, another tragedy struck. Dr. Robinson died in a freak accident in our barn.

Most of the farmers knew how to treat their livestock, so having no veterinarian on the island was not a big deal, but sometimes, if an animal needed stitches, Dr. Robinson would do it. Last week I'd been bringing in the cows and I saw that one of the calves had a nasty cut on its front leg.

I was just going into the house to get my dad when Dr. Robinson came out after checking on Mom. He followed me out to the barn to see if he could help. When he bent down to look at the calf, its mother kicked him in the head.

I'd helped him up, and he'd seemed fine at first. He'd ridden his bike home, had dinner, and gone to bed. Only he never woke up. Mrs. Robinson found him dead when she tried to get him up for breakfast.

I had spent the last week obsessing about this. It had made me more determined than ever to go and get my grandpa because he was a doctor and we had to have one on the island for Mom and the baby. We couldn't wait around for the province to do it, either, because it could take them up to a year to send us one. My grandpa was the obvious choice. It solved two problems at once: him being alone and the island needing a doctor.

The plane dipped hard and my stomach sank after it. "Hang on!" the pilot yelled back to us. "Gonna be rough for a bit."

I looked at the other passengers, hoping to see confidence in their eyes. A white-haired man across the aisle smiled warmly at me. "Just pockets of air," he said. "Nothing to worry about."

I must not have looked convinced. Especially when the plane sort of dropped and lurched to the left.

"Little planes move like this," he explained. "It's doing exactly what it's supposed to do."

"Okay," I said, hoping he knew what he was talking about and clinging to my fiddle for comfort anyway.

The turbulence lessened after a while, and we all relaxed back into our seats. Below, I could see the vast expanse of ocean. We flew over an island covered with trees, bisected by a long road. Tiny houses dotted the landscape, and I wondered if our island looked like that from the air. I imagined our farm. The sprawling log cabin that had been added on to twice. The red barn with its solar panels. The chicken coop would be a speck in the dust. And the fields would look like one of Mom's patchwork quilts.

"Beautiful, isn't it?" the man across the aisle asked.

"Yeah."

"Is that a violin?" he asked.

"Fiddle," I said, smiling.

"What's the difference?"

"Nothing. Just how you play it," I explained.

Inside the case, Jewels, my fiddle, was wrapped snugly in a piece of silk, her bow slack so the summer heat wouldn't snap the horsehair. My fingers ached to play because Poppy had rushed me out of the house before I had a chance to do my usual morning practice.

Mom had wanted me to leave Jewels at home for fear she'd get stolen, but there was no way I could go two weeks without her. That's how long Dad said I could expect to be gone. A few days of travel down, a week to help my grandpa get used to the idea of moving up to the farm and to sort out his things, and the trip back.

Even though I'd been traveling for two days already, first on a fishing boat from our island to Vancouver Island, then on foot to Nanaimo, and on a train from there to Victoria, I was barely out of the country. I still had to take a train from Seattle to Portland and figure out local transportation to a city called Gresham, where my grandpa lived.

Less than an hour after leaving Victoria, the man across the aisle said, "I love this view of Seattle. It still looks like a great city from the air."

Below us sprawled more roads and houses than I'd ever seen. They covered acre after acre. We began to rapidly lose altitude, and Lake Union came into view. Behind it, the towering skyline of Seattle showed itself, dim and gray in murky afternoon light.

When the floats hit the water, my queasy stomach pitched and I had to swallow hard to keep from throwing up. I couldn't believe it. This was the United States, and I was actually here. And then it really sank in. My mission was about to start for real.

2

I STUMBLED MY WAY DOWN THE NARROW METAL stairs onto the dock with Jewels in one hand and my backpack slung over my shoulder, trying to keep my balance in the high heels.

"Steady there," the pilot said, taking ahold of my arm.

"Thanks."

I looked around hoping to see Poppy's boyfriend, Tyler, but he wasn't there. The other passengers dragged small suitcases behind them, their wheels click-clacking on the wooden dock. When they got to the gate, they lined up and I watched the white-haired man who'd sat across from me hold up his passport to a scanner while looking into a black box. After a second, the gate clicked open and he went through. The woman behind him waited for the gate to shut, and then she did the same thing.

When all nine people had disappeared out onto the street, I wandered over to it, trying to look casual. Maybe I could just go out that way too. I wasn't sure what the little box did, but I thought it might be a retina scanner. In school we'd learned about how people had fought that technology, saying it invaded their privacy, but the U.S. had gone ahead with it anyway.

I scanned the docks again, looking for Tyler, but except for the pilot and a boy in a Hawaiian print shirt who had met the plane and helped tie it down, there wasn't anyone around. They were standing by the wing, the pilot smoking and looking out at the water, not at me.

I took my passport out of my pack and held it open like the other passengers had. There was a little beep, then a whirring sound came from the black box, so I stepped closer to it and looked right in.

Immediately an alarm sounded, flooding the docks with a piercing wail. I jumped back, twisting my ankle because of the heels, and dropped my passport. Two men came running out of a tiny shack onto the dock. A tall, thin one was in front, and a round, pudgy one ran behind him holding up a handgun.

"Stop!" he shouted over the siren, waving the gun in my direction.

"Don't shoot!" I yelled. I put my hands in the air just in case.

"Did you set off the alarm?" the first man screamed over the whine of the siren.

"I didn't do it on purpose!" I tried to tell them. "I was on the plane that just landed and everyone else just held up their passports so I did too but the siren went off!"

The thin guy was punching buttons on the scanner, but the siren continued to scream. He had brown hair flecked with gray, and a goatee. Based on Poppy's description, he could be Tyler.

"Bill," he shouted at the fat man, "could you turn off the siren from the main computer? The code changed last week, and I can't remember it with all this noise!"

Bill started to hand him the gun, but he waved him off. "I think I can handle her."

"If you're sure." He sounded doubtful, but he lumbered away towards the shack anyway.

"Are you Molly?" Tyler asked me.

"Yes!"

"We've got to get you out of here," he yelled over the noise.

"What happened? Why did the alarm go off?"

"You can only use that machine with an American passport. You should've waited for me. Sorry I got tied up on Cyber-Speak. I meant to meet you." He looked around, and I could tell he was desperate to get me out of there. "Bill will never let a minor into the country; we're just gonna have to break some more rules now."

Mercifully, the siren finally stopped blaring, but my ears were ringing. As soon as the alarm was silent, Tyler started punching more codes into the passport scanner.

"What's going to happen?" I asked.

The gate clicked open before he could answer. He shoved a piece of paper in my hand. "Directions to the train station," he said. Then he pushed me through the gate. "Run! I'll cover for you somehow."

I stumbled out onto the sidewalk, catching my heel. The gate clanged shut behind me, and I didn't waste any time getting out of there. I'm normally a good runner, but I could barely walk in Poppy's high heels, let alone run. I clomped along, looking over my shoulder every few seconds. My backpack thumped against me, and I cradled my fiddle in my arms like a baby. Long, low buildings, which had probably been warehouses, lined the wide, empty road. I'd only gone about three blocks when I stopped to check the map. Ahead of me, buildings towered even taller than the apartments I'd seen in Victoria, so I was pretty sure I was going in the right direction, but I wanted to be positive.

I ducked into an alley and slid down onto the dusty ground, kicking off my shoes and trying to catch my breath while I smoothed out the map. So far, so good. I just needed to keep going straight ahead and then to the left once I reached the part Tyler had labeled *downtown*.

I dug around in my pack for my sandals, but I couldn't find them. Dumping the contents out, I searched frantically. Where could they be? I couldn't go all the way to Portland in these shoes. If they weren't in my bag, they had to still be at Poppy's apartment. I must've accidentally kicked them underneath her couch last night. Oh, this was great. Just great! Now what was I going to do?

Slowly, I repacked my bag, trying to think. Finally, I slipped off the nylons. My feet were tough from gardening barefoot, but they weren't used to concrete. I took a few steps up and down the alley. Even though it was shaded, the pavement was still really hot and rough. I stuffed my feet back into the shoes, picked up my fiddle and pack, and peered around the building on the lookout for the man from customs. Luckily, the street was empty.

Our island was a little pocket of prosperity due to good farmland, planning, and hard work, but until I stepped out of that alley and took a hard look at Seattle, I hadn't really understood how blessed my small, simple life had been. Around me stood the crumbling shell of a great city, covered with obscene graffiti, littered with trash.

My parents had met at grad school in Seattle, and their stories of laughter, music, food, wine, and friends were a stark contrast to the empty, abandoned street that stretched out in front of me. After all the big governments had seized the last of the oil, which crashed the world economy and caused the Great Collapse of 2031, most people had left the city and moved out into the suburbs, where more than one family could share a house and they could grow food in their yards. It was like a giant broom had swept the streets clear of humanity, leaving only emptiness and wreckage behind. Cold fear made my heart pound.

It was close to noon, and the July sun beat down relentlessly, leaving me no shadows to hide in. I hurried along the street, checking over my shoulder for the man with the gun. As I neared the taller buildings ahead, I thought I heard footsteps behind me.

I threw myself into the next alleyway to hide. As I backed

into the narrow space behind an old metal Dumpster, I stepped on something that squirmed under my feet, exactly like when you accidentally step on one of the barn cats. As I stumbled, trying to right myself, a cold hand clamped onto my ankle and I screamed.

3

"WATCH WHERE YOU'RE GOING!" AN OLD WOMAN with matted hair and smeared red lipstick croaked. I tried to pull myself free, but she had a surprisingly strong grip. She was sprawled on the ground, dressed for winter, holding a sack tightly against her chest with the hand that wasn't clinging to my ankle.

"Let me go!" I said, shaking my foot.

I *could* hit her, but it seemed unfair to hurt someone lying on the ground like that.

"Give me your money," she said.

Was I being mugged? I'd heard that practically everyone in America was armed and you could be robbed right in broad daylight, but this woman, even though her hold was tight, didn't look strong enough to even get up, and I didn't see any gun either. Instinctively my hand went to the pocket on my pack where I'd stuffed the wads of American bills that my aunt had exchanged for me.

"It looks like a lot of money," Poppy had warned me, "but

it doesn't go far. Travel's really expensive, and it will probably take most of it just to get to your grandpa's house. He'll have to pay your way home."

I knew I couldn't spare any money, but the woman's eyes glowed with desperation and it made me feel stingy. Maybe she was hungry. "How about an apple instead?" I asked.

"No teeth. Money."

"I don't have any," I lied. Poppy had packed my bag with snacks and bottled water, and I had food to spare. "I'll give you a cheese sandwich."

The woman's hand slackened, and she licked her lips. I pulled the sandwich out of my bag and held it out to her. She let me go, grabbing at it and stuffing the food into her mouth like I might try and take it back.

I darted out into the hot street into the shadows of buildings, taller than the trees on my island. I finally saw some other people. I slowed down to catch my breath. I wouldn't call the streets crowded or anything, but at least there were witnesses now if the customs man appeared and tried to shoot me.

A few shops were open, selling fruit and newspapers, but I didn't see any shoes for sale. Not that I really could afford to spend any money before I got a train ticket. I'd look for shoes in Portland. Finally I came to the large public area that Tyler had marked on the map as Pioneer Square. There were two coffee stands, some old men deep in a chess game, and a few dirty kids running around in a dry fountain while their parents sat guarding a cart of belongings.

I couldn't tell from Tyler's map which side of the square I was standing on and was looking around for someone to ask when I saw a couple of policemen. I started to walk over to them, but right when I stepped out into the street, a teenage boy reached out and grabbed my arm, pulling me back.

"Hey!" I said, but then I realized he was just keeping me from getting run over by a long, black car that had come out of nowhere. "Oh, thanks!"

The car slid to a stop about half a block from us and four men in suits jumped out. I watched as they ran into the square, grabbed a rough-looking man, and dragged him back to the car. The man was yelling for help, but the people in the square just continued on with what they were doing, like nothing was happening. The old men kept playing chess; the parents on the bench dug through their belongings. Only the kids in the fountain watched what was happening.

I wanted to scream for someone to help him, but it was like I'd been frozen in place. By the time I could move, the men had already shoved their victim into the car and driven away. I ran over to the policemen on the corner. "Did you see that?" I asked. "What's going on?"

One of the officers turned towards me. He had a pale, expressionless face. "Best be on your way," he said.

"But–"

"Move along," the other officer, a short, stocky man about fifty years old, said.

And then they turned and walked away.

I told myself that I'd misunderstood what had happened. If the man had really been in trouble, someone would've stepped up and helped, wouldn't they? Still, my hands were shaking. I thought of Katie, who probably would've fainted, and I took a deep breath and made myself walk towards my destination. The sooner I got my grandpa and we were back home, the better.

As I got closer to the train station, I could see its brick walls were shored up with wooden planks and scaffolding. The whole thing looked about ready to fall down. I pushed through heavy double doors, and the first thing I searched for was the washroom. When I stepped inside it, I stopped, surprised.

It was bright and airy and made entirely of white marble. My heels echoed as I crossed the floor to one of the stalls. It would be so cool to play my fiddle in a room like this. The acoustics would be amazing. I resisted the urge and instead used the toilet, and then I changed my clothes.

I had to go barefoot because I couldn't walk around in shorts and a pair of navy heels, and the smooth floor of the station felt cool on my feet, almost like the creek back home. I smiled, relieved to be out of those horrible shoes. I moved what was left of my money into my front pocket and tucked my passport into the back one for safekeeping, pulling my shirt down over my hips. These were last year's shorts so they were nice and tight. No one would be able to pick my pocket, which was something else Poppy had warned me to watch out for.

In a cavernous waiting room, bigger than the island's community hall, a long line of travelers wound its way up to a wooden counter. One haggard-looking woman stood behind it, her dyed auburn hair falling out of its bun, a pencil stuck behind her ear. I took my place in line to wait.

Two hours later there were still fourteen people ahead of me. I'd had a lot of time to work it out, and on average, each

person spent four minutes getting tickets. Allowing for over-
ages, I still had an hour to go. The only book I had was my
dad's copy of *Uncle Ralph's Olde Time Farmer's Almanac.* This
was his idea of entertaining reading, and he'd insisted that I
take it along.

The last thing I wanted to do was haul a heavy book around.
Not to mention valuable, at least to my dad. Buying the collector's hardback edition, instead of an electronic one, was Dad's
big splurge every January. I'd begged Katie to let me take the
E-ZBook Reader, but she wouldn't part with it. Sometimes
she could be so selfish. I opened the almanac to today's date.

July 10th—Oaks fall, but bending reeds brave the storm.

I smiled. I guess Dad thought that if he wasn't around to
actually give me advice, the almanac was the next best thing. I
flipped through the pages, reading about when to plant spinach
and how to attract bees. It was all stuff I already knew by
heart, though.

When I finally reached the counter, I asked for a ticket to
Portland, but I wasn't good with money, so I ended up showing
it all to the woman and she picked out what she needed, which
was most of it.

"When's the next train?" I asked.

She shrugged. "Around ten o'clock tonight."

I looked at the clock on the wall behind her. It was just after
four. Great.

All the benches were taken up, so I found a spot against a
wall and sat down to eat an apple. I had Jewels next to me and
I couldn't stop thinking about that washroom.

Finally, the boredom and the need to play won out over

whether or not anyone would care if I practiced in there. The washroom was empty, so I took Jewels out and added a bunch of rosin to the bow. I ran it across the D string and the sound bounced off the walls, reverberated off the mirror, and sent a tingle of excitement up my spine! Ohhhh . . . this was going to be good. I started wrestling Jewels into tune.

A woman and two little girls in matching pink dresses came in, and the youngest one couldn't take her eyes off my fiddle. I knew exactly how she felt. Jewels was beautiful, honey colored and shiny, but with a gorgeous patina too.

While I waited for them to leave, I noticed in the mirror that my springy hair was sticking up all over. I set Jewels in her case and tried to tame my curls with some water and a rubber band. As soon as they were gone, I took Jewels and the rest of my stuff into the largest stall, the one with the wheelchair on the door.

It took me a full ten minutes to get her into tune, but even that sounded exciting to me in this room. I could hardly wait to play something for real! At home, I sometimes faced the large mirror in the dining room to get sound to bounce off of it, but this was beyond anything I could've imagined. It was probably like playing in one of those great halls from the old days.

I ran the bow lightly over the strings and launched into a warm-up, playing softly in case someone else came in. Not that you can hide the sound of a fiddle. I couldn't remember the last time I'd missed my morning practice, though, and my fingers were itching to play.

I let the bow bounce on the strings a little. Then, very quietly, I began to play "Turkey in the Straw." Quick notes danced off my strings, the sound bouncing back to me, filling me with music from my toes to the roots of my brown, frizzy hair. My fingertips vibrated and I tapped my bare foot on the cool floor, keeping time.

I'd started out as quietly as I could, but then, like a dam bursting, music overflowed, filling me, then the stall, then the entire washroom. I played one tune after another, rinsing the homesickness and worry out of my soul, the music a balm for all the stress of Mom's pregnancy and my silent grandparents.

I'm not exactly sure how long I played because the music had wrapped itself around me like a cocoon, but right in the middle of the "Cowboy Waltz," someone pounded on the stall door.

"Step out of there right now," bellowed a man's voice.

4

MY BOW DRAGGED TO A HALT ACROSS THE STRINGS.

"I said step out here," the man repeated.

"Coming," I managed to say.

This was bad. There was a man in the women's washroom. I must be in big trouble! When I bent over to put Jewels into her case, I saw about thirty pairs of feet, shoes of every color, and a pair of black boots standing right outside the stall. I snapped the case closed, grabbed my pack, and opened the door slowly.

A scrawny man in a burgundy uniform stood over me, glowering. He had the bushiest eyebrows I'd ever seen. Behind him was a sea of shiny, smiling faces. The women who had gathered in the washroom, presumably to listen to me play, broke into applause.

"Quiet!" the man yelled. "Come with me." He took me by the arm and pushed his way through the crowd.

"Your music was beautiful!" said a woman in a faded denim dress.

"Leave her alone," someone else shouted. "We liked her playing."

"Yeah!"

"I'm in charge here," he said.

An elderly lady with a long white braid attached herself to my other arm. "Don't you worry," she said. "He's all bluster, and I'll soon sort him out."

In the hallway, the man led me up to a wall where a sign hung that said NO BUSKING! He pointed at it. "Can't you read?"

"Busking? You mean like playing for money?" I asked.

"Exactly."

"But I wasn't. I was just practicing."

He looked confused for a second, his eyebrows scrunching together. "Well, no playing instruments in the train station," he finally said. "If you practice, then other people will want to, and the next thing you know . . . mayhem!"

"I didn't mean to break the rules," I protested. Tears welled up in my eyes and I swiped at them. "I'm really sorry."

"You just leave her alone," the elderly lady said. "Haven't you got better things to do, like worry about pickpockets? Your mother would be ashamed of you! Didn't you see all those ladies in there enjoying that little concert?"

"Well . . . yes, ma'am. . . ."

"And what were you doing in the women's bathroom anyway?" she demanded, drawing herself up to her full height, which wasn't even as tall as me. "I could sue you for sexual harassment."

"Well . . . I, uh . . . well–"

"That's a deep subject, mister!" she said. "Maybe we should talk it over with your supervisor?"

"No, I, uh . . . oh, never mind." He strode off like he had somewhere important to be. I think it was just as far away from me and this tiny tornado as he could get.

"Don't you cry," she said to me, leading me back into the main waiting area. "That was a beautiful concert."

"Thanks."

"I'm Jane," she said.

"Molly."

"How do you do?"

"Better now," I said, smiling.

I spent the rest of the evening chatting with Jane. It turned out that she not only loved Canada, but she'd even been to my island back in the "good old days" when people traveled for their holidays and the ferries ran all day, every day.

Talking to her about the island, even though she didn't really remember much about it because it'd been forty years since she'd visited, helped ease the homesickness that had taken root in my gut.

I knew it was weird, but I had to sort of look over Jane's shoulder when we talked because her face was so fascinating, I couldn't help staring. Her skin looked like paper that had been folded over and over again and then smoothed out. The largest wrinkles had smaller ones right over the top of them, branching out, like the roads on the Seattle maps hanging in the station's hallway.

Jane and I shared our food with each other. I gave her a sandwich, and she made me take half a dozen oatmeal cookies that the sister she'd been visiting had baked. Around ten fifteen that night, the train rumbled into the station. Nothing happened for almost another hour, but then they opened the big doors and we all swarmed out onto the platform. Jane and I managed to get seats in the first car and collapsed into them. I sat there with my eyes shut, resting my chin on the end of my fiddle case, my pack clutched between my feet.

Within minutes of our departure, the rocking of the car lulled Jane to sleep. I stared out into the darkness, thinking how odd it was that I had come this far. Only a handful of people I knew had ever left the island, and most of them had come back saying it was paradise on Earth.

The tall fir trees, the ocean crashing up onto the sandstone rocks, the eagles flying overhead . . . I hadn't thought about it being anything special until, well, right now. I'd always thought it was my family that made me feel happy and content to live there. And the farmwork. Growing our own food, working the fields, raising chickens for eggs kept us too busy to think about the real world much. But tonight, as the train carried me further from home, I longed to be back where there was silence and room to breathe. And where there were people who loved me.

Would the grandpa I didn't know, the one who had cut Mom off when she switched from premed to agriculture, be glad to see me? Mom said we'd met once when I was three, but I didn't remember. Katie had told me that my grandparents had complained about the farm the whole time they visited. And they thought the well water tasted disgusting. That's about all I knew of them.

The train jerked, snapping my head forward, making me realize that I'd dozed off. I tried to shake myself awake. The only light in the car was a kerosene lamp hung on a hook near the front. In the dim glow, I saw that Jane was awake and knitting.

"I can barely knit in the daylight," I said, impressed.

"When you've been at it as long as I have, you could do it with your eyes closed."

"Oh. I can now; it just doesn't look like anything," I joked, and she laughed. "How long have we been going?"

"Nearly four hours."

I couldn't believe it. I'd been asleep a lot longer than I'd realized. A rush of nerves washed over me. We must be getting close. "Do you know where we are?" I asked.

"Just south of Tacoma."

"That's it? I thought we'd be almost to Portland!"

"Takes a lot longer these days."

"Maybe I should go back to sleep," I said.

"Why not?"

The train began to move again and Jane's clicking needles soothed me. I was bone tired, but I was too awake now to sleep again. After a while, the train slowed and eventually squealed to a stop. A scratchy voice sounded over the speaker. The more he repeated himself, the more people drowned it out with, "What? What did he say? Did you hear what he said? What's going on?"

When nothing happened, the passengers began to doze off and then the crackling voice made another announcement that woke everyone up, and the mutterings started all over again. Eventually a door slid open at the end of the car and a conductor stepped into the crowded aisle.

"Sorry, folks," she yelled. "Everyone off the train! You're going to have to walk!"

5

WHEN NOBODY MOVED, THE CONDUCTOR SHOUTED again for us all to debark. She was wearing the same burgundy uniform as the security guard in the station, and her long blond ponytail caught the light from the kerosene lantern, glowing like gold.

"Come on, people!" she shouted, frustrated. "Let's move!"

"Why? What's the deal?" a man bellowed from somewhere in the dark.

"Track's washed out by a mudslide," she said. "You're all going to have to hoof it the two miles to Olympia. If you hurry, you can make the train going south from there."

I did a quick calculation in my head. Two miles was just over three kilometers. In shoes that would be a breeze, but could I walk it barefoot?

"Is there really a train to take us to Portland?" I asked.

"Yeah," she said. "And I have to walk it myself, so will you all please get off the train!"

Jane shrugged and got up. "What can you do?" she asked me.

The others resigned themselves to hiking too, and we shuffled down the stairs into the cool summer night. The weather was just like at home. Hot during the day but cold as soon as the sun went down, and I shivered when a breeze rustled through the woods surrounding us. I pulled my sweater out of my pack, and my hand touched a small bundle in a zippered pouch.

"Wait a sec, Jane," I said.

We stepped out of the way of the passengers and I pulled a Crank Light flashlight out of the emergency supply pouch Dad had given me as a travel gift. I twisted the end of it around and around, and it made a satisfying clicking noise as the beam of light grew brighter and brighter.

"It doesn't do much in vast darkness like this," I said. "But we've got the moon too."

"Yep. Almost full tonight. You better go on ahead," Jane said. "I'll just slow you down."

"I doubt it. I don't have any shoes."

"None at all? I thought you just weren't wearing them because they pinched or something."

"Nope. I lost them."

"Well, then, I guess we stay together."

She sounded cheered by the thought, and I was too. The train track was in a little ravine, and we had to climb up and walk along a path that bordered the woods because the slide area was unstable. On our left, a forest of fir trees melted into the darkness; below us on the right were the tracks.

"Why do you think there's a path up here?" I asked Jane.

"Probably for the maintenance crew. These trains and the track are so bad that they're always having to work on them."

The damp earth soothed my blistered feet, but unfortunately, just when I would relax, a sharp stone would find the tender part of my arch, making me wince in pain.

"This used to be a great train line," Jane told me. "I think it was about 2015 or so that they extended it down to Mexico and up to Vancouver."

My heart beat faster at the mention of Vancouver. Maybe when I traveled back with my grandpa, we could just take the train all the way up there and then get a ferry home! Jane caught her foot on something, and I reached out to steady her.

"I'm fine, I'm fine," she said, but she locked her hand in mine and we guided each other along. Her dry skin felt smooth against my rough palm.

As we walked, Jane told me about her little house in a place called Kelso. "It's just a cottage, really. My late husband and I bought it back in nineteen seventy-four."

"Nineteen seventy-four! How old are you?" I exclaimed. She laughed. "I'm sorry . . . that was rude. . . ."

"You shouldn't ask a thirty-year-old woman how old she is, but I'm past worrying about that. I was born in fifty-two," she said proudly.

"So you're . . . eighty-nine?"

"Last April the thirtieth," she said.

"Wow."

It's not like eighty-nine is ancient exactly. We had a few old-timers on the island. But they mostly sat around and gossiped. I didn't think any of them could walk two miles.

"Are you as shocked by the U.S. as you are by my age?" Jane asked. I could hear the smile in her voice.

"It's different than home, that's for sure," I said. "We're kind of insulated from the rest of the world because they cut back ferry service years before the Collapse. That forced us to form a self-sufficient community."

"No bread lines?" Jane asked.

"What's that?"

She laughed. "It's an old term, like soup kitchens. A place where hungry people can get a meal."

"Oh, we have poor people on the island, but the church makes sure they have enough to eat. We're almost all farmers or fishermen, so food's not really an issue."

"Are there many fish?" Jane asked, surprised. "I thought they'd been pretty much cleaned out by commercial fishing."

"After the Collapse, the big boats couldn't get any fuel," I explained. "So they stopped fishing. It'll never be like it was because of all the pollution, but the fish have come back in surprising numbers. My family still doesn't eat them, though, because my parents are worried about mercury."

"Yeah," Jane agreed. "There's a boy in my neighborhood who catches them and every once in a while he'll bring me one. At my age, I'm not that worried about mercury. As long as it doesn't have two heads, I fry that sucker up and enjoy it."

Jane cracked me up! We talked more about my home, and I told her about the men in suits in Seattle and how they'd pulled that man into the car. Jane explained that the police had ignored it because it probably had to do with illegal gambling.

"But if it's illegal, why didn't they stop them?" I asked, confused.

"Because the police are on the take–bribes," she said, "to look the other way."

"Oh."

That didn't really make me feel any better about what happened, but at least I didn't have to worry about men jumping out of cars and grabbing me. At least, not if what Jane said was true. We fell silent, shuffling along the path. A burst of wind whipped a branch and the tips of the needles brushed my face; the smell of pine floated around me.

Eventually, faint streaks of light began to turn the edges of the sky a dull gray. "Dawn already," Jane said. "Boy, will I be glad to get home."

"Me too. But that won't be for a while."

Only a few stragglers were behind us now, and as the sky lightened, a pinkish hue showed me that Jane's mouth was hanging open, and her cheeks were flushed. Even with bare feet I'd been walking too fast. I immediately slowed down.

"No, keep going," she said. "You'll miss your train."

"It'll wait."

"I doubt it," she argued. "You better hurry on ahead. You need to get off your feet."

My soles were caked with mud, and they were so cold I couldn't feel a thing. I didn't want to miss it, but I couldn't leave Jane behind either.

"Look," she said, pointing. "You can see the train. You go and I'll probably make it anyway."

"I don't–"

"Just go."

She gave me a smile and a shove, and I hugged her quickly and lumbered off as best as I could on my frozen feet. My hand felt empty and alone without her warm one enclosed in it, and my heart ached for home. Ahead of me there was a long platform crowded with people, and a tiny station with a cracked sign hanging at an angle that said OLYMPIA.

The maintenance path sloped down to a concrete platform, and I hurried across it, hoping to get a seat. There were new passengers streaming through the station doors too, so the already-crowded train would be packed. I slipped my wiry frame through the crowd and placed myself by the door to one of the cars so I could jump on if I had to but I could also see if Jane was coming.

I watched a man in a horrendous plaid suit struggle out the doors of the station and make his way through the crowd with a woman in a wheelchair. Her skirt was made of the same yellow plaid. I couldn't take my eyes off either of them because I'd never seen anything so ugly. When he got to the train, he lifted the woman out and handed her to a conductor whose knees buckled under her weight.

"My wife can't manage herself," he told the conductor, who carried her aboard.

I stood on my tiptoes, trying to see if any of the last few people coming down the path were Jane. Where was she? If we sat here for even ten more minutes, she'd probably make it. I watched the plaid man fight the wheelchair, trying to collapse it so he could take it on board.

Of course! I turned to him. "Can I use your wheelchair?" His plaid jacket was even more blinding close up.

"What? No! Of course not."

"I'll bring it right back. Please? My friend, I mean, my grand-mother, my *great*-grandmother is going to miss the train if I don't borrow it."

"And if you don't make it back, then what will I do for a wheelchair?"

"Please? Please?"

The man grimaced and held on tightly to the handles. I fished around in my pocket for what was left of my money. "Here! Take this as security. I'll bring your chair back. I promise."

"It's worth a lot more than that," he said, grumbling but eyeing the money. He grabbed the bills and shoved the chair towards me.

From further down the platform, I heard a conductor shout, "Two minutes! All aboard!"

I raced across the concrete, pushing the wheelchair. I had to get Jane, no matter what!

6

I SWERVED AND DODGED, DODGED AND SWERVED. The pavement tore at my bare feet. Little kids shrieked, and parents screamed at me to be more careful. I didn't care. I was so close now! I found Jane picking her way down the slope of the maintenance trail. Leaving my fiddle in the chair, I ran up the path and just as I reached her, something punctured the ball of my foot, momentarily crippling me.

"We've got to hurry!" I said, swallowing back the pain. I scooped Jane up into my arms–her tiny body almost as light as one of our chickens! I ran down the slope, deposited her into the chair and she clutched my fiddle to her chest. Then I spun her around like a top.

"Whoooheee!" she whooped.

"Is the train moving yet?" I asked.

"Can't tell."

We hit a bump, and I grabbed her shoulder to keep her from flying out. "Hang on!"

She gripped the arm of the chair with one hand, her knuckles white. There were still stragglers everywhere, and I wove recklessly through the crowd. When I got to the train, I screeched to a halt, nearly catapulting Jane out of the chair.

"All aboard!" yelled the conductor.

"Wait! We're coming!"

Jane jumped up and hobbled towards the door, still holding my fiddle. Her long white hair hung loose to her waist, floating behind like cobwebs. I kicked at what I thought was the release mechanism on the wheelchair, but I couldn't get it folded up.

"Leave the chair!" the conductor shouted as he helped Jane aboard.

"I can't!" I said. "It belongs to that man in the plaid suit."

"No it doesn't," he yelled. "It belongs to the station!"

The train began to move slowly away.

"Come on," Jane shouted.

I couldn't believe it. That man had tricked me out of my money! Jane was still holding Jewels, and I abandoned the chair and limped painfully alongside the train, my backpack thumping against me. It was picking up speed, nearing the end of the platform. I made a last-ditch leap onto the train step and fire shot through my feet all the way up my legs. Jane and the conductor pulled me aboard just as my knees gave out.

The conductor was really annoyed when I told him about the plaid man and my money, and he helped me search the car. The man must've ducked into a washroom and changed his clothes, though, because we never did find him, and you couldn't exactly miss that jacket. His wife had mysteriously moved to a different seat too.

"Sorry," said the conductor, rubbing his temples. "Just one of those things. I have to get back to work now."

"Okay . . . thanks."

He left me standing in the corridor of the train. What was going to happen to me now? I had messed up this whole trip. I'd gotten Tyler into trouble, and maybe Poppy too. No one had stamped my passport, so I probably could get arrested any second if someone asked to see it. I had trusted a stranger with all my money and been robbed. What if I got to Gresham and couldn't find my grandpa? What if not only had my grandma passed away from the stroke, but my grandpa had died of grief? Old people did that. Especially ones who had been married for a long time.

As far as I could see, I only had one choice. Dad had made me bring the Solar Fone for emergencies, but it was so old and the battery so decrepit that it only held a charge that lasted about thirty seconds. There was no guarantee it would recharge again, either. Each time seemed like the last. He said to use it if I had to, but I'd really only brought it for one reason: to call when I arrived and let my family know about my grandparents. Instead, I was going to have to use it now to call Dad and admit how stupid I'd been.

"There you are," Jane said, coming into the corridor.

I rubbed my eyes like I was just tired, so she wouldn't notice the tears.

"Come here. I have a surprise for you." I followed her back, and everyone turned in their seats to look at me and smile. "We took up a collection," Jane said, handing me a wad of bills.

"Oh, no . . . ," I told everyone. "I can't–"

"You were the one playing the violin in the bathroom, right?" a bald man asked me.

"Fiddle. Yeah, that was me." I could feel the blush creep up my face. Had they heard me even out in the waiting room? Probably. Fiddles were loud!

"Well, open up your case, then, and play us a waltz. If you can't take the money, you might as well earn it."

"You don't think I'll get in trouble, do you?" I asked.

He said, "We'll protect you. Just play!"

I'd never performed for money before, but the idea was a lot more appealing than charity.

"Okay," I said when I finally got Jewels somewhat in tune. "Here's the 'Peekaboo Waltz.'"

The train lurched, and I braced myself against the arm of one of the seats. With the first slide of my bow across the string, my body relaxed into the music. I closed my eyes and leaned into the sway, the notes ringing throughout the train car.

One, two, three, one, two, three. . . . In my mind I saw my friends and family waltzing in the community hall, couples whirling, bodies close, smiles and dreamy expressions across their faces. Up and down went my bow, smooth as silk, even with the movement of the train. In fact, it was as if the music and the train melded together.

I drew out the last note, long and clear, and everyone clapped, snapping me back to reality. "How about a little 'Whiskey Before Breakfast'?" I asked.

When they all cheered, I looked up at my audience for the first time. Across the aisle was a young, rosy-cheeked mother with a toddler whose hands she was holding while he tried to stand on the seat. And an older couple sat up front. They looked exactly like their shaggy gray lapdog, which the man held in his arms. Behind them, crowding into the aisle and even kneeling on seats to get a better view of me, were men and women, dusty with travel. Worry lines creased their foreheads even though they were smiling, and they all looked hot and tired.

I dove into the tune with quick, short strokes, my fingers flying. Some people started clapping along and despite my sore feet, I couldn't keep my toes from tapping with the rhythm. One tune flew off my bow after another, and I was starting to think that if we had room, we'd have a full-fledged dance right here.

I played for almost an hour while the train moved along at a pace that my dog, Black Bart, could've outrun. After a while, my audience had that sort of glazed look that people get from too much fiddle and I knew they'd heard enough. Fiddle music is like that, so I packed up Jewels and sat down with Jane. Only diehards like me and my dad can listen to it endlessly.

Somewhere in the middle of nowhere, the train stopped for almost three hours without explanation, and then it started up again. Jane had a deck of cards, and she taught me to play rummy. She tried to help me, but it was hopeless, and I lost every hand.

Just before noon, the train pulled into Jane's hometown of Kelso and the conductor came through the car and told us we'd be there for two hours, so we should get off and enjoy the sunshine.

"If I lived a little closer, you could come to my house and we could find you some shoes," Jane said, "but I think you should wait here in case the train leaves early."

"Oh, yeah. I'm staying right here," I said, sitting down under a leafy dogwood tree.

Jane gave me a hug good-bye, and I tried not to cry. My dad told me that one of his favorite things about travel had been meeting new people, but I hadn't really understood until now.

"If you need a place to stay, or a meal on your way back, stop by," she said. "I'd be happy to see you anytime, dear. Good luck with your grandpa." She handed me her address on a scrap of paper, and I hugged her again. I watched her hobble off until the crowd swallowed her up.

Jane had given me a pair of purple knitted slippers from her small shoulder bag. I used a little of my water to clean my feet off and then I put them on. The soft wool cushioned my sore feet, but they were really warm on a summer day.

Just over two hours later, the conductor called "All aboard," and the rest of the southbound travelers got back on. Around four thirty, I saw a bridge ahead of us and I just about lost it. No one said we were going to have to cross a bridge! They'd been falling down all over the world ever since the Collapse, when tax money to repair them had dried up. Before I could find a conductor to ask if this really was a stable bridge, the train groaned across it and below us a wide green river snaked on its way.

I clamped my eyes tight, and I swear I held my breath all the way across. I'd seen a bridge in Victoria, but I'd never, ever been on one. All I could think about was it cracking under our weight, sending us plunging down into icy water. When we crept over a second, equally shaky bridge, I thought for sure I was going to faint, but then we were on solid ground again and after a few minutes, the train slowed and stopped.

"Portland, Oregon!" called the conductor. "This is Portland, Oregon!"

7

EVERYONE STREAMED THROUGH THE MUSTY STATION, out big doors into the early evening heat, and walked away in one direction. I limped after them because Dad had said that I needed to take the electric train called MAX and most people would probably be going that way. I had to ride it to Gresham, Oregon, a city about twenty-five kilometers away.

"It's really just a suburb of Portland," Dad had said. "You won't be able to tell when you cross from one into the other. Should be pretty easy."

He'd run his hand through his hair then, tugging at it. When he was worried, his curly hair stood up like a clown's wig from doing that, but I pretended not to notice he was nervous about me making this trip. Even though I'd been scared at the time, I'd liked being the chosen one for a change, instead of just James's and Katie's little sister. Now I wasn't so sure.

This part of the city looked a lot like the deserted bit of Seattle. Buildings had big condemned signs posted on them, and colorful graffiti decorated everything. I saw the rosy-cheeked woman with the toddler pushing a stroller, and I hurried after her.

"Is this the way to the MAX train?" I asked.

She smiled. "Yep. We're going that way too."

"I need to get to Gresham."

"MAX will take you there. Hopefully a lot faster than that stupid train from Seattle. I catch the one going the other direction, but I'll show you."

"Thanks."

The MAX station turned out to be just a narrow road paved with crumbling red bricks, and two tracks. People crowded together on both sides of the street, huddling in the shade of the buildings. Rivulets of sweat trickled down my spine under my backpack. I had a feeling my hair looked like my mom's after she'd cooked a big meal. Humidity in the kitchen made her long, frizzy hair bush out even worse than my dad's clown hair.

"You catch your train across the street," the woman said. "Good luck. And we really loved your music."

"Thanks."

My dad had told me to buy a ticket from one of the machines before I boarded. I saw a big dispenser with cracked red buttons and a little screen. The entire thing was covered with graffiti. There was a spot to put money in, but a strip of metal had been screwed over the top of it so you couldn't use it.

A guy with sandy hair and a sunburned nose stood leaning against the machine, watching me. I pushed a button just to see if maybe the screen would light up, but nothing happened.

"Those machines haven't worked since the Collapse," he said.

"Oh."

"The MAX is free for anyone who lives in the county. It's a social service," he explained. "You just apply for a pass and they send you one every month in the mail.

"How do visitors pay?"

"You buy a pass at Pioneer Square."

I was totally confused now. "In Seattle?"

"No. Downtown."

"Oh." Did every city in the U.S. have a Pioneer Square? "Can I walk there?"

"Sure. It's not far, but it's kind of confusing. I'll take you there if you want," he said, smiling.

He looked normal enough. He was clean and wore shorts and a T-shirt, and I didn't think his pockets were big enough to hide a gun, but he could have a knife. I was done trusting strangers. Getting burned once today was enough.

"That's all right," I said. "I can find it. Just tell me where it's at."

He studied me for a second, then shrugged and started giving me directions.

"Stop," I said after about fifteen seconds. "You were right. I'm already lost. Are you sure you don't mind taking me there?"

He laughed. "No problem."

We walked down the street, under a bridge where more people waited at another stop, and then turned right and headed up towards the heart of the city. I studied the guy out of my peripheral vision. He was definitely older than me, but not by much. Maybe early twenties.

Everything about him was average, from his sun-bleached hair to the light sprinkle of freckles across his nose. He had an athletic build, strong and lean, tall enough, but not too tall. He was wearing shorts, and his tanned calves were thick and hard with muscles, which probably meant that he rode a bike. I liked the way he looked, and it made me want to explain my own disheveled appearance.

"I lost my shoes," I said.

"I noticed."

"I was barefoot and my feet were bleeding and someone gave me these slippers. I'd take them off but the pavement's really hot."

He smiled.

"Normally I don't wear slippers outside. Or at all, really. I mean, in the winter I do because it's cold. But not in the summer. It's just that I-"

"Lost your shoes. I know," he said.

"Do you think there's anyplace to buy a used pair?" I asked him.

"Mmm . . . Maybe tomorrow. I think all the shops are probably closed by now."

"Oh."

We walked in silence for a few blocks while I tried to think of something else to say. Finally I burst out, "I'm from British Columbia." I said it like it was some amazing feat, like I'd come from the moon or crossed a desert. "I'm here to get my grandpa and take him back home with me."

"I've been thinking of moving up to Canada myself," he said.

"You mean to live?" I asked.

"Sure."

"I don't think you can. Unless you have relatives up there. Do you?"

"Nope," he said.

"I don't think they'll let you in, then, except to visit."

"Yeah . . . well, I know people who know people. They'd help me get in."

"Unless they're family—"

He smiled. "They'd have to catch me crossing the border."

"What do you mean?"

He leaned towards me a little and said quietly, almost as if he thought the brick buildings could hear him, "There are ways to sneak in, you know? Boats go places where they don't expect you to cross. Or I could probably get through the Rockies. Or I could just go for a visit and stay the rest of my life."

"Oh."

I wondered if a lot of people were sneaking into my country. With just a little help and a bribe, it really hadn't been that hard for me to sneak into the U.S., so it probably went both ways.

"This is a nice city," I said. "My dad thought it might be really run-down."

"Portland's built on two rivers, which helps with transportation of goods," he said. "So there are still some jobs."

We walked down a tree-lined street with sidewalks made of brick until we came to a large plaza. I saw more MAX tracks on either side of the square and big crowds of people waiting for the trains.

"In there," he said, showing me through a double door into a cavelike room. I turned to thank him, but he was gone. I spun around and searched the square. It was like he'd become invisible. I shrugged and went inside. Behind a glass window sat a woman with enormous purple-framed glasses, chewing on an apple and reading an E-ZBook Reader by kerosene lamplight.

"Excuse me? I'd like to buy a visitor's pass for the MAX."

"For what day?" she asked, looking up from what she was reading.

"Today."

"I've sold the allotment." She flipped through a little file box. "I have one left for tomorrow and twelve for the day after that."

"But I don't have anyplace to stay tonight."

"Sorry, but they're trying to control crowding on the MAX, so I can only sell fifty a day, and I'm sold out."

"Where will I go?"

"There's a mission by the train station," she suggested. She gave me directions back to where I'd just come from and reminded me to buy tomorrow's ticket before I left since she only had the one.

"How does it work?" I asked, letting her choose some bills.

"Just have it ready to show the fare inspectors when they get on the train."

Maybe I could sneak on with tomorrow's ticket, I thought.

"Today's is orange," she told me, reading my mind. "You can get on, but they'll fine you if you're caught, and if you can't pay"—she paused, leaning forward for maximum effect—"they'll arrest you."

"Arrest me?"

"Yep."

"Wow. Well . . . thanks for the warning," I said. I accepted the lavender ticket marked for tomorrow. She'd sounded so dramatic that I wondered if she was just trying to scare me into doing the right thing, but I couldn't be sure.

Outside I blinked in the bright sunshine, and my bruised and battered feet begged me not to walk all the way to the shelter. I was so close to getting to my grandpa's house. I scanned the square for the sunburned guy, hoping he'd have a suggestion, but I couldn't find him.

There was a big crowd waiting to get on the MAX, maybe as many as two hundred people. How could the fare inspectors possibly catch me with all those people onboard? I hobbled across the hot bricks to the eastbound platform and stood near the waiting crowd. We could hear the MAX horn long before the train got to us, and we pressed our hot, sweaty bodies into one another, trying to be closest to the edge without being shoved off and run over.

I weighed my options one more time. I could sleep in a corner of this square, go to the shelter, or get on the train. The first two choices seemed infinitely more frightening than sneaking aboard. After all, I'd already stowed away on a government flight and crossed the border illegally. If I had to, I would just tell them I was a foreigner and I hadn't understood how the system worked. It was just a local train. How much trouble could I get in, anyway?

8

AS SOON AS THE DOORS OPENED, PEOPLE PUSHED and shoved, and I rode a wave of smelly bodies up into the train car.

"Move," a woman shouted from behind me, pressing on my pack and sending me staggering forward into a guy with shaggy dreadlocks. All the seats were instantly taken, so I grabbed a ring hanging from a bar to steady myself, my hot feet throbbing, my backpack pulling at my shoulders, and Jewels in my other hand.

The doors shut, and the train slid forward. I saw a map above me of the route, but instead of helping, it confused me more. The city of Gresham had six stations. How did I know which one was mine?

The train stopped every few minutes to let people off and after about half an hour, I found a seat. From the wide windows I could see an old highway on one side, rutted with potholes and so overgrown that saplings had struggled through the cracks. A few people walked along it, and I saw a couple of carts and horses, and more cyclists than we have on our entire island.

There was also a group of boys, dressed in black and white, riding together. I noticed them not just because of their unusual clothing, but because they wore bike helmets. Nobody had helmets on our island because the whole point was to feel the wind in your hair.

I studied the map trying to figure out how long it would take to ride to the end, but nothing seemed to be to scale. I was so absorbed in my worries that the train's doors had shut behind two burly men in gray uniforms before I even noticed them.

"Fares, please!" they shouted.

All around me there was the rustle of people getting their wallets out. I clutched my visitor pass, heart thumping. I should've known this wouldn't work. When the inspector got to me, he held out a meaty hand. He wore two gold rings, one wedding and one pinkie, and his palm looked soft and pink. He'd never held a pitchfork in that hand, that was for sure. I showed him the lavender pass.

"This is for tomorrow," he said. He sounded really happy that he'd caught someone. "Do you have one for today?"

"Oh, that's the wrong one?" I asked, feigning innocence. "I have today's in here somewhere." I dug through my pack like I was looking for it. "I, ummm . . . I must've lost it. It's orange, right?"

"If you don't have the correct pass, then we'll be stepping off at the next stop. There's a fine, you know," he said gleefully.

He took a handheld computer out of his back pocket and began to type something into it.

"I'm from Canada," I said. "I didn't know . . . I mean . . . I don't have any money to pay—"

"If you can't pay the fine, you'll get free accommodation for the night," his partner said. He had crumbs in his beard, and some of them flew off when he laughed.

It wasn't funny to me, though. This was just great. I really had thought the ticket lady had only been trying to scare me with the threat of jail.

"What's your name?" the man asked.

"Ummm, Mol—"

"Hello, sir," I heard a voice say behind me. I turned in my seat and saw the guy who helped me find the MAX office. "I hate to interrupt," he said, "but I don't think you checked my fare."

He held out an open brown leather wallet, showing off his pass and a photo ID. Then he nodded at me. "You don't want to give her a citation. She's my guest."

I saw a shadow cross the fare inspector's face as he looked at the guy's wallet. He tugged at his beard. "Oh, right," he said. "She's your guest. No problem."

The first inspector quickly stuffed his computer back in his pocket. "Okay. Sorry about that."

They hurried down the aisle, calling, "Fares, please!"

"What just happened?" I asked the guy.

He shrugged. "Nothing."

"But they were going to give me a ticket."

"The transit company has an arrangement with my employer," he said. "Our guests don't have to pay."

"Ummm . . . well . . . thanks."

"No problem."

I scooted over into the seat by the window and he sat next to me. I was grateful, but curious too. Why had the inspectors looked . . . almost scared of him? I'd definitely seen their fear. Still, he was kind of cute in that boy-next-door way, so I decided not to worry about it too much.

"I tried to buy a pass for today," I explained so he wouldn't think badly of me. "But they were sold out. I kind of had to sneak on."

"You're bold. I like that," he said.

I smiled. If he only knew about how I'd gotten into the country, he'd probably be highly impressed. One thing about him that I noticed as we sat there was that he didn't really look at me. His blue eyes never stopped scanning his surroundings, which made me even more nervous.

"I was just wondering," I said, "I've got the address where I'm going, but I don't know how to find the house."

I handed him the paper, and he examined it. "I'm not really sure. Anyone know where Creekside Way is in Gresham?" he called out.

"It's that housing development out past Burnside," someone answered.

"Oh, yeah. The ritzy one that's not so ritzy anymore."

There was a general agreement. "Get off at the last stop, then," he said. "That's my stop too. You'll have to walk about two and half miles. Will your slippers hold up?"

"My slippers probably will, but I'm not so sure about my feet."

"Can anyone draw her a map?" he asked.

A man in faded blue jeans and no shirt drew a rough sketch of my grandpa's neighborhood on the piece of paper for me. "That's about right," he said. "I think so anyway."

At the last stop, we stepped off the train and the evening air blew hot in my face, reminding me of the woodstove in winter. I stood around while the guy unlocked a bike from a rack, hoping he'd say something more, but then I saw he was just going to leave, so I blurted out, "My name's Molly."

"Nice to meet you, Molly," he said. He rode off with a quick wave, and I was more disappointed than I should've been because it wasn't like I was ever going to see him again.

Just over thirty hours after Poppy put me on the plane, I was finally getting close enough to my destination to believe I might actually make it. I checked the map and headed down a paved road, cracked from weeds pushing through. Three-story apartment buildings lined the street on either side, and residents sat around on cement porches. A couple of darkly tanned boys kicked a deflated basketball past me, and two little girls played with a jump rope on a scrap of grass.

I limped along for about ten minutes until I came to a wide road, which intersected the one I was on at an angle. Across the street I saw an old building with a faded Fred Meyer sign on top. That was my landmark, and I crossed the empty street to a parking lot that was now an outdoor market.

Men and women were dismantling tents and canopies, loading boxes into carts attached to bicycles or horses, and generally laughing and shouting while they closed for the day. I skirted the market and found the road that ran behind it and climbed a long, winding hill that normally would've been a breeze but was no picnic in a pair of slippers. A few houses were set back off the road, the lawns overgrown, garbage piled in the yards. Occasionally people passed by on foot, or a person on a bike dragged a cart up the hill, but no one seemed to notice or care about me.

Big rustly maples lined the street, and the branches hung heavily overhead, nearly touching in the middle, forming a dark green tunnel. The map told me to turn at the top of the hill onto a side street. There weren't any big trees on this road, and the last of the evening sunshine poured down on me. I stared in amazement. Giant houses stood in neat rows, so close together they were practically on top of each other. They were built of wood or brick, and all looked alike. Wide driveways led up to two- and three-car garages, and cracked pathways wound through the weeds to massive, carved front doors.

The streets were deserted, but I could hear people calling to each other, their voices floating on the summer air. I had an eerie feeling, like people were watching me and then ducking into the shadows of their doorways quicker than I could turn and see them. I tried to shake off the feeling of being out in the open, being vulnerable, being observed.

I made my way through the neighborhood checking the weathered green street signs on the corners. Some of them were missing, but there were enough to keep me on track. I found Creekside Way and turned down it. These houses were even larger, and all of them had low stone walls in front of them. Halfway down the short street, I found the house. I stared at the building, fear looming up inside me. It was a massive soulless place, and all the ground-floor windows were boarded up.

Could Grandpa still be living here, or had he gone away after my grandmother died? I tried brushing off my clothes, but travel had made me dusty, and it didn't help much. With each step towards the front door, my heart thundered in my chest and the pain in my feet shot up through my legs. What would I do if I'd come all this way and he was gone? The little money that Jane had collected for me wouldn't get me back home, and my mother needed my grandpa. He had to be here. I raised my hand, tightening my fingers into a fist, and knocked.

Nothing happened.

I tried again in case he hadn't heard. A moment later, the door creaked open, but instead of my grandfather, a woman answered. I stumbled backwards, thinking I was seeing the ghost of my mother. The woman's face was lined and creased, and her gray hair was frizzy and out of control just like Mom's. Her big doe eyes stared out at me. I clutched Jewels to my chest and staggered backwards down the two porch steps.

A voice boomed from inside the house. "Katharine? Where are you?"

Katharine? Had the voice inside really called out for Katharine? It wasn't a ghost! The woman was my grandmother. She hadn't died after all. She'd been *discharged* from the hospital just like we'd tried to tell my mother. All these months of worry and she was standing right there, very much alive!

"Grandma? It's me. Molly McClure. Your granddaughter."

She didn't say anything.

"Brianna's daughter," I tried.

I thought I saw a tiny flicker in her eyes and then they returned to dull staring.

"Can I come in?"

"Katharine? Why do you have the door open? Who's there?" demanded a man's voice from inside. "We don't want any! Go away!"

A skinny hand pulled my grandmother back into the house and slammed the door shut. I heard a bolt slide into place.

9

I STARED AT THE CLOSED DOOR IN SHOCK FOR A second and then knocked again. I thought for sure Grandma would tell him it was me, but the door stayed firmly closed. This could not be happening. I set Jewels and my pack on the steps and banged on the door.

"It's me! Molly McClure!"

No answer. Tears of frustration and anger dripped down my face as I pounded so hard my hands began to feel bruised. "Fine!" I shouted. "Be that way!"

But I hadn't come that far to give up. Especially now that I knew Grandma was okay.

I unzipped my pack and pulled things out, flinging them all over the porch. The Solar Fone was in there somewhere, and I'd been saving my one call for something really important. This was it. I found the phone in the bottom and pulled it out of its case.

"Call home," I told it.

I knew my family would be on the porch, enjoying the evening air while sitting in rocking chairs, probably listening to Dad play the fiddle. I hoped that they would hear the phone. Of course, I should've known they'd be waiting for it.

"Molly?" Dad's voice asked after half a ring, the connection crackly.

"Grandma is alive!" I said. "She seems okay." That was what they were waiting to hear, and I had to get it out before the phone died. I could hear my family's cries of joy as my dad relayed the message.

"How are you?" he asked. "Everything go okay?"

"No! Everything did not go okay. I'm on their porch–" The phone chirped, signaling that it was about to die.

"What?" Dad said. "You're fading–"

And then the stupid Solar Fone beeped twice, and the miles between me and home became insurmountable. I threw the useless piece of crap onto the cement porch and heard it crack open.

I had slept on a train last night, and tonight I wanted a bed. I pounded on the front door again and when no one came, I decided to try to get in another way. Every house had at least one back door. I walked out onto the dry, overgrown lawn, and it crunched under my feet. The front yard just had the low stone wall, but the back was enclosed in a high cedar fence, and the only gate was padlocked shut. I gave it a kick just because I was mad and was instantly sorry because all I had on were the slippers. I collapsed onto the grass, massaging my big toe, tears leaking down my cheeks.

The last of the sunset deepened into blue twilight as I sat there, crying into my hands. What could I do? How could I prove to them that I was their granddaughter so that they'd open the door and listen to what I had to say?

I limped back to the porch and saw Jewels sitting there, her case looking like a black lump in the fading light. Music. That's what I needed. I would block out my problems by playing Jewels. I sat on a step and took her out of her case. Once I was in tune, I did a few scales to loosen my hands. The sun was gone now, but I could play Jewels in the dark even better than Jane could knit. It was starting to get cold, though, and I knew it wouldn't be long before my fingers would be clumsy on the strings.

I shook out my left hand to get the blood flowing and then launched into "Stony Point," hoping something fast would keep me warm. The bow dashed over the strings, dancing in my hand. I tapped my sore feet in spite of the pain. It only took a minute for me to get lost in the music.

I was plowing my way through a really difficult French-Canadian tune, taking my frustration out on the strings, when I thought I heard the creak of the door behind me. Swaying my body with the music, I turned slightly and saw out of the corner of my eye that I was right.

Someone was there, listening. Was it my grandma? Did my grandfather know she was there? I pretended not to notice and kept going, wishing I was playing something I knew better. I rushed through to the end and dove into the "Peekaboo Waltz." That one I could play both in the dark and in my sleep. Maybe the comforting notes of a waltz would draw Grandma out on the porch.

I pushed myself painfully to my feet, still playing, and turned towards the open door, smiling. My grandmother stood there, holding a candle, wax dripping dangerously close to her fingers. Her mouth hung slightly ajar, and her eyes glittered in the flickering light. I noticed her foot was tapping ever so slightly as I started the tune again. I was on my third time through it when my grandpa stepped out of the shadows and into the doorway.

"Who are you? What do you want?" he asked.

"I'm Molly," I said, still playing, but softer. "Molly McClure."

"Bri's daughter?" he asked.

I nodded in time to the music. "Yes."

"Breee," said Grandma.

Grandpa noticed the dripping wax and took the candle from her. "Where is she?" he asked. He held the candle up and peered out into the yard like maybe I'd hidden Mom in the bushes.

"She's in Canada," I explained. "I came by myself."

I finished the tune and put Jewels under my arm. It was hard to believe this was my grandfather because he was the only person in my family that didn't look anything like us. His face was pinched, his body slight; gold-framed glasses perched on his thin nose. In the dim light I could see a halo of gray hair circling his mostly bald head.

"You are Jack Buckley, aren't you?" I asked, just to be sure.

"Yes . . . yes . . . of course I am," he said.

"Come," Grandma said. She reached out and started pulling me inside.

"Wait a minute," Grandpa said. "How do we know she's actually Molly?"

I really needed to sit down, so I set Jewels in her case and started picking up all the things I'd thrown out of my backpack.

"Why would I lie?" I asked.

"Why, indeed? Who wouldn't want to live in this big house?" he asked. "Practically everyone in the whole neighborhood is a filthy squatter these days." He glared at me over his glasses.

"What's a squatter?" I asked, stuffing the remains of the Solar Fone into the pack.

"Homeless people who move into abandoned houses," he explained.

"Oh. Well, I'm definitely not homeless."

"Hmmm . . . Well, I think you should prove that you're Molly."

"How?" I asked. I swatted at the mosquitoes that were swarming around me, biting my bare legs.

"Do you know 'Brianna's Reel'?" Grandpa asked.

I smiled. "Like the back of my hand!" I tucked Jewels under my chin and began the tune Grandpa had written for my mother on the piano when she was a little girl. Mom played the piano too, and she'd taught me the melody when I was about six years old.

When I was done, Grandma said, "Breeee. Come now." She took my arm again in her thin, bony hand. Grandpa stared at me hard, considering. Then he shrugged and picked up my pack. I stuck Jewels in her case, snapped it closed, and followed them inside.

The single candle didn't allow me to see much more than shadows.

"This way," Grandpa said, leading me to a staircase. "Katharine, you stay down here. I don't want you on the stairs."

"Okay," she said.

"We don't have electricity," Grandpa told me, "and I can't spare the candle, so you might as well get some sleep and we'll talk in the morning."

I wanted to tell him everything right then, talk him into leaving as soon as possible so we could get home to Mom, but I was also completely exhausted, and the relief of getting here overrode any desire except sleep.

He deposited me into a room at the top of the stairs, showed me the bed and where the washroom was, and then said good night. I collapsed onto a mattress big enough for both me and Katie to sleep in without ever touching each other, so unlike our tiny double bed at home. Part One of my mission was complete, but I had a feeling the hard part was still ahead.

10

July 12th–Pray you now, forget and forgive.
–William Shakespeare

I SLEPT WELL PAST DAWN FOR THE FIRST TIME IN years. I found a dusty bunch of purple grapes in a bowl by the sink that was some sort of fancy soap, but once I was in the shower, I kept dropping it. The bunch broke apart into individual grapes, and I rubbed one purple ball awkwardly all over my head to wash my matted hair. The frigid water stung the open cuts on my feet, and I gulped in pain as I dug the soap into my wounds to get them clean.

I got out, shivering, and inspected the damage to my feet. Eleven blisters, one puncture wound on the ball of my right foot that looked red and inflamed, and a raw spot on each heel. I found a comb in my pack and pulled it through my hair. Then I quickly made one lumpy braid down my back.

Grandpa must've heard me coming because he was waiting at the bottom of the stairs. "Follow me," he said.

I hobbled after him through a wide archway. He led me into a giant room that opened onto a black and white kitchen, towering ceilings, a huge dining area with an empty space where the table and chairs should've been, and a sitting area with a bunch of once-elegant furniture. Grandma sat on a worn settee staring off into space.

"Sit," Grandpa ordered.

I chose one of the swivel chairs.

"What happened to your feet? Don't they have shoes in Canada?"

"I lost them."

"How do you lose shoes?"

"Long story."

"Well, we can't have you bleeding all over the hardwood floors," he said. "Wait here."

He returned a minute later carrying a bowl of water, a clean cloth, and a small bag. He also had a pair of old-lady sandals. "Probably too small for your big boats," he said, tossing them at me.

"Ummm . . . thanks." I wasn't sure what to make of his gruff manners. Was he mad at me for something? I started to put them on, but he waved his hands at me.

"I better have a look first," he said.

"I already washed them really well."

He ignored me and dragged a chair over. He lifted one foot in his thin hands, and I saw the long piano fingers that my mother had told me about. His nails were rough, but his hands were smooth and soft. He examined my foot thoroughly and then set it gently back on the floor, picking up my right one and looking at it.

He wet the cloth and began to dab at the puncture wound. "What brings you to the U.S.?"

"It's my mom. She's pregnant and–"

"Again? How many kids is she planning to have?"

"Well . . . I don't think this one was exactly planned. . . ."

"They have ways to control pregnancy these days," he said. "But she probably wouldn't know about that, since she dropped out of premed."

I swallowed hard as he poked at my sore foot. Dad had warned me that the fact that Mom could've been a doctor was probably going to come up.

"Anyway," I said, wincing from his examination, "she's really stressed, mostly because we thought Grandma was dead, and she's worried about you–"

"Why would she think Katharine was dead?"

I looked over at Grandma to see if she was listening, but she seemed to have dozed off on the couch. "That's what the hospital said. Or at least what we thought they said."

"Well, she's clearly fine, so your mom can stop worrying."

Grandma was not fine. She had spoken to me, and she seemed to know who I was, but there was that staring off into space and falling asleep right now when Grandpa and I were discussing important things. The stroke had obviously messed her up a little, if not a lot.

"Mom wants you two to come back up to live with us," I explained. I hoped he couldn't hear the nervousness in my voice.

"That's just another one of your mother's lamebrained ideas. Like marrying a Canadian in the first place."

I knew my grandparents blamed my dad for Mom switching to agriculture, which was just stupid because they didn't even meet until grad school. For some reason, Grandpa thought that if my dad was any kind of man at all, he would've convinced her to go back to medical school.

"My parents are very happy," I said. "We all are."

Grandpa shook his head at me, unconvinced. "Raising chickens and kids? Is that what I educated Brianna for? She was premed, for God's sake!"

"Breee!" Grandma said, suddenly, startling us both.

I looked over at the couch where she was sitting wide awake and alert now. Grandpa was wiping my foot with the cloth, and the more we talked about my mother, the harder he rubbed. I gritted my teeth so he wouldn't know it hurt so much.

"She uses her education," I told him.

"Farming? Huh. She could've been a doctor," he said. "Your mother was smarter than anyone in her class. Who knows what medical discoveries she might've made if she'd followed through?"

"Look," I said in the voice I use when I'm trying to get Little Jackie to be reasonable about something, "I know you wish she was a doctor, but she's not, and she needs your help. Her blood pressure is out of control. And the island doctor was killed last week."

"Killed?"

I didn't want to explain. I didn't want Grandpa to know that it was my fault for not separating the calf from its mother. "There was an accident," I said. "And he died."

"So what? I thought your mom preferred a *midwife*." You could hear the contempt in his voice for midwives everywhere.

"She does, and Mrs. Rosetree is looking after her as best as she can, but this time Mom's health is really bad. She needs a real doctor."

He didn't say anything.

"And Mom misses you both," I continued. "When she thought Grandma had died and you hadn't made up . . . well, she almost went crazy with grief. She really needs you."

He studied my punctured foot, not meeting my eye.

"They need my help on the farm," I said. "And I want to go back right away. Will you both please come?"

He shook his head. "Nope. Your mom made her own bed, she has to lie in it."

"But she won't," I said. "Dr. Robinson ordered her to nap two hours a day, but she's being stubborn. My dad thinks you're the only one she'll listen to."

He laughed then, a big, rolling, bitter version of my mother's usually joyful one. And then his face softened. "Molly, I'm sorry that circumstances have made it so we haven't gotten to know our grandkids, and you're welcome to stay for a short visit, but I think you should head back pretty soon so you can help your mom."

"I can't help her," I said. "Only you can. Besides, I can't just go home anyway."

He pressed the bottom of my foot and I flinched. "Why not? What's stopping you?"

"I don't have any money," I admitted. "At least not enough for train fare."

He looked up at me, his eyes wide behind his glasses. "You came all the way down here to take us back and you don't have any money?"

"Mom said–"

"Mom said," he mimicked me, suddenly bitter. *"Mom said* we have all the money in the world, did she? What do you eat up there in Canada without any money? Stone soup?"

He had let go of my foot so he could root around in his bag, and I jumped up in indignation.

"Sit down," he said, his voice gentle. "You've got something deep in your foot."

I sat back in the chair, but only because it hurt so much to stand.

"This is going to be painful," he said, "but I'll be as quick as I can." He used sharp tweezers to dig into the tenderest part of my foot. A little yelp escaped in spite of my efforts to hold it in.

He leaned in close, squinting. "Don't move. I've almost got it."

White-hot pain burned through my whole body, and wooziness washed over me, making me sink back into the chair.

"There," he said, holding up a piece of green glass with the tweezers.

I let out a long, slow breath. "Thanks," I gulped. "Listen, all we need is train fare–"

"You don't get it, do you? There isn't any money."

"There has to be enough for train fare," I argued. "We can sell something."

"Do you think we'd be sitting here without electricity if we had anything left to sell?"

"But Mom said you're rich. And whenever we talked to Grandma on CyberSpeak, she said you were fine."

His tone had softened, but his eyes flashed with anger. "We were getting by until a couple of months ago, but a few weeks in the hospital wiped out our entire savings and the pension fund dried up last year. I had to sell everything I could just to buy food."

He'd sold his possessions to buy food and he had the nerve to be mad at Mom for becoming a farmer? I didn't understand him at all. I took a hard look at the room and saw that it really was much shabbier than I would've expected from my mom's descriptions. The chairs were threadbare, and the china cabinet was empty and covered in a layer of dust. They'd obviously been hard up for a lot longer than he was even willing to admit. Grandma saw me looking around and gave me a lopsided smile. Had she followed the conversation or not?

"None of us are going to Canada," Grandpa said. "If you don't have any money, then you're stuck here, too."

11

A HALF HOUR LATER, AFTER GRANDPA HAD USED THE supplies from my emergency kit to bandage up my feet, we were all sitting there absorbed in our own thoughts. I knew I should be concentrating on ways to raise some money, but honestly, all I could think about was food. I'd finished all of Poppy's snacks the night before, and my stomach was growling.

"Ummm, Grandpa?" I asked.

He looked over at me.

"Is there . . . I mean . . ." This was hard. I'd been raised to wait for someone to offer food.

"What?" he asked.

"Did I . . . ummm . . . did I miss breakfast?"

"You're hungry?" he asked.

"Starving!"

He stood up. "Come on. I'll see what we have."

I hobbled after him to the kitchen counter and climbed up on a bar stool. I wasn't expecting much, nothing like home, but when he took out a cutting board and knife and chose two battered tomatoes out of a ceramic bowl, I got a little worried. Tomatoes for breakfast? He sliced them nice and thick, just like my mother always did. I didn't have the heart to tell him that if there's one thing I hated, it was tomatoes. I figured I'd just force them down.

"We're out of pepper," he said, sprinkling the slices with salt.

He handed me three on a saucer. On another plate he placed one slice, and on the third, he put two slices, which he cut into tiny pieces and took out to Grandma. I limped behind him, back to the chair, and sat with my food balanced on my knees.

"Three is too many," I said to him. "Have one of mine. I'm not that hungry."

"You said you were starving."

"Figure of speech."

"I'm not a charity case," he said, but he didn't stop me when I slid a tomato onto his plate.

The food situation was clearly worse than I thought. They both looked skinny, but because I didn't really know them, I wasn't sure if that was just how they normally were or not. If he was willing to accept my food, though, things must be pretty bad. I slipped a bite into my mouth and swallowed it whole.

"Did you grow these?" I asked.

"They come over the fence."

"What do you mean?"

"Most days the neighbor throws vegetables over the fence," he explained. "Not just tomatoes, though. Sometimes there's zucchini. We used to get a few strawberries, but not anymore.

I guess strawberries are done for the year. And once we got a couple of onions and some pretty small carrots."

Was that all they had to eat? Grandma inhaled her tomatoes and stared ravenously at mine, so I cut them into small pieces and when Grandpa got up to take his plate to the sink I slipped them to her. She stuffed the bits into her mouth all at once with her fingers, and I hoped she wouldn't choke. The last thing I wanted to have to do was tell Mom I'd killed her mother.

"Show me this fence," I said, when Grandpa returned.

He led me out through French doors onto a huge covered deck and down some steps into an overgrown yard. "Wow. You've got more land than I expected," I said.

"Goes all the way down to the creek," he said. "Half an acre."

"You'd never know it from the front."

He shrugged. "Hey, look." He pointed to where half a dozen tomatoes lay on the ground along the bottom of the fence. "Lettuce too!" he shouted, grabbing up a small head of romaine with brown edges.

I handed him a couple of bruised tomatoes. "Have you ever tried to talk to the neighbor?"

Grandpa's smile vanished. "Leave well enough alone, Molly."

"I don't have enough money to get us back to Canada," I said, "but I have a little left over from busking. Maybe if I offered to pay him, he'd give us more." And better quality, I thought.

"Just forget it, okay? He might think you're one of the squat-ters and shoot you."

"What? Are you serious? With a gun?"

"Of course with a gun. Listen, I'm not saying he's a bad guy, and he probably wouldn't shoot you, but you can't be too careful. If he wanted to be friendly, he would've come over. He knows we're here. Come inside."

"I'm just going to walk down to the creek," I said.

"Stubborn like your mother," Grandpa said, but he didn't sound angry, or even worried, so I didn't think he was too scared of whoever lived next door.

"I just want to see what the garden looks like," I said.

Shaking his head, Grandpa took his cache inside, and I waded through the tall, dry grass. My mom always says gar-dens are like a magnet to me. Every time we visit friends, I have to check out theirs to see if I can learn anything. I had to see this one too.

When I got to the end of the yard, I was met with a solid wall of blackberry bushes. I found a place near the fence where they were a bit thinner and peeked around the end into the neighbor's yard. The man had cleared the entire lawn and turned it into a huge vegetable garden, but he was obviously not a serious farmer because the place was overrun with weeds. He'd be lucky if he didn't lose his whole crop.

Bracing myself for scratches, I pushed through the briars to get a better look. Green corn rustled in the light breeze, and weeds choked the stalks, but the plants looked like they could be saved with some care. The tomatoes stood tall and bent to the ground under their own weight. Someone should stake them up to keep the slugs from getting them.

Carrots, potatoes, and other root vegetables grew helter-skelter, and I could barely figure out what was what because of the weeds suffocating everything. Pumpkin and zucchini vines had taken over at least 20 percent of the garden and needed to be cut back.

The place actually looked abandoned. Whoever the gardener was, it had to be someone totally overwhelmed, completely clueless, or very lazy. As I stared at the overgrown vegetable patch, my hands itched to get in there and go to work. I could see dozens of healthy green weeds, just a foot away, that I longed to pluck from the ground and toss onto the compost heap. I wanted to feel the soil against my palms and under my nails, just to remind myself that home still existed. I was hungrier than ever, and it was all I could do not to rip the young corn from the stalk and eat it right then.

I stood in the garden, leaning against the fence for a really long time, breathing in the fresh scents of plants and dirt, thinking. There were a lot of things in life I didn't know, but the raging hole in my stomach made me absolutely certain of one thing: We needed more food, and we needed it today. I could try to buy it from the neighbor, or I could just take it at night and . . . and what? Leave the money I had to pay the owner back? No, that was stupid. I needed a better idea.

What would my dad do in this situation? I laughed to myself. Knowing Dad, he'd get his farmer's almanac out and open it randomly, looking for advice. Maybe I should do that. But suddenly I didn't need to because I remembered Dad's favorite quote from the book.

A *competent farmer rarely goes hungry.*

Of course! Whoever had planted this garden didn't know the first thing about keeping it under control, but I did! Not only could I show my competence, but I could make myself totally indispensable. And I knew exactly how to do it. Assuming I didn't get shot in the process.

12

*July 13th–Jesus said to his disciples, "The harvest is
truly plentiful but the laborers are few."*
–Matthew 9:37

I HAD TO WAIT A DAY TO PUT MY PLAN INTO EFFECT
because I was so tired, I couldn't even think, let alone pull
weeds. I spent most of afternoon sleeping, had a dinner of lettuce and tomatoes, and then slept long and hard all night.

The next morning I was in the garden right at dawn, though.
It wasn't long before the sun started getting strong and the
vegetable beds were steaming around me, the emerald leaves
glistening with dew. Morning in the garden is one of my favorite places to be on Earth. The fact that it wasn't my garden–
and I'd probably have to do some fast talking when the owner
came outside–didn't really bother me because I had my hands
deep in the soil.

Even though I don't like to eat tomatoes, I love their
fragrance; that sort of bitter-fresh scent smelled like everything
good to me . . . soil, dew, plants, food . . . the farm, so I started
weeding around the thick green tomato stalks.

I scooted along the row on my knees, letting the monotony
of pulling weeds relax me and bring me the first real peace I'd

known since leaving home. I was running a tune through my head, deep in my own private world of music, when I noticed movement.

The house looked almost exactly like my grandparents', and up on the deck a little boy and girl were watching. They moved closer and peered out at me through tangled dark hair. Their smudged faces were in need of a good washing, but their matching blue eyes sparkled. They both had such skinny bodies it made me queasy. The girl walked over to me and plopped down onto the damp ground. "I'm Brandy," she said. "Who are you?"

"Molly. Nice to meet you." I held out a muddy hand and she giggled.

"That's Michael," she said, pointing at the boy. "He loves worms. What are you doing?"

Making myself indispensable!

"Weeding," I answered.

"I'm six. My brother's four. He doesn't know what weeds are, but I do. This is a carrot." She yanked a spindly carrot out of the soil. "This is a weed," she added, pointing to a plant next to it and leaving it in the ground.

"Yep. You're pretty smart for six."

"I know."

More movement near the house made me look up. In three quick strides, a tall man was towering over us. Luckily, he didn't seem to be armed.

"What in the hell is going on out here?" he said. "Who are you?"

Brandy jumped up and ran back to Michael. I stood, brushing my hands on my shorts, and then I got my first good look at the man and almost staggered back in surprise. I don't know what I was expecting, but it definitely wasn't young, blond, and handsome! Well, youngish. He must've been about thirty. His hair curled around his ears where it had pulled loose from a thick ponytail that hung halfway down his back. His face was tan, and his arms were chiseled muscles.

"Ummm . . . h-hi," I stammered.

"Hi? Is that all you have to say? What are you doing in my garden?"

"Well . . ." He glared at me, and I took a step back. "I, ummm . . . I'm staying next door . . . with my grandparents . . . Jack and Katharine Buckley–"

"And?" he demanded.

"And so they were telling me about the food you give them. You know, throw over the fence. And so I was looking at your garden–"

"And you thought you'd just help yourself?"

"No! No, not at all! The thing is," I said rushing on, "I live on a farm in Canada, and the kitchen garden, it's all my responsibility. It looked like you needed some help over here, and since you've been giving my grandparents food, I thought maybe I should come over and, you know, weed for you."

"Did it ever occur to you to ask first?"

"I guess I should've," I admitted. "But I was up at dawn and you weren't around . . . so I just started. Look at the tomatoes! Don't they look great?"

He gave them a cursory glance. "Slugs are getting them."

"I know, but I can help you with that. We can stake them up, and–"

"I don't need your help."

"It's no problem. Really."

He continued to glare, and even though he was extremely good looking, he also had a hardness about him. There were deep lines in his forehead and a flinty look in his eyes. I wasn't so sure this was the best idea I'd ever had.

"It's pretty overgrown," I said.

"We've had a lot of rain this year for some reason," the man grumbled.

"So . . . is it okay if I just keep working for a while?"

He stared at me for a minute and then walked back to the house. "Do what you have to do," he said over his shoulder. "But I'm not my sister, and I'm not planning on feeding the whole neighborhood like she used to do, no matter how much you work."

I should've been disappointed that he wasn't more enthusiastic about my help, but I wasn't. Not yet, anyway. Weeding the garden so he'd give us more food was worth a shot. Plus doing something productive helped keep me from breaking down into tears every time I thought about how I couldn't get back to the farm.

I knelt onto the ground to weed. After a while, Brandy wandered back to my row and sat down.

"What's your daddy's name?" I asked her.

She giggled.

"What?"

"He's not my daddy!" she said, laughing. "He's my uncle."

"Oh. Well, what's his name?"

"Uncle."

Eventually I got the story out of her. At least the story she knew. This was her parents' house, but they were both in the ground. Not this ground, though, so we shouldn't be afraid to dig because we'd never dig them up. I thought that maybe Uncle should explain things a little better, but I had a new respect for a guy who'd taken on someone else's kids too.

There was no way I was going to live in the U.S. forever, but seeing this garden made me think that maybe, if I really was stuck here for a while, I should try and plant some things at my grandparents' house. Then I ditched that idea as absurd. We had to get back. It wasn't a question of if, but how.

Brandy stayed by my side all morning, and once when I found a worm, I held it up for Michael. He came and took it from me, but then ran off without a word. Like on the island, the air had been cool in the morning. However, by noon it was already hotter than we ever got. After a couple of hours of weeding, you could see a little progress, but nothing to write home about. My back ached and my fingers were grimy and rough, but I felt good.

"Hey, farmer girl, are you planning to weed all day?" the guy asked from the sunporch where he was tanning himself, watching me work.

"Actually, I was just going to stop. My name's Molly."

He grunted.

"What should I call you?"

"Mr. Edwards."

I nodded. "I'll be back tomorrow, Mr. Edwards."

"If you're trying to soften me up, you're wasting your time."

"I'm not. I just can't see a garden without wanting to get my hands on it."

I smiled to myself as I walked around the end of the fence into Grandpa's yard. He stood there, fists on his hips, waiting for me.

"You've been over there for hours. What were you doing?"

He actually sounded a little worried. I smiled, trying to reassure him. "I was just helping him weed and talking to the kids."

I heard a giggle from the other side of the fence, and I had to dodge a giant zucchini, three tomatoes, a head of lettuce, four cucumbers, and a handful of green beans. Grandpa and I scurried around gathering our lunch. Most of it looked to be in a lot better shape than the stuff Mr. Edwards usually threw over.

"Don't eat all this," I told him. "I want to make soup later."

He grasped his bounty against his chest. "You don't put lettuce and cucumbers in soup."

I laughed. "Fine. Eat those."

"I will." He strutted off to the house.

The day was just starting to heat up, and I knew I better get going down to the market pretty soon. Jane had inadvertently shown me a way home, and now I had to see if it would work. If it did, hopefully we'd all be heading for Canada by next week.

13

AS SOON AS I STEPPED OFF THE STREET AND INTO THE market, I began to doubt my plan. Grandpa had told me that I could find produce and other goods for sale, but instead all I saw were men crowded together inside tents and under canopies, drinking, smoking, and playing cards. I heard a few whistles, and from inside a tent someone called out, "Hey, baby!"

I like to think I'm brave, but my insides twisted, uneasy. I considered just going back to the house, but I had to earn some money, so I made myself keep walking. Eventually the tents full of cardplayers gave way to food stalls and produce stands. I found a spot near a pile of old tires, and I opened my fiddle case and took out Jewels. By the time I had her tuned, a small crowd of kids had gathered around.

"You gonna play?" one asked.

"Yep." I nudged the case casually with my foot, so it was out in front of me a bit.

I started with something simple that people might know, "Turkey in the Straw." Before I'd finished, a few adults had wandered over to listen. The next one I played was called "Rosin the Beau." It was an old tune Dad and I had learned from a Cape Breton fiddler. After that, I played a couple of Irish reels and a few people started a sweaty dance right out in front of me.

I'd been playing for a half an hour before I finally earned something. A man in dingy jeans and a faded work shirt leaned down and dropped four small onions in the case. I smiled at him and he shrugged apologetically, but my heart leapt at the idea of something besides tomatoes and lettuce. Onions could really liven up a meal too.

A woman, dressed nicer than anyone I'd seen so far, nudged her two sparkling-clean kids forward. They each put a little money in the case and gave me wide smiles. I grinned back and nodded my thanks. After that, the listeners added half a loaf of bread, two cucumbers, and some cherries. When an old farmer in overalls set a whole pie down next to my case, I smiled big. My grandparents would be excited to see that!

After an hour, I wiped at my dripping forehead with the back of my bow hand and said, "I think I'm about done." The heat of the day pressed down on me and couldn't be good for Jewels either.

"Play one more!" someone shouted.

I ran my bow lightly over the strings, in a thinking sort of way, and tried to come up with something good to leave them with. The fiddle music made me ache for Dad and our evenings playing on the porch together, and I decided on my name-sake song, just for him. Even though everyone at home likes to tease me when I play it, calling me Handsome Molly, no one here knew my name, so I didn't think twice. What did surprise me was that two or three people started singing right away.

> *I wish I was in London*
> *Or some other seaport town*
> *Set my foot in a steamboat*
> *And sail the ocean 'round.*

> *While sailing around the ocean*
> *While sailing around the sea*
> *I'd think of handsome Molly*
> *Wherever she might be.*

The crowd grew larger, and a few more people joined in on the singing. They seemed to know all the verses, so I just kept playing. Finally, we got to the end.

> *Sail around the ocean*
> *Sail around the sea*
> *Think of handsome Molly*
> *Wherever she might be.*

"I know exactly where handsome Molly is," I heard someone say as I drew out the last note. I looked up, saw the guy from the MAX train, and felt a little flutter in my heart. I gave him a big grin, and he shook his sandy hair out of his eyes and smiled back.

And then he placed an icy bottle of root beer next to my

fiddle case. Everyone else had clapped and wandered away, but he came and sat on the tires. I grabbed the pop and collapsed next to him. Not the smartest place to sit, hot tires, in the middle of a summer's day, but I was curious about him.

"Wow," I said. "I haven't had pop in . . . well, I don't know how long. Where'd you get it?"

"Ask me no questions, I'll tell you no lies."

He grinned and I opened the bottle. "You're the best," I said.

"So I've been told." He smiled, and then in a mock-serious voice he said, "Are you lost? Walk straight in that direction and you'll run into Canada eventually."

I laughed. "Oh, you know . . . ," I said, not completely willing to spill the family secrets to a virtual stranger, even a cute one. "I'm visiting for a while before we travel."

He was smiling, but the way his eyes moved around, looking over my shoulder, lively and always scanning the crowd, I had the feeling he was only half with me and already on his way somewhere else.

"What about your big move to Canada?" I asked him.

"Oh, maybe," he said. He took a long swig of his pop. "You never know. Business is good right now."

"What business?"

"Ask me no questions—"

"Yeah, yeah . . . you'll tell me no lies."

"You're a quick one," he said.

"I wish my *cash* business was better." I nudged the fiddle case with my toe. "I'm really glad to have the food, but we could use the money for the trip."

"People save their cash for emergencies. The market's mostly the barter system."

"Same as on our island."

Suddenly he stood up. I followed his gaze. A small man in a suit and tie was making his way through the crowd towards us. "I gotta go," he said, "but maybe I'll stop by your grandparents' house sometime."

The fact he knew where we lived shocked me a little. "You remember the address?" I asked. The guy seemed nice enough, but I couldn't forget the fear in the fare inspectors' eyes when he'd shown them his ID or whatever it was.

"Never forget a face," he said. His cheerful smile relaxed me a little. "Never forget a place or, well, anything, really. Part of the business. See you around, Handsome Molly."

"Okay. Thanks for the root beer."

As he and the small man crossed paths, they nodded hello to each other but didn't speak. The man continued past him and walked up to me, a friendly smile on his face. I pressed the cold bottle against my sweaty forehead. He eyed my fiddle and then my case full of produce.

"Finished playing?" he asked.

"For today." I packed up Jewels while he watched and was about to scoop up my take when he leaned over and picked up the pie.

"I'll take that," he said.

"Oh, that's okay. I've got it."

"You're new around here, right?" he asked, still holding my pie.

"Ummm, yeah."

"Well, let me introduce myself. I'm Randall." He held out his hand and I shook it tentatively. "And one of my jobs is to make sure everyone knows the rules. You see, this market ain't exactly public, if you know what I mean."

I shook my head.

"It's a private enterprise," he said. "And as a private enterprise, the Boss takes a fair share of any profits the vendors make. In other words, the house always wins. Get it?"

"I guess." He was taking my pie as a commission for my being allowed to play at the market?

"A word to the wise," he told me. "You don't play here without clearing it with the Boss first."

"Are you the Boss?"

He laughed. "Oh, no. Not me."

"Well, how do I clear it with the Boss, then?"

"Let's just say you don't."

He tipped his hat and walked off with the pie. I stared after him. My big plan had been to busk every day until I had enough cash to get us home. If I couldn't play here, I was back to square one without any idea what to do next.

14

July 14th—Sow fall vegetable seeds.

THE NEXT MORNING I DID SOME MORE WEEDING, and when I got back to the house, I found my grandparents in the yard, sitting under a knotty lilac. Grandpa seemed to be saying something to Grandma, and she was repeating it, but when I got closer, they stopped talking.

"Do you mind if I look around the house?" I asked them.

"Why not?" Grandpa said. "Maybe you'll find the family silver and save the day!"

"I'm pretty sure that must've gone first," I said. I actually *was* hoping to find something he'd overlooked, though. "I just wanted to check out your house. It's so huge."

Grandpa's thin mouth widened into a big smile. "Four thousand twenty-two square feet."

"What?"

"The house," he said. "That's how big it is."

"Amazing."

What in the world did two people need four thousand square feet for?

After searching the whole upstairs and coming up empty, I went downstairs. At the bottom, you could go one way to the front door, the other way to the living room, or straight ahead to a door that looked different from the others. It was metal, for one thing. Maybe it led outside?

I tried the knob, and the door opened on silent hinges. I stepped out into the most amazing room of all. An almost entirely empty three-car garage. Smack in the middle of it sat a car like I'd never seen before. Well, maybe in the movies that we watched on the computer, but only the really, really old ones from last century.

The car was painted a shimmery blue-green with silvery trim. The back and front windows curved in a way that glass usually doesn't, and something that looked like a streaking silver bird sat on the hood, glimmering in the bit of light that came through the garage windows.

"She's a beauty, isn't she?" Grandpa asked from behind me, making me jump.

"What kind of car is it?"

"A nineteen-fifty-nine Studebaker Lark."

"Wow. That's almost a hundred years old."

"Eighty-two, actually."

"It's gorgeous."

"Yep. And don't even ask about selling it. I've already tried. No one has money for collector cars."

We stared at it, me taking it in, Grandpa reliving his days out on the open road. His shoulders straightened and he seemed to shed twenty years. I imagined him grinning as he drove along, people stopping to turn and stare admiringly.

"Get in, Molly." He opened the passenger door and I slid inside, and then he walked around and got behind the wheel. "There's nothing quite like a Studie."

The bench seat was covered with stiff fabric and trimmed with vinyl. The interior was painted a deeper blue-green, the dials and knobs were glittering chrome, and it smelled of a past I couldn't quite imagine. "It's so clean and new looking," I said.

"Yeah . . . well, I can't let her rot here."

"What do you mean?"

He caressed the dashboard. "I take care of this sweetheart."

I gave him a quizzical look. "Do you think the government will release oil to the public again or something?" I asked.

"What do you think I am? An idiot? Of course they won't. Besides, she doesn't run on gas anymore."

"She doesn't?"

"In 2015, I had her converted to electric, and then in 2027, I upgraded her to a Super Seven Solar battery."

My heart leapt! "We could drive her back to Canada!" I said, bouncing in my seat, making the car rock.

"Stop jumping around! We can't drive her to Canada."

"Why not?"

He glared at me. "Mostly because your grandmother and I aren't going anywhere, but also because her battery's dead."

"But you said it was solar. Can't we charge it?"

"You can only charge them so many times and then they're no good."

I knew all about that because of the Solar Fone.

"This one's a goner," he said. "I'll show you."

We got out of the car and walked to the front. His skinny, undernourished arms shook under the weight of the heavy hood, but he managed to hold it with one hand and prop it up with a little rod. Instead of an engine, there was a gaping hole, a handful of wires, and a small square battery. "See that?" He pointed to the end where the wires were still hooked up. "It's black. That means it's dead beyond hope."

"Maybe we could get a new one."

"And pay for it how?"

"Well, what do you polish the car for," I asked, "if you're never going to drive it again?"

He sighed. "Something to do, I guess. Retirement's kind of boring."

"You know"–I was scheming now–"if you came to Canada with me, there's lots to do. There'd be work on the farm, or fishing, or you could even be a doctor again."

"Molly, I have been stubborn all my life, and to be perfectly honest, it's worked out pretty well. But I *am* sorry about one thing."

"What?" I asked.

"I hate that I passed on that trait to your mother and then she passed it on to you."

"But–"

"I am not sure how to make this any more clear to you," he said. "We're staying here."

"But my mom needs you. And she wants to see Grandma."

He pulled the brace out from the hood and let it slam. "Do you not understand what a trip like that would do to Katharine? She's not well, Molly." He ran his hands through the little hair he had left. "How can you ask me to take that chance?" He pushed past me and headed for the house.

15

July 16th—Gardening is not a single act, but a series of experiences.
—Katherine Gordon

FOR TWO DAYS, I'D BEEN WEEDING IN THE GARDEN from dawn until about noon. Mr. Edwards hadn't said much, except to ask me to please stop calling him mister.

"I was just being adverse when I said that," he told me. "Call me Doug."

We didn't talk much, even when he weeded right next to me, but I had Brandy to keep me company. She was a chatterbox, and I liked it because it kept me from worrying about Mom, wondering about Katie's wedding plans, and hoping someone had taken over my garden chores so that we'd have a good harvest this year. It also kept me from worrying whether I'd ever figure out how to get enough money for train tickets.

When the sun was right overhead, I stood up and stretched. Brandy had been following me like a shadow all morning, but Michael had spent his time in the shade, playing with a box of dirt and a bunch of slimy worms.

"Hey, Brandy, guess what?" I said.

She jumped up, bouncing around like a puppy. "What? What? What?"

"I have reeeeeeallly itchy fingers."

"You do?" she asked, her blue eyes growing wide. "How come? Did you get bit by a mosquito?"

"Noooo," I said, taking her grubby hand and leading her over to the deck. "They're itching to play the fiddle! Let's have some music!" I tickled her with wiggling fingers, and she squealed.

"Yay! Can I play the fiddle too? Can I?" she asked.

"I think I need someone to *dance!*" I said, nixing that idea.

I'd left Jewels on the deck in the shade, and I unpacked her from her case. She was still close to in tune from my morning practice session, but the E string had definitely slipped. "This is a dancing song," I said, making the adjustment and running the bow over the string. "Can you move your feet like this?" I tapped my bare foot on the deck.

"*Yes!*"

"How about you, Michael?" I called.

He looked up from his worms, uncertain about whether he wanted to come over or not, but he stayed put. I can't really dance and play at the same time, but I am able to do the steps if I'm sitting, so I plopped down into one of the deck chairs. My feet were still sore, but getting a lot better.

A second later, I was in tune and ready to go. Quick, sharp movements across the strings sent the notes flying into the air. One foot kept time and the other did the steps while Brandy jumped and bounced around on the deck, her bare feet slapping against the warm wood.

As soon as I'd started to play for real, Michael had dropped his worms and come right up to me. But he didn't dance. Instead, he stood there, about two feet away, staring at my fingers and the bow, his eyes wide and his mouth in a little O. Brandy tried to pull him away, but he was frozen in front of me. I knew exactly how he felt. There was nothing like a fiddle!

Brandy danced herself around, squealing with laughter. "Faster!" I yelled, picking up the tempo. She spun and jumped up and down. "Now, slower!" I changed to a waltz. She didn't know how to waltz any more than she knew how to dance a reel, but it was fun watching her change her steps and move slowly to the timing of the music. I'd been playing for about fifteen minutes when she collapsed in a heap of giggles onto the deck, panting.

"Too hot," she gasped.

When Michael realized I was finished, he walked silently back to his dirt and started digging again. About half an hour before that, Doug had disappeared down to the creek with a pair of rusty shears, and now he came up through the garden to us.

"I have to go to the market," he said.

"What about the kids?" I asked.

"They're fine. They know not to go anywhere."

"You're joking, right?" He wouldn't leave them there alone, would he?

"We always stay home by ourselves," Brandy said. "I take good care of Michael. Don't I, Uncle?"

"You sure do," he said. He ruffled her tangled brown hair and she beamed at him.

I didn't know what to do. I considered taking them back

with me, but I had to hand-wash all our clothes and hang them out to dry, and then Grandpa and I had to try to find some firewood somewhere. Brandy and Michael were his kids, after all. He should know if they'd be okay or not.

"Well . . . all right," I said. "See you guys tomorrow."

When I got down to the end of the yard, I saw that Doug had cut the blackberry bushes back away from the fence, leaving an easy path into my grandparents' yard. Sitting in the grass was a large, neat pile of produce too. Doug hadn't said much about my help, so it was nice to see he actually did appreciate me.

It was a balancing act carrying the squash, lettuce, tomatoes, green onions, spinach, and Jewels, but I managed. Grandpa was dozing in the shade, and I hated to wake him up, but I didn't know where Grandma was and I needed someone to open the door.

"Hey, Grandpa," I said. "Look what Doug gave us."

"What? Huh?" He sat up and adjusted his glasses.

"Could you open the French doors for me?"

"Sure."

He pulled himself up off the blanket he'd spread on the lawn and led the way up the steps. It took a second for our eyes to adjust to the dimness of the cool, dark living room, and when it did, we were both too surprised to speak.

Sitting on the couch chatting away with my grandma was the guy who had walked with me to Pioneer Square and brought me the root beer at the market.

"Hi, Handsome Molly," he said, smiling.

16

GRANDPA STEPPED FORWARD TOWARDS THE GUY.
"Who are you?" he demanded.

"I'm a friend of Molly's," he said.

He smiled, stood up, and held out his hand, but Grandpa
was looking at me for confirmation. "You know him?" he
asked.

I nodded. "Yeah . . . he's the one I told you about that helped
me on the MAX."

Grandma started talking to the guy again. A lot of the time
she could say single words very clearly, but sentences seemed to
elude her, and when she tried, her conversations sounded more
like gibberish mixed with the occasional swearword. Today, she
was animated, and the guy looked enthralled, even though I
couldn't understand anything she was saying. Was he just being
polite? I was starting to get the idea he was pretty nice, and it
made me want to know more about him.

"What are you doing here?" I asked, finally breaking into
the conversation.

"Nice to see you too, Handsome Molly," the guy said.

The sunburn had faded, and his nose was peeling.

"Well, yeah. . . ." I could feel myself blushing. "That's what I meant. I was just surprised. I see you've met my grandma."

"Yep."

He smiled and I blushed harder for some stupid reason. He acted like a nice guy, but I wasn't really sure how I felt about him memorizing my grandparents' address just because I'd shown it to him on the MAX. That seemed a little creepy.

But he was here now, so I decided to be polite. I set the produce on the end table and wiped my dirty hands on the back of my shorts. Then I reached up and undid my ponytail, letting hair fall around my face. I hoped it wasn't too sweaty and gross.

"Come," Grandma said to me. She took my arm and led me to the kitchen counter. Grandpa and the guy followed us. With shaky hands, she unwrapped a small brown-paper package and then she peeled off an inner layer of HyperFoil. She smiled at me as I gazed at a slab of some kind of red meat, the ice crystals still clinging to the marbled fat.

"What is it?" I asked.

"Beef," the guy said.

"You brought this?" I asked him.

He nodded. I stared at him. "Ummm, that's very nice of you, but–"

"You don't have to be afraid of it," he said. "This is organic, free-range. I know the farmer personally."

It wasn't that I didn't trust him, exactly. It just seemed risky. Practically the whole world had given up beef back in 2031.

Millions of herds had been slaughtered because cattle had developed an unstoppable virus that had caused over two hundred thousand human deaths. I was not going to eat beef, and I didn't want my grandparents to either.

The only cows on our island were milk cows, so it hadn't affected us, but even I remember seeing worldwide riots on the web news, calling for the governments to do something. It had destroyed the fast-food industry overnight and caused unprecedented unemployment. Even though it had been labeled the Second Factor in the Great Collapse of 2031, some people thought it was an even bigger reason for the Collapse than the First Factor, which was when the government took over petroleum. Only organic farms were spared, and even a lot of those lost their herds.

"The truth is," I said, trying to sound diplomatic, "I don't have any idea what to do with it."

"Ever cook a chicken?" he asked.

"Well . . . ours are mostly for eggs, but I've made chicken stew," I said.

"Same idea," he said.

We were smiling at each other, but I was pretty sure I was going to throw it away after he left, and somehow I got the feeling he knew that.

"Why don't we sit on the deck?" Grandpa suggested. "Your grandma looks tired, and she can lie on the blanket under the tree."

"I really have to go," the guy said.

"What's your name?" I finally asked, since he still hadn't offered it up.

"Ever read *The Borrowers*?" he asked.

"Of course!" Grandpa exclaimed.

"Yes!" I said. "I love those books."

"Remember Spiller?"

"The guy who brings the family meat?" Grandpa asked.

"That's the one," he said. "Just call me Spiller."

Grandpa and I started laughing. Grandma tried to say it, but all she managed was "Spillllll."

"Hey, I like that better," he told Grandma. "Spill it is. I really better go now."

I kind of liked this guy. I mean, he'd read *The Borrowers*! But how strange was it he wouldn't tell us his name? Maybe it was something horrible like Herbert or Reginald. I was torn. Part of me wanted to get to know him, but I was still a little concerned about how he'd just knocked on our door like we were old friends. What had he told Grandma to get her to let him inside? Or would she just open the door to anyone? If she did, that would explain why Grandpa had slammed it on me that first day.

"You could stay for dinner," I suggested.

He gave me a small smile that said he could tell it was a halfhearted invitation, which made me kind of embarrassed that I hadn't been more enthusiastic.

"Maybe next time," he said. "I really have to go now, though."

"I'll walk you out," I offered.

"Hey, wait a minute, Molly," Grandpa said. He pulled me off to the side. "If this guy can get beef, he's obviously got connections. You should ask him if he can get you on CyberSpeak. To let your parents know you're okay."

"Nah," I said. "I already called them on the phone."

"But they need to know . . . well, our . . . circumstances."

"I've got it under control," I said.

This Spill guy was nice enough, but I already felt weird about him bringing us meat as a gift. Plus there was something oddly secretive about him. I was not going to ask for favors.

"Spill?" Grandpa said. "Do you know anyone on Cyber-Speak? Molly needs to talk to her parents."

"I'll handle it myself," I said to Grandpa, giving him a bug-eyed look.

"Sure," Spill said. "Well, actually, maybe not CyberSpeak, but email. Do you know anyone with an email address?"

"Of course she does," Grandpa said.

"Yes," I answered, glaring at him.

"Next time I have to make a delivery out this way," Spill said, "I'll stop by and pick you up. Okay?"

I was annoyed with Grandpa, but I forced myself to smile. "That would be great. Thanks."

The two of us went outside. As I watched him unlock his bike, I was hit with a wave of longing. "I wish I had my bicycle," I said.

"If you had it, you could ride it back to Canada. There's a great trail all the way from Portland to Seattle."

I laughed. "I can just see myself hauling my grandparents behind me in a little trailer like yours all the way back to B.C."

"When are you leaving, anyway?" he asked.

"Well . . ." Did I really want to admit to him that we were broke? I guess it wasn't a crime or anything. Lots of people were poor. "We're a little short on the train fare," I said. "I just need to find something to sell."

"Really good booze is about the only thing you can get cold, hard cash for," he said.

"What do you mean, *really good*?"

"Imported. Rich people like the good stuff."

"Well, no luck there. We don't even have the bad stuff."

Spill got on his bike.

"Just so you know," I said, "you don't *have* to take me to send an email. I'll figure something out on my own."

"It's not a problem. But you do have to promise me one thing."

"What's that?"

"You can't tell anyone where I take you."

"Ummm, okay. I promise. But you won't get in trouble, will you?" I asked.

"Only if we get caught."

As I watched him ride away, I wondered where he would be taking me that was such a secret.

17

GRANDPA AND I WERE PICKING OUR WAY ALONG
the creek that ran behind the house. I wanted to make a stew,
and Grandpa had suggested I build a fire in his stone fountain
on the sunporch, but we needed fuel. We'd scoured the underbrush close by for anything we could burn but hadn't found
much, so we were expanding our search.

"It's those squatters," Grandpa mumbled. He pushed his
glasses up the bridge of his sweaty nose. Even in the heat he
was wearing pants and a button-down long-sleeve shirt.

"What do you mean?" I asked. I added a few small branches
to the burlap sack. We'd found it in the garage and were using
it to hold anything we were lucky enough to get.

"When times got tough," he explained, "most of our neigh-
bors moved away to live with their grown kids. For a while,
your grandma and I were practically the only ones on the
whole street. Now squatters live in almost every house. And
they've already collected all the firewood."

"Are they . . . dangerous?"

"Oh, probably not." He added a long, skinny branch to the bag and it stuck out the top. "They're just homeless, I guess. But you should be careful. Don't talk about the garden to anyone. You don't want Doug to have to defend it."

"Really? Would he have to?"

"Well," Grandpa said, "that's why he came here last summer. His sister and her husband asked him to because they *said* they needed a guard at night."

"Wow."

"I don't think they really needed one, though," Grandpa explained. "His sister, Courtney, she knew Doug was down on his luck, but he wouldn't take her charity, so I think she made up a story about people stealing from the garden at night."

From what I knew about Doug, that sounded about right. He would've wanted to seem useful if he was going to live off his sister. Grandpa added a few pinecones to the bag to use as fire starters while I sat on a boulder and dug a stone out of my sandal.

"His sister and husband lived here last year?" I asked. "You mean they died that recently?"

For some reason, I thought it had been a while. I guess because of the way Brandy talked about it like it was no big deal. Of course, when you're six, even a few months is a long time. I picked up some sticks for kindling.

Grandpa nodded. "Flu," he said. "Over the winter. Both the husband and wife, and the baby too. I guess Doug didn't know I was a doctor. He never asked for help."

"That's just awful," I said. My nose prickled in that funny

way like when you're about to tear up over something sad but you're not actually going to cry. "He never told me."

Grandpa put an arm around my shoulder and gave me a squeeze. "Yeah, well . . . he used to be a lot more friendly. We talked some last summer, but since they died . . . he keeps to himself. At least he did until you forced your way into the garden."

He smiled at me, so I knew he was just teasing. We'd reached the end of the housing development and the creek disappeared into some woods. There was a big sign that said PRIVATE PROPERTY and three strings of barbed wire blocking our way.

"Can you get through the fence if I hold the wire up?" Grandpa asked.

"Probably, but I don't want to get shot or anything."

"Ah, don't worry about it. I know the guy who owns this land."

He grabbed the top wire and lifted it, and I scooted in between, grazing my calf.

"Ow."

"You're fine," he said.

"Gee, thanks! Are you coming?"

"No way. I'm too old to run if we have to make a quick getaway." He saw the shocked look on my face and laughed. "I'm kidding. I'm kidding. Ben Jamieson was a doctor at the hospital with me. He's pretty good with a golf club, but I doubt he's ever shot a gun. Besides, he lives way on the other side of the property. Just go look in the underbrush for a few logs."

I sighed. I hoped Grandpa knew what he was doing. Or

rather, what I was doing! I walked along the creek into the deep shadows of the fir trees. Silence enveloped me, and the scent of pine made my heart churn with homesickness. If only I knew how Mom was doing . . . Maybe now that she'd heard Grandma was alive, her mind had eased. I hoped so.

The squatters had obviously ignored the PRIVATE PROPERTY sign too and weren't concerned about getting shot because there was a beaten footpath along the creek and not much wood in the brush. What was there was mostly too big to haul away. Off the path I found enough branches to fill the bag until it was too heavy to carry. We went back for three loads before we called it quits. In the yard, Grandpa and I collapsed on the blanket next to Grandma, hot, sweaty, and exhausted.

"Wait," she said, getting up.

"Oh, we're not going anywhere," I told her.

She came back with two tall glasses of water, and Grandpa and I drank them down gratefully. Then I got up to stack the wood somewhere dry. The sky was so empty and blue that it didn't look like it would ever rain again, but you couldn't be too careful.

"Just leave it on the grass," Grandpa said. "Your grandma will stack it under the eaves."

"Oh, that's okay," I said. "I can take care of it."

"No," he said. "I want her to do it as part of her physiotherapy."

"What do you mean?" I asked.

"Me," Grandma said. "I'll do it."

I watched her pick up a few sticks in her scrawny arms and carry them towards the house.

"For a while," Grandpa said, "she was making really good progress. We did physio and speech therapy every day, but then she just lost interest. I think she was depressed. She seems happier now that you're here, and I'm determined to get her doing stuff again."

"Well . . . all right. If you say so."

I smiled to myself. I couldn't help thinking he might just be getting Grandma in shape to make the trip back to Canada.

It wasn't quite the eleventh hour when we sat down to steaming bowls of vegetable stew, but it was close. Grandpa didn't think we should eat the meat either, and he'd thrown it in the burn pile he had going on the other side of the creek.

"Who taught you to cook?" he asked.

"Mom."

"Breeee," Grandma said.

"Is the stew all right?" I asked.

"It's okay," he said. And then he laughed. "It's great. Thanks."

The spoon gave Grandma too much trouble because of the paralysis on one side of her mouth so she slurped hers directly from the bowl. She managed to get down two full servings, which said exactly what she thought of it, and my heart soared. I couldn't take care of my own mother right now, but I could feed my grandmother to help get her strong and restore her health.

We'd been outside all afternoon and evening, but I hadn't heard Doug or the kids through the fence like I usually did. He had to be home from the market by now, didn't he? I decided to take them some stew, and I made my way through the garden by moonlight. Doug's electricity was turned off too.

"Brandy? Michael?"

"Molly?" answered a tiny voice.

"Yeah, it's me. Where are you guys?"

By the time I got to the French doors, they were standing there peering out at me. "How come you don't have a lantern? Where's your uncle?"

"He's not back yet," Brandy said.

Michael stood silently by her side. He still hadn't said a single word to me in the week I'd been here, no matter how I'd tried coaxing him. In fact, I hadn't heard him talk to anyone and wondered if he could.

"Come out here and have some stew," I said. "I'll get some bowls from inside."

The house was laid out almost exactly like Grandma and Grandpa's, but the only furniture was a lumpy-looking couch and two cots where the kids obviously slept. I found some bowls, spoons, and a lantern in the kitchen and took it all back outside, where I dished up warm stew.

"Have you eaten anything?" I asked.

They shook their heads as they spooned the food into their mouths, chomping like starving animals.

"Is your uncle usually gone this long?"

Brandy shrugged. "Sometimes."

"When you're finished, I think you should go to bed."

"I don't want to," Brandy whined.

"If you crawl into your cots," I said, "I'll run home and get my fiddle and play you some tunes to help you sleep."

"Really? Okay!" she agreed.

"Into bed, then."

For all her protests, Brandy was sound asleep when I got back with Jewels. I played a few quiet lullabies, but Michael lay there, wide-eyed, watching me. Some people can't sleep when there's music playing, so I quit after a while and settled onto the couch to wait.

I must've fallen asleep because, when something crashed in the hallway, I woke up disoriented and confused. A second crash brought me to my feet. The lantern was still burning, but very faintly, and I looked around for something to defend myself with. Brandy turned over on her cot, but didn't wake. Michael sat up, startled. I'd just picked up my fiddle case to use as a weapon when Doug stumbled into the room. I could smell the booze on him from where I stood.

"Shhhhhh," he said really loudly. "They're sleeping." And then he swayed forward and crumpled to the floor.

18

July 21st–Never refuse any advance of friendship, for if nine out of ten
bring you nothing, one alone may repay you.
–Madame de Tencin

DOUG NEVER MENTIONED COMING HOME DRUNK, so I didn't either. After a week, I'd found myself in a daily rhythm. I'd weed each morning, and sometimes he'd join me—other times he wouldn't. Then I'd go back to my room and lose myself in music, playing Jewels for two or three hours. It was impossible to worry about Mom with the notes running through my mind.

One night I had a horrible dream that my mother had died, and the next day, even the music wouldn't block out the image of my sister Katie weeping and telling me I'd failed my family. I packed Jewels in her case, feeling angry that she'd let me down somehow.

I didn't want my grandparents to see my bad mood, so I walked down to the market in the lazy afternoon sunshine. I'd never really explored it, except the produce stalls. This time I wandered down a row of stands selling goods, things like over-alls, fabric, and yarn. Most of the material was sturdy cotton, used for making work dresses and shirts, but at one stall, a woman sat in a chair and all around her drapes of silky fabrics floated colorfully on the breeze.

"These are beautiful," I said.

She nodded. My hand reached out and touched a piece of sky-blue silk. It was exactly the color that Katie had been talking about me wearing at her wedding. So far I had refused to believe I might not make it back in time. I had to be there. You don't miss a family wedding. Especially your sister's. Tears welled up in my eyes. The idea of not being at Katie's wedding combined with my horrible nightmare was just too much. I had to get home, and I had to do it soon.

"Hi, Handsome Molly," Spill said. He'd come around the end of the aisle. "I've been looking for you everywhere."

His eyes were so warm, like he was happy to see me, and his look washed away a bit of my homesickness. I tried to smile back, but I knew it looked forced. "Hi."

"You okay?" he asked.

"Yeah, sure." I brushed at a tear. "Just dust in my eye."

He looked at me like he knew the truth, but he didn't press me. "I went to the house to get you," he said, pushing his hair away from his face, "and your grandpa said you were here. I have to make that delivery now, and I was hoping you could come along."

This was exactly what I needed! A chance to tell my parents I was okay, and maybe there'd even be a message from one of them. "I don't want to get you in any trouble," I said, "but it would be so great to email my parents. I know they're worried. I've been gone almost two weeks already."

"No problem," he said. "I just need to get my bike and cart."

We wove our way through the market into the scary part and walked past one of the tents where men were playing cards. I thought I saw Doug, but I didn't stop to double-check. It wasn't like I was going to talk to him if he was there anyway.

"I don't really like this section," I told Spill.

"You're okay as long as you're with me." I moved a bit closer to him. "Why were you crying just now?" he asked.

"I wasn't."

"You *were*."

"Okay, I was. But . . . it's just . . . I'm supposed to be in a wedding, maid of honor for my sister . . . and that blue silk reminded me of it."

"When's the big day?"

"Not until the end of September. The thing is, I'm good at farmwork, but I'm a really slow seamstress. I'd pretty much have to start making my dress now in order to have it done."

We'd reached the edge of the market, and Spill stopped at a white tent. "Wait here," he said. A few minutes later he came out pushing his bike. He'd replaced his usual small trailer with one that was much larger than I would've thought you could pull with a bicycle.

It had high sides and was wide enough that I bet you could put two big bales of hay in it. Of course, then it would be too heavy to move without a horse, so it wouldn't do you much good. Mysterious things bulged under the tarp.

"You'll have to walk," he said. "I'll let you ride on the way home."

"That's fine."

He rode up the hill towards my grandparents' house, and I followed on foot. In spite of the hill, and his load, he kept up a good clip.

"Okay," I panted after a few minutes. "Just tell me where we're going and I'll meet you there."

"Sorry," he said. "I was trying to go slow. I guess maybe you'll have to ride in the trailer after all." He stopped, peeked under the tarp, and then told me I could sit on one of the crates he had near the back.

"Are you sure?" I asked. "I don't see how you can pull it at all, and with me in there–"

"It's a military trailer," he said. "The tires are a special design, extremely high pressure, and made to have the least amount of rolling resistance possible. You want to try pulling it?"

So instead of getting in, I took a seat on the bike while Spill jogged alongside me. The trailer was definitely heavy, but nothing like what I'd expected. It rolled along so smoothly, without any friction, making the load feel like it was propelling itself. We definitely needed one of these for the farm. After a few minutes, he took over riding again, and I sat in the back. The road twisted and climbed through more neighborhoods with overgrown shrubs and trees crowding together.

"Spill? Can I ask you a question?"

"I might not be able to answer it."

"It's not about you. It's about my grandparents."

"I definitely won't be able to answer it, then," he said, laughing. "I hardly know them."

"I'm just wondering why if they were rich enough to buy such a nice house, and my grandpa was a doctor for so long, they don't have any money."

"My guess is no liquid assets."

"What do you mean?"

Spill was pulling us up a pretty steep hill, but he never lost his breath at all and continued to talk normally. "People with old money are still rich," he explained. "And there have always been, and always will be, the poor."

We reached the top of the hill, and the road flattened out into open countryside.

"For a while," he continued, "there were people like your grandparents, who earned good salaries and reinvested their savings in technology and real estate. They made money fast, but it was mostly on paper. They were rich in assets but usually had a ton of debt. When the Collapse came, they lost everything."

"Oh."

"The truly rich knew that the oil was almost gone and that the governments of the bigger countries would have to make a move of some sort," he continued. "People with money were connected. They had inside information and knew once the oil was gone, everything would collapse. It was pretty obvious the U.S. would be hit the hardest because all the way through the twenties we still had an oil-based economy."

This all sounded vaguely familiar. Maybe I should've paid more attention in school instead of thinking about music all the time.

"The smartest thing the wealthy did," Spill said, "was trade their U.S. dollars for gold and euros. Everyone knew Europe would fare better after the impending crash."

"Because they'd been preparing for it for fifty years, right?" I said. I guess I had been listening a little in history class.

"Right."

We'd gone about eight kilometers when Spill turned down a gravel road. Ahead of us stood a monster house! This must be what Mom and Dad call a Pasture Palace. It was pale-pink brick with arched windows and two chimneys that reached up to the sky. I stared at it in awe. This house was at least twice as big as my grandfather's four-thousand-square-foot castle.

The gravel gave way to a long brick drive that led almost to the front of the house but then curved to the left. We passed through an archway and came around to the back. In the distance was a lake. Not a pond, but an actual lake in their backyard.

"Okay. Here's the deal," Spill said. "Mr. Polodichuck probably won't come down because he doesn't like to talk to 'the help,' and Mrs. Polodichuck is usually resting in her room at this time of day. Mrs. Miller is the housekeeper, and she'll let you inside."

"To use the computer?"

"Well . . . actually, you're going to have to be sneaky about it because there's no way they'd let you use it. That's why you can't use CyberSpeak. It keeps a record of your conversation. Email's more secure because you have to sign in to your account."

"Are you sure this is a good idea?" My stomach already had butterflies.

"Come on," he said. "Don't worry." He pushed the bike and trailer up close to the back door. "Once you're in the kitchen, there's a little built-in desk for housekeeping stuff. I used the computer once to check on an order, so I know it's there. Okay?"

"I guess. . . ." This did not sound good.

"Just use it quick and get out of there."

"Won't she notice?"

"I have to stack everything outside the door, and Mrs. Miller stands out here with me, checking things off the list."

"What happens if we get caught?"

"We're not gonna get caught. Be bold, Handsome Molly."

I took a deep breath for courage. I could do this, I told myself. I'd done a lot scarier things in the last two weeks.

"Okay. Let's go."

He took the tarp off the trailer and handed me a large wooden box. I'm strong, but my knees buckled under the weight. "My God, what's in here?"

"Sherry," he said.

I set the box down beside the pile he had started by the door. Sherry? Hadn't Spill told me that booze was really hard to get? He'd said he was a delivery boy, but I was starting to worry about who he might work for.

"If anyone asks, say you're with Quinn," he told me.

"Ha! Now I know your name."

He just shook his head. "Like these people know my *real* one."

"Oh." How many names did he have?

I straightened my sweaty shirt while he knocked on the kitchen door. A woman in a long, black housedress answered, and a whoosh of cold air streamed out of the doorway. Unbelievable. They actually had air-conditioning. I'd heard of it, but I didn't know anyone who could afford it.

"You're late, Quinn," Mrs. Miller said.

"Sorry. I'll unload quickly."

"I'll get my clipboard," she said.

"Wait. Mrs. Miller? This is my cousin Miranda. I was just wondering if she could come inside for a minute and sit down. The heat's really getting to her."

I made my face go kind of slack to look like I didn't feel good.

"Oh, I don't know, Quinn," she said, looking over her shoulder. "The rules—"

"I know, but . . . I thought the air-conditioning . . . well, never mind. Maybe she can just go down to the lake and splash some water on her face."

"No, no . . . that's not a good idea. Mr. Polodichuck wouldn't like her down by his boat." She studied me. "All right, come in for just a minute, Miranda."

I smiled feebly and followed her inside.

"Sit there," she said, pointing to the little desk chair. "I'll get you some water."

Spill was standing in the doorway, and I gave him the thumbs-up. The air was as cool as the creek in the spring! I gulped in satisfying deep breaths. She handed me a glass of water with ice in it, and then the two of them went outside and shut the door. I was in! I turned to face the desk, but I couldn't see a computer anywhere. Would they have moved it? Spill seemed so sure this would be easy.

Think, Molly, think.

Of course! It was built into the desk. I ran my fingers under the edge and found the power button. An infrared keyboard appeared instantly and the wall lit up, showing the desktop. High-definition projection. Wow! The color was so strong and three dimensional that I wanted to reach out and grab the spinning apple and take a bite.

Spill's voice outside the kitchen snapped me out of my daze and reminded me to hurry. I typed in my info to bring up my email program, but nothing happened. The apple continued to spin, antagonizing me. Did I need a password? How could I possibly guess?

"Damn," I said aloud.

"May I help you?" asked a smooth computer voice.

I jumped. It was voice activated. "Zippee email site," I whispered.

"One moment."

The screen instantly changed to Zippee and the sign-in page. I typed my name into the box, but nothing showed up.

"What the—"

"May I help you?" asked the computer's cool voice again.

"Quiet!" This time when I tapped a few keys and swore the computer asked in a quieter voice if it could help. "Keyboard," I growled, realizing how stupid I'd been.

Keyboard is now active ran along the bottom of the projection.

I signed in. There were a few old emails from some school friends, but I didn't have time to read them. Quickly I typed in email addresses for Mom, Dad, Katie, and Aunt Poppy, and then I wrote my message.

> I'm all right. Still with Grandma & Grandpa. Will rtn
> ASAP. No $. Working on it. Don't worry. Love, M
> P.S. Tell Mom to stay in bed.
> P.P.S. Delay the wedding! PLEASE!!!!!

I hit send, and relief washed over me like the air conditioner, but then I heard a noise in another part of the house. Footsteps! I quickly typed *shutdown,* and the computer's projection and the keyboard disappeared. I jumped up and ran for the door, slipping out and closing it quietly behind me.

"Everything okay, Miranda?" Spill asked.

"Fine. Everything's fine. Thanks."

"Glad to hear it," he said, winking at me.

I looked at the stack of boxes he'd unloaded. Sherry, fruit, a freezer box with HYPERFOIL FOR ALL YOUR NEEDS printed on the side, which was probably full of meat. I kind of admired that he could get things the average person couldn't, but it also scared me a little. Who was this guy? And did I really want to owe him?

19

July 29th–Don't throw away the old bucket until you know
whether the new one holds water.
–Scandinavian proverb

ONE MORNING DOUG AND I WERE FILLING WATER
jugs at the outside tap when Grandpa showed up with a surprise.
He stood there, grinning, with a green garden hose in his hand.

"Maybe this would help," he said.

"Do you know how hard hoses are to come by?" Doug
asked.

"Well, yeah . . . that's why I didn't want to lend it to you.
In case it got ruined . . . but, well"–Grandpa wrinkled his nose,
which I'd noticed he did when it was hard for him to admit
something–"you've helped my family out quite a bit, and . . . I'm
grateful."

The kids came running over from where they'd been exam-
ining Michael's worm colony.

"What is it?" Brandy asked.

"Oh, let me show you!" I grabbed the hose from Grandpa
and hooked it up. Water squirted out the end, and I sprayed it
in an arc, laughing. "This is great! Thanks!"

"Yeah, thanks," Doug said, and he actually smiled.

"Watch out! You should never trust a teenager with a hose!" I turned the water on Grandpa's legs and he laughed, and jumped around like a chicken.

"Spray me! Spray me!" yelled Brandy.

"Me too!" Michael said.

I was so surprised Michael had spoken I accidentally dropped the hose, and it flipped around like a snake getting all our feet wet. He *could* talk! I picked up the hose and squirted their legs. Brandy took Michael's hands, and they danced in and out of the water.

"Time to get back to work," I said, after they were sufficiently drenched.

At lunchtime, Doug suggested that we celebrate our high-tech irrigation system with cheese and bread to go with dinner. He went off to the market to get it, but six hours later, he still wasn't back, so we ate without him. By nine o'clock, Brandy's and Michael's eyes were drooping with sleep, but I didn't want to take them back to an empty house.

"I guess they could sleep upstairs with me," I told my grandparents.

"I'd rather they were on the ground floor," Grandpa said. "I don't want them getting confused and falling down any stairs. Let's put them in our bedroom."

"All right," I agreed.

Grandma and I made up the foldout couch for them in the master suite, and we tucked the kids in together, and then I played Jewels for them for a while.

In the morning, I went to water the garden, but the hose was gone.

I was so mad I was just sitting on our deck with my arms crossed when Grandpa came outside.

"Don't you need to water?" he asked.

"I don't feel like it," I snapped. And then I explained about the missing hose. The thing was, the thought of all those thirsty plants relying on me made me feel too guilty to just sit there. "Fine," I said. I stormed over to the garden.

Grandpa followed me to Doug's and helped me water in silence. After a while, Grandma came around into the garden for the first time ever, led by Brandy and Michael, who were each holding one of her hands.

Grandma seemed to want to work, so I gave them a job and watched from across the beds as they picked bright red cherry tomatoes, dropping them into a basket. Ever since we'd played in the water with the hose, Michael had started talking to us all, and the three of them were giggling like crazy together. I worked my way across the hills of squash until I was close enough to hear. It was as if Grandma was speaking a foreign language that only the children could understand.

Grandma: *Something totally incoherent.*

Brandy: *"I like that part too, but my favorite is when Pooh gets stuck in Rabbit's hole."*

Grandma: *More mumbling that made no sense to me.*

Michael: *"I love that story!"*

All three of them burst into laughter. How was it the kids could understand Grandma so well, but I couldn't? When I tried asking Brandy about it later, she just opened her wide blue eyes and stared at me like I was the one speaking in tongues.

We didn't see Doug for two days, and when he did finally straggle into the yard, he was unshaven, dirty, and had a black eye. He staggered into the house and didn't come out. I took the kids home with me that night too because I hadn't seen him again. If he noticed they were missing, he didn't come looking for them.

"So, are you a drunk, or what?" I asked when he wandered out onto the patio the next morning.

"Lay off, Molly," he said. "I have it under control."

"Oh, well, excuse me for taking care of your kids while you just disappeared for forty-eight hours."

"They're not my kids."

I looked around for something to throw at him. There were a lot of things to choose from, all of them ripe. Tomatoes, runner beans, squash, zucchini, peppers. How about a thunk across the head with an ear of corn? Instead, I took a deep breath and let a fiddle tune run through my mind to calm me down.

"I'll make you a deal," I said.

He sighed and laid his head on the patio table. "What's that?"

"I'll help you get the harvest in, preserve it, store it, whatever you want to do, and you give me half."

"Molly?" he said, and then he groaned. "Could you leave me alone? My head hurts."

"Do we have an agreement or not?"

"If I say yes, will you go away?"

"Sure."

"Yes. Fine. We have a deal."

"But you have to stay sober until the job's done."

"Whatever. Okay?"

"It's a deal, then?"

"Yes, yes, yes." He raised his head. "Did you want to shake on it or something?"

"Nah . . . I trust you," I said. Although I wasn't sure why I did.

Even though Doug had made me mad earlier, I practically danced through the rest of my work that day. This was it! It meant a longer delay in getting home than I wanted, but the prospect of having half the harvest to sell thrilled me. This was our ticket back to Canada for sure. And even though it would take weeks, Mom wasn't due until the first of November. If my dad could keep her calm and maybe even in bed, we could make it. And I could use the time to convince my grandparents to come back home with me.

20

August 8th—Uncle Ralph says,
"Hot enough for ya?"

IDEALLY YOU PLANT THINGS SO THEY DON'T ALL ripen at once, but there's still a time called peak harvest when you have to work fast, no matter what big plans you have. Anyway, one day we were picking *bits of this* and a *few of that,* and the next, we were overwhelmed with all we had to do as soon as possible.

Zucchinis the size of my thigh covered the ground, tomatoes in every stage, from green to perfect to rotting, called for our attention. Corn bulged on the stalks, ripe and sweet, most of it ready at once because Doug hadn't known to plant it in stages. Cucumbers that would've been perfect for pickles grew too long and too fat to fit in jars. Still, they could be sliced or made into relish as long as we got to them soon. Our real problem was how to save the food for the winter.

It had been a muggy week since Doug's last disappearing act, and he seemed normal and cheerful, so I decided not to worry about it. We'd worked all morning, and I'd gone home to make my grandparents' lunch, leaving the kids with Doug, feasting on fat blackberries that they'd picked down by the creek. When I came back, the three of them were playing cards.

"What's your bet?" Doug asked Michael.

Michael studied the playing cards in his hands. "Four blackberries."

"You're bluffing," Brandy said.

"Are you in or out?" Doug asked her.

"You're teaching them to gamble?" I asked.

"I wasn't *teaching* them," he said, laughing. "They already know how. Are you in for the next hand?"

I shook my head. "No, thanks. I hate cards." I didn't tell him that it's mostly because I'm not a good loser.

"I'm winning," Brandy said.

"Well, I think you better just eat those blackberries because Doug and I need to walk the garden and make a plan for preserving this food."

She stuffed a handful of berries into her mouth and smiled at us, showing purple teeth. Doug laughed and then got up and followed me over to the corn. I peeled back the green husk and silk. "Looks pretty ripe. Do you think we can get some jars?"

He smiled big. "Today's our lucky day. I have a pretty nice wad of cash."

"Really? Where'd you get it?"

He smiled and raised his eyebrows at me. "I don't always play for blackberries."

"Oh. Right."

"So if I can find the stuff, do you know how to can the food?"

I burst out laughing. "You've got to be kidding! I've been preserving food since the cradle. Don't you know how?"

"Why would I?" he asked.

"Well, you've planted a pretty big garden. What were you going to do with it all?"

"I'm not really sure," he admitted. "My sister and her husband were the gardeners. They built all these beds a couple of years ago." Doug's face tightened, the little lines on his forehead deepening. "Over the winter–"

"Grandpa told me what happened," I said, cutting him off so he didn't have to explain. I kicked at a clod of dirt with my bare foot, not looking at him.

"Yeah, well . . ." Doug shook his head like he was trying to clear away the memories. "I figured I better plant the garden so we'd have something to eat this year, but that's about as far as my plans went. My brother-in-law had a job, so they mostly ate fresh food in the summer and gave the rest away to the squatters."

"Doug, I'm really sorry." I reached out to touch his shoulder, but he stepped back.

"Okay . . . well." He dug a rubber band out of his pocket, ran his fingers through his long blond hair, and pulled it into a ponytail. "Guess I better go to the market and see what I can find."

"The thing is," I said, glad he'd changed the subject because thinking about his dead family reminded me of my mother and made my stomach ache, "I don't have any money to contribute for the jars."

"I said I'd cover it."

"I know, but . . . we're supposed to be equal partners. I'll pay you back if I can."

"Trust me, if I get jars, you're gonna earn them," he said.

Grandpa and I were in the garden when Doug came home almost five hours later. His clothes were rumpled and he smelled a bit like whiskey, but he seemed steady enough. I knew I couldn't change him and so I tried to just be glad he'd come back.

"Did you get the stuff?" I asked.

"You can't buy jars for love or money," he said.

While Doug had been gone, black clouds had rolled in on a stiff wind. Sunset was still two hours away, but it had gotten significantly darker, and the humid air was almost too thick to breathe. I could hardly wait for the rain to start and cool me off. A gust of wind whipped at my hair, pulling strands loose from the braid.

"My farmer's sense says we better start picking some of this food and get it inside," I said. "Hail could ruin us."

"Okay," Doug said. "You're in charge."

Grandpa brought out emptied kitchen drawers, laundry baskets, cloth bags, and two wooden boxes to put the food in. Before we'd even started, the skies opened up all at once, drenching us and turning the topsoil into a muddy puddle in less than five minutes. We could hardly see each other through the sheets of water, let alone see what we were trying to pick.

"Help me lift this!" Grandpa called from the corn rows.

It took both of us struggling through the mud with the

heavy wooden box of corn to get it into the garage. The hail burst down on us, stinging our bare arms and legs and covering the already beaten-down plants. I scooped up as many of the slippery yellow squash as I could manage, using the bottom of my shirt as a sort of basket, and ran sloppily to the garage. Over and over, I hurried with armfuls of cucumbers and green peppers. Doug slogged past me with zucchini and tomatoes. At least the root vegetables were safe in the ground.

I stopped Grandpa from cutting the cabbages because I figured they'd survive. Plus, they weren't mature yet anyway. I think we must've been trudging around in the rain and mud for an hour or more when I did a head count and realized there were four of us working.

"What're you doing here?" I asked Spill.

He laughed. "How come you always ask me that instead of saying hello?"

"Sorry!" I couldn't help smiling, even though I knew I looked like a drowned rat.

He grinned back, water running down his face. "Came to hear some fiddle music."

"You'll have to wait."

"I'll take a rain check."

"Ha-ha!"

Grandpa shoved a pile of bean plants that he'd torn out by the roots into my arms. I didn't have the heart to tell him they probably would've been fine left in the ground. Plants bounce back pretty well—it was the ripe produce I was worried about. Eventually it was too dark to see, and we fell exhausted onto the garage floor, surrounded by piles of vegetables, wondering if we'd saved more than we'd lost.

"Well, that was a bust," Doug said.

"Are you kidding? We did great," I said. "Besides, there's still lots out there that will be fine."

"Yeah . . . maybe," he said, determined to be a wet blanket.

"Check it out," I said. I turned slowly, swinging the lantern, trying to get Doug to look at all the food, but instead he noticed Spill and gave an involuntary jump.

"I know you," he said. "From the market. You work for–"

"Yeah, that's right," Spill said, cutting him off. "I know you too."

Doug flinched. Spill's eyes narrowed, and his voice was hard and cold, sending a shiver through me.

"Yeah . . . okay," Doug mumbled, not making any sense.

Spill dragged his gaze from Doug to me. "You going to preserve all this, Molly?" he asked, friendly again.

"If we can get some jars."

"I can pay," Doug told him.

Spill nodded and they exchanged a look that I didn't understand. I raised my eyebrows at Grandpa, but he just shrugged and looked away.

The next day, we'd decided to take advantage of the softened ground and try to dig a root cellar in the dirt by the compost pile. Even if we got jars for canning, a cellar would provide way better storage than the garage. Underground, the temperature would stay consistently cool, even in the summer, and the food wouldn't freeze in the winter either.

Grandpa, Doug, and I were taking turns with the one shovel we had when a man rapped on the fence and called out, "Someone order canning supplies?"

"Uh, yeah. I did," Doug yelled back to him. "You can unload in the driveway."

The man grunted. Doug chose a key on the ring he'd taken from his pocket, unlocked the padlock on the gate, and the three of us stepped through. The man who'd taken my pie at the market that one day stood next to a horse and large wagon.

"I know you," I said. "You're not the Boss, but I can't remember your name."

"Randall," he reminded me. "And I have a package for you."

"Really? Who's it from?"

He just winked and gave me a large, soft brown-paper parcel. Then he crawled up into the wagon and started handing down crates to us. Randall lifted down one to Grandpa and he staggered under the weight, his skinny arms betraying him. We all pretended not to notice, but when he came back for another, Randall asked him to steady the horse instead.

"She gets a bit nervous with all this activity around her," he said. "If you could just hold her bridle and talk to her . . ."

I saw Grandpa's cheeks flush, but he went over and stood next to the horse anyway, speaking softly to her. When the last crate was unloaded into the driveway, Grandpa went home to tell Grandma about the delivery and Randall climbed into the wagon, tipping his hat to us as he drove away.

"I thought you said we couldn't get canning supplies," I said to Doug.

"Your friend Spill has connections. I paid him last night, and he arranged it."

"Really? What kind of connections?"

"To the Organization," he said. Doug was digging through a crate looking for something, and I saw him pull out a small, unlabeled bottle and slip it into his back pocket.

"What's the Organization?" I asked, sitting down and unwrapping the brown paper on my package. Inside were yards and yards of powder-blue silk. I couldn't believe it!

"You know," Doug said. "The Organization. It runs things. Like the market at the bottom of the hill. And the gambling and booze trade. Organized crime."

I tore my eyes away from the beautiful silk. "Spill's not involved in all that. He's just a delivery boy."

"Yeah, for the Organization."

"He is not!" I shouted, surprising us both. But even as I said it, I knew I was kidding myself.

21

August 9th–Do not protect yourself by a fence, but rather by your friends.
–Czech proverb

DOUG AND I WERE ON MY GRANDPARENTS' DECK,
inspecting what was left of the woodpile. We were going to
need serious amounts of firewood to do all the canning. I'd put
the kids down for a nap in my grandparents' bedroom while
we brainstormed.

I was actually still mad at Doug for saying Spill worked for
the Organization, but he didn't seem to notice. The truth was,
I might've been a little angry at myself because I wanted to
trust that Spill was as nice as I'd always thought he was, but
doubts were running through my mind now.

I thought back to how he had told me business was good
but wouldn't tell me what the business was. And how he'd
given me ice-cold pop, which was hard to find. And brought
us meat, and now the blue silk. And he made me call him by a
nickname instead of telling me his real one. Still . . . part of
organized crime? That couldn't be true. Could it?

I knew from school that the U.S. government was techni-
cally still intact but that they hardly had any money because

no one could afford to pay taxes. That weakness was all orga-nized crime had needed to become as big as it had been a hundred years ago when alcohol had been illegal and a guy named Al Capone had run Chicago.

"There's not enough wood here," Doug said, bringing me back to the problem at hand.

"Do you have any money left?" I asked. "Maybe we could get the electricity turned back on."

"No dice. I owe them a small fortune from before they turned it off, and I'm betting your grandparents do too."

I looked over at Grandpa and Grandma, who were sitting in the shade of a gnarled lilac tree, working on speech therapy. He was probably right. Doug had a woodstove in his living room, and even though the surface wasn't that big, I was pretty sure we could cook on it. The problem du jour was we needed something to burn. We stood there leaning against the house looking for the answer in the cloudless sky.

"No furniture left either," Doug said. "Burned most of that last winter."

"Well, we've got furniture, but I doubt that would fly with Grandpa."

"Darn right," Grandpa called across the yard. I'd noticed before that he had excellent hearing.

I suddenly felt so tired. The work here was just like on the farm and didn't bother me much, but I wasn't used to being the problem solver too. At least not for every single issue. It was wearing me out. I slid to the ground, the warmth and strength of the house supporting me. And then I saw the answer.

"The fence!" I shouted.

"Talk about obvious!" Doug said. "There's a lot of wood there."

"What?" Grandpa asked. He jumped up, leaving Grandma under the tree and hurrying over to us. "Oh, no you don't. You are not tearing down my fence."

Doug and I ran down the deck stairs to the fence and he thumped on it excitedly. "Oh, come on," Doug said. "The world needs fewer fences."

"No way! Use your own fence."

"I would, but the squatters pretty much stay out of the garden now," Doug said. "If I take down the fence on my side, it will be like rolling out the red carpet. But if we use the one between us, we're still pretty secure. I'll get my crowbar."

"And a sledgehammer."

"Over my dead body!" Grandpa shouted. "This is very expensive cedar fencing! You can't get this stuff anymore."

"You have another one on the other side," I joked. "We may need that eventually too."

"Never!" He placed his scrawny body spread-eagle against the fence, his face set, determined to stop us.

"Grandpa . . . we'll cut around you."

"Just try it! I'll sue you. I'll call the police! You are not taking down this fence."

Maybe in Grandpa's day you could call the police for something insignificant like a fence dispute, but after what I'd seen in Seattle, I knew it was an empty threat. Doug made the first chop on the other side and Grandpa's shoulders sagged. I put my arm around him and led him back to the lilac. I sat on the blanket next to Grandma and she put her hand on my shoulder—a hand that felt exactly like my mother's. I snuggled into her despite the heat.

"Grandpa, come on. Sit down," I said. "We're not trying to ruin your house. We just need to can this food so Doug and the kids can get through the winter."

"What about us?" Grandpa snapped. "Hoping we don't last that long?"

"You'll be with me in Canada."

"Like hell we will!"

I pulled him down to the ground so we were facing each other. "You can't stay here. You'll starve."

"What about all this food you're supposedly canning?" he demanded. "Don't we get our share?"

"Well, yes. To sell." I tried my sympathy card. "Plus, my mom really needs you."

Doug's sledgehammer cracked against the planks.

"Molly, I don't know how many times I have to tell you, but we are not going back to Canada with you."

I looked at Grandma, hoping she'd somehow take my side. She was gazing at me, but she didn't say anything. I tried another tactic. "Even if you have the food, what will you do for heat?"

"We'll burn the goddamned fence," he said.

I giggled. He laughed a little too. Even Grandma smiled. But as my laughter died away, tears prickled in my eyes and my nose had that funny tingling you get right before you sneeze. Or cry. "I can't go back to the island without you." I stared at the blue cloudless sky to keep the tears from coming.

"Your mom will be fine," he said. "And at this rate, the baby will be born before we could get there anyway."

"She's not due until the first week of November," I reminded him. "As long as she doesn't have it early, we could still make it back." The tears were edging out around the corners of my eyes, and I sniffled. I felt Grandpa's bony hand touch mine, sort of patting me reassuringly, and I burst into tears.

"Molly . . . come on, sweetheart," he said, pulling me close. He scooted around so he was next to me, and Grandma leaned into me too. The air was filled with the sounds of splitting wood as Doug pried the first planks away from their posts. "Don't cry. It's okay. . . ."

I squeezed my eyes shut. The thing was, I was tired of crying. It wasn't going to save my mother.

"Look," I said, straightening up and pulling away from them both, anger flooding me. "I'm sorry that you seem to hate Mom so much that you won't even go up there and try and save her life, but she's my mother! If she dies, my brothers and sister and I won't have a mom anymore. That may not be a big deal to you, but it's huge to me!"

"Molly, you have no idea what you're saying—"

"I do!" I shouted. My anger and frustration had finally heated up to the boiling point. "I know you said that Grandma couldn't make the trip, but look at her!" I stood, pointing at Grandma. "She's fine! Well, maybe not fine, but we'll be on a train. And we'll take it easy. Whatever we have to do. I just don't understand how you can let a stupid twenty-year-old argument over medical school come between you and Mom when it's life or death."

Grandpa's expression was unreadable, but he took off his glasses and rubbed his eyes, and I knew my words had stung him somehow.

"She needs a doctor," I yelled.

Grandpa put his glasses back on and stood up, looking right at me. "Well, I'm sorry, Molly, but it can't be me."

"It has to be you."

"It can't be. I'm not a doctor anymore."

"Of course you are."

He sighed and looked at Grandma for help, but she turned away from him. The silence hung in the air. "I haven't been a doctor since the twenties," he finally said.

"But you worked at the hospital until last year," I argued. "Mom said you did."

"I was an administrator." His look was sullen.

"But you got that glass out of my foot."

He shook his head. "Anyone could've done that."

"You've been helping Grandma," I said.

"Yes," Grandma said. "Yes."

"You *like* being a doctor," I said, "I know you do."

He shook his head, but there was a bit of light in his eyes that I hadn't seen before. Grandma held her hand out to me to be helped up, and when she was standing, she grabbed Grandpa's hand. I could tell she was squeezing it tightly.

"Breeee," she said, looking hard at him. "Breee!"

"Well . . ."

"Yes!" Grandma yelled.

Grandpa sighed and turned to me. "I guess, if you come up

with the money. . . . But there has to be enough to get us there without the travel killing us."

"I know."

"And . . . and I'll do what I can for your mother," he said, "but I'm not making any promises about taking over as the island doctor."

I threw my arms around him, and Grandma wrapped hers around us both. "Thank you," I murmured into his shoulder. It was the first step I'd made towards home since I'd left.

22

August 25th–To know the feeling, /
play music at once, with heart / and ears wide open.
–Bob Deck

AUGUST BLAZED ON, AND WHEN THE TWENTY-FIFTH finally arrived, my family was on my mind all day because I'd never spent my birthday away from them before. We'd been so busy–keeping a hot fire going in Doug's woodstove about ten hours a day to sterilize the jars, cook the food, and preserve it–that it had snuck up on me, and when my grandparents didn't remember, I didn't say anything.

Grandma and I had also sliced a lot of vegetables to dry between old window screens in the backyard. Grandpa wanted her to use the knife in her right hand as therapy, but whenever he wasn't around, she used her left. If he came by, she'd quickly switch hands, smirking at me with her lopsided grin. In between all those jobs, I took my turn digging the root cellar too.

When we'd thought it couldn't get any hotter, a fierce, dry wind had come up from the east, roasting us. While everyone else dealt with it by having a nap in the middle of the afternoon, I was too hot to sleep.

I wanted to sew my dress, but I was afraid of leaving sweaty fingerprints on the silk, so I only worked on it at night or early in the morning. Inside the package, there'd been a note from Spill.

> *Molly, I know these patterns are really old, from the 1980s or something, but Aunt Lili says wedding fashions don't change that much, and they're back in style now. I hope there's enough fabric.*
>
> *Spill*

And even though I was grateful, the whole connection between the fabric and how he'd probably gotten it made uneasiness flare up inside me every time I held it in my hands. Besides, even though I'd been making doll clothes since I was four or five and my own clothes since I was about ten, there was no way I could finish this dress without a sewing machine. All I could really do was cut it out and pin it together.

I thought about playing Jewels, but was afraid I'd wake everyone up from their naps, so I decided to go for a walk. I was halfway down the stairs from my bedroom when I heard piano music. I stopped, my ears perking up, listening. It was coming from somewhere inside the house.

At the bottom of the stairs, there was a door that I'd noticed before but always assumed was a coat closet. It was open, and when I peered into it, I saw a wide, thickly carpeted stairway leading down into a basement. How had I never realized we had a basement before?

The music floated up the stairs to meet me as I made my way down into a huge, low-ceilinged room. Cobwebs hung from all the corners, and spiderwebs encased every piece of furniture. Grandpa sat at a grand piano, a candle flickering on top of it, his eyes closed, his fingers dancing on the keys, the music filling his entire body. He was the most peaceful I'd ever seen him.

The music was something classical that I didn't recognize, but it seemed familiar too. Maybe my mother or Katie had played it on our upright piano once at home. I didn't want to disturb Grandpa, but the music was drawing me in closer to him like a moth to candlelight.

"Come here," he said, not opening his eyes. I jumped a little, not realizing he'd known I was there.

"I thought you must've sold your piano," I told him.

He continued to play, but his eyes were open now. "Can't get it out of the basement," he said. "The builders put it down here before they finished all the doorways in the house so it's pretty much stuck here."

I sat on the hard bench next to him, and for a long time he played and I just listened. I'd missed the sound of someone else making music. Sometimes, when you're a musician, it's so nice to just listen. It's like my mom says about cooking. She loves to cook, but when someone else makes the food, even if it's just an egg sandwich, it tastes so much better because she didn't have to do it herself.

After a while, he stopped. "Do you play piano too?" he asked.

"Not really," I said. "Mom gave me lessons when I was little, but I never got that excited about it. Katie is the one who can really play."

He nodded. "Yes . . . I remember from when we visited. She was just a little girl, but she had a spark."

"Yep."

"Like you with the fiddle," he said, smiling.

"Thanks."

We sat there for a while longer. He played something jazzy, and we let the notes float around us. "I quit the piano when your grandmother had her stroke," he said. "It was like she'd been cheated out of happiness, and I thought I shouldn't have any pleasure if she couldn't. I probably should've played *more* instead of stopping. It would've helped me get through it."

"Music makes me feel better when I'm missing home," I agreed.

"You practicing every morning made me realize I was only hurting myself," he said.

I smiled. "Can we play together?"

"Sure. But right now, let's go upstairs and find something to eat."

"We just had lunch," I said, bumping his shoulder and laughing. "Are you seriously hungry?"

"I'm awake, aren't I?" he said.

We got up, and he picked up the candle. In the fluttering light I noticed a long granite-topped bar with a mirror behind it and bottle after bottle of liquor. My heart leapt at the sight.

"Hey! We could sell all that alcohol," I told Grandpa.

"Empty," he said.

I sighed. "Figures."

We went upstairs together, and in the dining room we

stopped, dazed and a little blinded by the daylight. All of a sudden, everyone jumped out from behind the furniture. "Happy birthday!" they all yelled, including Grandpa.

"You were playing music just to get me out of the way!" I said when he hugged me.

He laughed. "Worked, didn't it? I'm like the pied piper, only with a piano."

Everyone swept me up into hug after hug. First Grandma, then Doug, the kids, and, surprisingly, Spill! He touched me kind of awkwardly, like he wasn't sure if he should or not and then we both stepped back, embarrassed, but smiling.

"Come outside!" Brandy squealed, grabbing my hand and pulling me behind her. A pink cake covered with luscious-looking blackberries sat melting in the heat. Fresh flowers drooped in small jars placed sporadically around the deck.

"We weren't really asleep!" Brandy shouted.

"We pretended," Michael added.

"We decorated all by ourselves," Brandy said.

"It's beautiful," I gushed.

I knelt and squeezed their small bodies to me. They'd put on some weight, and I could barely lift Brandy anymore. Michael was still as light as a puppy, though.

"Spill brought the cake," Brandy said. "Can we eat it?"

"I'm with Brandy," Spill said. "Let's eat."

"Get Jewels first and play 'Happy Birthday' so we can sing," Grandpa suggested.

"I have to play 'Happy Birthday' to myself?"

"Well, who else is going to do it?"

"You are! On the piano."

"Can't haul the piano upstairs, though, can we? Get your fiddle, and we'll play later."

I ran upstairs and got Jewels. Everyone sang and Grandma cut the cake into eight slices. In about thirty seconds we all sat staring at our empty plates.

"For Molleeee," Grandma said, pointing at the last piece.

Grandpa had disappeared right after we'd eaten, and now he came out through the house wheeling a shiny green mountain bike. "Happy birthday, Molly." His face was glowing.

"Oh, my God! Where did you get that? I thought you sold everything."

"I had it in the attic. I'd totally forgotten about it until the other day. It was your grandma's."

I ran my hands over the seat, inspected the tires, and squeezed the brake levers. "It looks brand new."

"Yeah, I think she rode it once about twenty years ago," he said, laughing. Grandma thumped him on the arm, but she was smiling too.

"Spill got it some new tires," he said.

I looked at Spill, pleased. So Grandpa seemed okay with his job. . . . Maybe who Spill worked for didn't really matter. If Grandpa thought it was all right, then I could probably live with it too.

Grandpa told me to take the bike for a spin, but I wanted more music.

"I'll try it later," I said. "Now it's time for the piano. Let's move the party downstairs and play together."

We trooped down to the basement, and Doug's eyes immediately traveled to the liquor bottles on the wall.

"Empty," I told him.

"That's okay. Got my own." He patted his back pocket.

I pretended like I hadn't heard him and moved towards the piano, where Grandpa was running his fingers lightly over the keys. He kicked off with "Oh, Susannah," and I jumped in with Jewels. Before long, Spill and Doug were swinging Grandma and the kids around, and everyone was laughing. We had so much fun that after dinner we all went back downstairs for more music.

It was getting late, and Grandpa was playing a soft lullaby for Brandy and Michael, who were almost asleep in the corner. Spill and Doug and I sat in dusty leather chairs listening, half asleep ourselves, when the music was broken by a loud rapping noise upstairs. We all froze. It sounded like someone was trying to knock the door down.

Spill and I ran up the stairs. By the time we got to the front door, the knocking had stopped. I looked through the peephole. A small man in a suit was stepping off the porch and walking towards a bicycle.

"I think it's for you, Spill," I said.

He unbolted the door and opened it. "Hey, Randall."

"Oh," he said, turning. "Sorry to interrupt, but the Boss wants to see you."

"Right. Okay," said Spill. "I have to go, Molly, but . . . here." He'd taken a wooden box out of one of the bags he had attached to his bike. "Happy birthday."

"Oh, you didn't have to get me anything," I said. I could feel my face flushing.

"Of course I did. It's a birthday party."

He held the box out, and I took it. "Well . . . thanks."

"See you soon," he said.

I watched them ride off together. The Boss wanted to see him. So Doug had been right after all, and I couldn't deny it any longer. Spill was not simply a delivery boy.

Later, when I was alone in my room, I pried open the lid of the box and inside I found a beautiful pair of hand-stitched leather work boots. I slipped on the right one and it fit like it had been made just for me.

The next morning I went to the basement to collect my fiddle off the piano. As I passed the bar, I saw a door that I hadn't noticed before because it was part of the mirrored wall. I ran my fingers along the edge and caught the clasp. The door sprang open.

I think I was hoping for piles of gold, or all the family valuables, because my heart sank down to my new boots when all I discovered was an old storage cupboard. Table linens and extra glasses lined the shelves. Cocktail napkins, mixers, and boxes of candles all sat neatly in rows. The candles were a real find, and I lit a fresh one from the stub I was carrying.

Mostly the closet was empty, but as I turned to go, a box tucked deep in a corner caught my attention. Setting the candle down, I moved over to it and tugged. It was so heavy I had to put my legs into it and I dragged it out behind the bar where I could see better.

Using a bottle opener, I pried open the top. As I reached into the crate and grasped the first bottle, I knew exactly how a prospector felt. I'd struck gold! In the flicker of the candle I read the words I knew would take us all the way back to Canada. Back home.

Jameson Gold Irish Whiskey.

I didn't know anything about whiskey, but this was from Ireland. It *had* to be the "really good booze" Spill had been talking about. I did a little Irish jig with the bottle for a partner. When I heard Brandy calling my name from upstairs, I quickly shoved the crate back into the closet, into the darkest corner, burying it under some tablecloths. If Doug found it, my lifeline home would be gone before I could play a single note of "Oh, Canada"!

23

September 14th–Cabbage: A familiar kitchen-garden
vegetable about as large and wise as a man's head.
–Ambrose Bierce

OVER THE NEXT THREE WEEKS, I WAS ABOUT READY
to explode from both excitement and frustration over the
whiskey. I hadn't seen Spill once, which really bothered me for
a couple of reasons. I kind of missed him, but more importantly,
even though I hated to ask for help, I knew I needed him to
sell the whiskey for me.

Not only was Mom's due date creeping closer, but Katie's
wedding was less than two weeks away. Getting my grandparents back to the island and Mom's health were the most
important factors, but I didn't want to miss the wedding if I
could help it, either. I finally decided I couldn't wait any longer
for Spill. I would try selling two or three bottles, just to see
how much I got. If it went well, then I'd sell the rest, buy our
train tickets, and we'd go. I hoped we would see Spill again
sometime, though. I'd found myself daydreaming a little too
often about his blue eyes and friendly smile to just walk off
without saying good-bye.

On a misty morning, I packed three bottles wrapped in one

of Grandpa's old shirts into my backpack and headed for the market. I wore a pair of old jeans I'd found upstairs, with a denim jacket, and I let my hair hang loose so it was kind of wild. I'd even smudged a bit of dirt on my cheek too, hoping I'd look like I belonged there, like I was tough.

I stopped on the street just before the entrance, slid one of the bottles out of my pack, keeping it wrapped in the shirt. Men sat at tables, playing cards, smoking, and drinking out of coffee mugs. The aroma of beer was strong, even though it was only ten in the morning. If I couldn't get Spill to sell my whiskey to the rich people, then these were my customers, but I wasn't sure how to approach them. They, however, had no qualms about talking to me.

"Hey there, baby. You're a sweet thing," a scruffy man who could use a good wash said.

"What's a lovely little thing like you doing around here?" his pal with a mangy beard asked.

"Ummm . . . I have . . . I have something to sell," I managed to squeak out.

"You don't say?" He raised his eyebrows and let out a wolf whistle.

Everyone laughed, and I felt my face flush. Then a group of about six men, moving like a pack of wild dogs, got up from a table. As they shuffled towards me, I skirted around another guy who could've been one of their ugly brothers. I held on tight to the bottle, still wrapped in the shirt.

"What you got in your hand?" asked one of the men from the pack. He was crowding up to me, close enough that I could smell the reek of cigarette smoke on his flannel shirt.

In a matter of seconds, I was surrounded by a scraggly lot.

"Nothing," I said, trying to back away. I'd changed my mind. This was not a good idea, and I had to get out of there fast. "Just my grandpa's old shirt." I edged to my right, and the circle of men moved with me.

"Let me see it." A big hairy paw reached out. When I jerked back, the two bottles in my pack clanged together.

"Sounds like bottles," one guy said.

I decided to come clean. Maybe I could start a bidding war or something. I unwrapped the Jameson Gold and held it up like an auctioneer.

"Who wants to buy this bottle of fine old Irish whiskey?" I asked a little too loudly. Suddenly every man within fifty meters descended on me.

"Buy it? Why would we buy it?"

"Seems like it's there for the takin'."

"No! Wait! Stop it!" I shouted as a man reached for it.

"There's more in her pack. I can hear 'em."

"No there's not! Keep your hands off me!"

Someone tried to snatch the bottle out of my hand, but I held on with all my might. I'd been shoveling and digging all summer, and my grip was strong. As I yanked my arm away, I lost my balance and the bottle cracked against the head of the guy standing next to him. The whiskey was intact, but the man dropped to the ground.

"Hey! She killed Weasel!"

"Oh, my God!" I cried.

"He ain't dead," the man in flannel said, laughing. "Takes more than that to kill him. Look, he's still breathing."

Everyone laughed around me, and the scruffy guy nudged the fallen Weasel with his boot. His chest was definitely moving up and down, and for a second I was relieved, but then I felt a tug on my pack. I swung around, trying to hit whoever it was, but the man behind me was ready, and he grabbed my wrist, clenching it so hard tears welled up in my eyes.

"Let me go! Please! Please let me go!" I screamed. "You're breaking my arm."

In spite of everything going on around me, only one thing flashed across my mind. If he broke my wrist, I might never be able to play Jewels again. Or at least not very well.

"I'll give you the whiskey," I said. "Just let me go!"

"Oh, now you want to bargain, huh?" the bearded man snarled. "Too late, missy!"

He had the bottle, but he didn't let me go. Instead, he started dragging me into the tent.

"Help!" I screamed. "Help me!"

That was when I saw Doug. He stood on the outer circle, bleary-eyed, his hair matted. He clearly hadn't been to bed the night before. At first I thought he didn't see me, but then our eyes met and relief flooded me.

I'd planted my feet as best I could to make myself as heavy as possible, but my sandals slid on the gravel, and my wrist was hot with pain. The more I resisted, the tighter the man held on, twisting it. I collapsed onto the ground, making myself dead-weight, and then I kicked at him, but he wrenched my arm harder, and I screamed.

"Don't try that with me, little girl."

"Doug!" I yelled. "Please! Doug! Help me!"

The bearded man pulled me to my feet, and when I looked where Doug had been standing, he was gone. "We'll have your whiskey," the man hissed in my ear, "and we'll have you too, if we want."

"Or you could let her go," a steely voice beyond the crowd said. "And then I won't have to kill you."

24

THE MAN INSTANTLY DROPPED MY WRIST, AND THE others around the edges of the group began to shuffle off as if they'd just been passing by. The way the crowd dispersed, I'd been expecting a giant, but instead, Randall stepped through.

Even though the bearded man towered over Randall, he stepped back, obviously worried. In a somewhat shaky voice he said, "You've got no right. We found 'er first. We've got no quarrel with you."

"And I don't want to have one with you, because the house always wins," Randall said.

He was wearing the same suit he'd had on the day he'd taken my pie, and also the day he'd delivered the canning stuff, a dark one with stripes. And his felt hat stood at a jaunty angle. He looked cool and calm.

I stood there too scared to even massage my aching wrist. I'd forgotten all about the Boss. Randall had told me not to busk at the market, and if I couldn't busk, I definitely shouldn't be selling whiskey.

"Well . . . ," Scruffy told the man, "there's more of us than you."

He hadn't even gotten the words out before the few remaining men slunk off, leaving him standing alone. Unless you counted the unconscious Weasel, who lay at his feet, and I didn't think you could.

"Doesn't look like your pals are staying," Randall said.

Scruffy backed away about three or four yards and then he turned and ran, leaving Weasel passed out on the ground.

"Th-thank you," I stammered.

"Molly, Molly, Molly," Randall said. "I'm very disappointed."

"I'm sorry," I squeaked. "I guess I shouldn't have–"

"You better give me that whiskey, and I'll see that Robert gets you the money. After a small commission, that is."

I handed him the rest of the bottles.

"And then you better get outta here," he said. "I told you once before about this not being a public market, remember?"

I nodded.

"In the future, if you've got anything else to sell, let Robert do it for you."

"I will."

Randall didn't even bother to hide the bottles as he walked off. I ran in the other direction and out onto the street towards home. My swollen wrist burned, and my shredded dignity floated behind me in tatters. How was this Robert going to find me? I was halfway home before I put one and one together.

Robert was Spill.

. . .

After what Doug had done, or not done, to help me when I needed him, I was highly tempted to never set foot in the garden again, but what choice did I have? We had to eat. After making sure he wasn't there the next morning, I went over to check on the fall crops. I was squatting next to the kale, dreaming about music, when Spill burst through the gap in the fence.

"Molly! Where are you?"

I stood up, brushing my hands on my shorts. "Right here. Hi!"

"Are you crazy?" Spill shouted. "What were you thinking?"

He stood over me, hands on his hips, his face as red as his sunburned nose had been that first day we met.

"Wait a min–"

"You could've been killed!"

"Would you stop screaming?"

Grandpa stepped through the gap. "What's going on? Why're you yelling?"

"You know, for some stupid reason, I thought you were smarter than that," Spill continued to rant. "What the hell were you thinking? If Randall hadn't heard the fight, you'd be dead! If you have something to sell, you bring it to me!"

"How can I bring it to you when you don't come around?" I asked coldly. I glared into his flashing blue eyes. "I haven't seen you in a month!"

"It hasn't been a month!"

"Well, three weeks, then," I said. "I was getting desperate. We need to get home!"

"What made you think you could sell whiskey without get-ting killed?"

"Sell whiskey?" Grandpa demanded. "Who's selling whiskey?"

"Your granddaughter!" Spill spit out the words like poison. "She waltzed into the market yesterday waving around bottles of whiskey. If Randall hadn't known who she was, she'd prob-ably be in a ditch somewhere."

"Where'd you get this whiskey?" Grandpa asked.

Uh-oh.

"Ummm . . ."

The two of them glared at me.

"Well?" Grandpa demanded.

"Your basement."

"My basement? Not Jameson's Gold?"

"I found it in that storage closet behind the bar."

"You stole my whiskey?"

"I didn't steal it! You said if I could find anything to sell in the house, I could have it."

"Well, I didn't know there was whiskey!" Grandpa shouted.

"I'm sorry," I said to both of them.

Spill had come into the garden through the gap in the fence between my grandparents' house and Doug's, and he turned and stormed off back the way he'd come. I ran after him as he barreled right through the house, nodding politely at my grandma, and out the front door.

"Wait, Spill. Come back."

"Here," he said, turning to me. "I almost forgot why I came." He thrust a huge wad of money into my hand.

"What's this for?"

"Your whiskey."

"Three bottles brought this much money?"

"I told you, imported whiskey is hard to get around here. This is your share minus Randall's commission. And a ten percent tip for saving your life."

I fingered the money. "Spill. I'm sorry. Really."

His face softened. "I'm not mad. I was just—"

"What?"

"Scared for you," he said, his voice low.

"I'm sorry. Really. Tell Randall thank you."

He nodded.

"It's just that my mom, she needs a doctor . . . and my sister's wedding is a week from Saturday." I smiled at him, trying to make him understand. "I had to try. . . . I'm really sorry."

"Don't be. It was partly my fault. I shouldn't have just disappeared. It's . . ." He unlocked his bike without looking at me. "Look, Molly, we both know who I work for, and I'm just not sure that you should be hanging out with me. The Boss isn't that happy about me fraternizing with civilians, either, which is why I haven't been coming around."

I giggled. "Fraternizing with civilians?"

"The Boss prefers if we aren't too friendly with the public," Spill explained. "It's safer for everybody that way."

"Oh, well, I don't really care what you do. . . ."

And I realized as I said it, I didn't. Spill was a nice guy. So what if he delivered black-market sherry to the rich? It's not like he was killing people or anything.

"Well, you should care," he said.

"Well, I don't, and you can't tell me what to think." I smiled at him and tilted my head, forcing him to meet my eye. Finally he smiled back. After a long silence, he took one of my hands in his, and my heart did a flip.

"I do have to go, Mol," he said. "Try not to do anything else that stupid, okay?"

"Gee, thanks!"

He laughed.

"There are nine more bottles of whiskey," I said. "Is that enough to get us home?"

"Should be. I'm not sure exactly when I can help you, though," he said. "But it'll be soon. I promise."

"Thanks, Spill. You've been really great, and I . . . well . . . thanks." I looked at the ground instead of him, suddenly aware of how messy my hair must look after all morning in the garden. "Listen," I said, "if you think I'll get enough for the whiskey, I guess I'll leave the food with Doug. You know, for the kids."

"About Doug . . . ," he said.

"What?"

He shook his head. "Oh, never mind."

"No, really. What?"

"Nothing. I can't talk about it." He looked over at Doug's house. "It's just . . . you can't take the kids with you, can you?"

"And what? Sneak them into Canada in our suitcases?"

He shrugged.

"It's not like I haven't considered it," I said. "But don't you think I have enough responsibility right now just trying to get my grandparents back home with me?"

"Yeah. Never mind."

"Is Doug in some sort of trouble?" I asked.

"I gotta go."

I reached out and touched his arm. "Spill. Seriously. You can tell me."

He opened his mouth to say something, but then he stopped himself. Instead, he reached up and covered my hand with his. "Molly," he said, "it's too late for Doug. Just . . . just try not to take on his problems too, okay?"

I scowled. "After yesterday," I said, "you don't have to worry about me trying to help him."

He squeezed my hand. "I know," he said. "But he's in over his head this time, and he might try to . . . I don't know . . . play you for sympathy. Stay clear of him or he'll take you all down with him."

25

I FOUND GRANDPA IN THE GARAGE, LOCKING THE doors of a big metal cabinet.

"The whiskey's in there," he said. "I don't want Doug to find it."

I didn't tell Grandpa that Doug had left me to fend for myself at the market. We still had to live next door to him, and I was afraid how Grandpa might react if he knew.

"I'm sorry I took the whiskey without asking," I said.

He shrugged. "You meant well. I didn't realize we still had any, though, or I would've sold it. Your grandma is the whiskey drinker in the family, and I never even thought to look."

"Lucky for us, then," I said.

He put his arm around my shoulder and squeezed. "I guess so."

We were on our way inside when I noticed the car was covered in a thick layer of dust.

"Guess I've been keeping you busy, eh?" I said.

He ran a finger over it, leaving a streak. "I guess so. It doesn't seem so important anymore. Hey, get in. I'll teach you to drive."

I laughed, but he was serious, so I climbed in the driver's side. Grandpa went around to the other door and slid in onto the bench seat.

"So the first thing you do," he said, pointing to a pedal, "is pump the gas five or six times."

"It's electric," I reminded him.

"We're going back to nineteen fifty-nine," he said.

"Oh, okay." I pumped the pedal a couple of times.

"Then you start the ignition."

I pretended to turn the key. "Vroom, vroom!" I said, imitating cars from the movies.

"Don't flood it," he said seriously.

"What?"

"Never mind. It was a joke. Okay, so now what you do is check your rearview mirror to make sure nothing's behind you."

"You mean like the garage door?"

He laughed. Using both hands, I made a big show of adjusting the rearview mirror. Then I pursed my lips at my reflection, like I was checking my makeup.

"Oh, yes, quite the glamour girl," he said. "Now, this is an automatic, so you just pull the gearshift in towards you and then slide it all the way over to R for reverse."

I started to pull on the handle and he stopped me. "You can't really do it, Molly. We're playing."

"Oh, right."

Grandpa walked me through pretending to back up, then shifting to D for drive, and then we were out on the open road. "Canada, here we come!" I yelled.

"B.C. or bust!" Grandpa shouted.

Maybe he was more excited about seeing my mom than he'd let on. We rolled down our windows, and I hung my left arm out. "Ahhhh, the wind's in my hair. . . ."

"Smell that sea breeze," Grandpa chimed in.

"Farmland and mountains are flying by!" I shouted.

"Watch out for those cows!" Grandpa yelled, laughing.

I laid on the horn, and it surprised us both by blasting out loud and clear. Not thirty seconds later, the door leading into the house opened and Brandy, Michael, and Grandma stood there looking at us like we were totally nuts.

"Get in!" I called to them.

The kids ran across the garage, with Grandma right behind them. They all climbed into the backseat, slamming the doors, yelling, and laughing.

"Molly's a crazy driver," Grandpa said. "She almost ran over a whole herd of cows."

We were still goofing around fifteen minutes later when we heard a thud against the garage door behind us. For a second, I thought the car had somehow slipped into gear and we'd rolled back.

"What the hell was that?" Grandpa asked.

We all scrambled out of the car and ran through the house to the front door and out into the yard. I was the first to round the corner into the driveway. Doug sat slumped on the ground, leaning against the house as if he'd slid down it.

When he saw me, he mustered up a wan smile. "Hey, Mol. Is the doctor in?"

And then he passed out.

26

HE WASN'T UNCONSCIOUS FOR LONG, AND GRANDPA and I managed to get him on his feet while Grandma took the kids into the kitchen. At first, we thought he was drunk, but the way he howled when we tried to help him stand made us realize he was injured.

"Owww! My ribs, my ribs!" he shouted. "Don't touch my arm, either!"

In the end, we let him shuffle along, and we walked on either side to make sure he didn't fall. We took him into the master bedroom and eased him onto the edge of my grandparents' bed. Then we cut his T-shirt off because he couldn't raise his left arm more than an inch or two. I gasped when Grandpa peeled the cloth away and exposed skin that was already turning an ugly shade of purple.

"What happened?" I asked.

Grandpa had gotten his doctor's bag out of the closet and was listening to Doug's heart.

"Fight," Doug said.

"Fight or beating?" Grandpa asked.

"What's the difference?" he mumbled.

Grandpa gave him a long look I didn't understand and then he poked and prodded at Doug for a while, not saying much except "Does this hurt?" which Doug usually answered with "Hell, yes!"

"Take a deep breath," Grandpa told him. "Any trouble getting air?"

"Not really."

"I don't think it's too serious," Grandpa finally said. "Your vital signs are strong. The main thing to worry about is a punctured lung, but your breathing seems okay, so I think you've only bruised or cracked a couple of ribs."

"What about my arm?"

"A bad sprain. Did you get hit in the head at all?" He shone a tiny light in Doug's eyes.

"I don't think so."

"Good. Well, there's no sign of a concussion."

"Don't you think he should go to a hospital?" I asked.

"Like I could pay for that," Doug said.

"They won't do anything for broken ribs," Grandpa told us. "They'll just tell you to rest, Doug, so I'll leave you to it."

Grandpa took my arm and led me out into the hallway. "Molly, I don't like this at all."

"Me either," I said. "I don't want to take care of him." I knew I sounded mean, but after Doug had abandoned me at the market, the last thing I wanted was to be his nursemaid.

"What I mean," Grandpa said, "is Doug is bad news. It's not

safe for us to have him in this house. We need to get him on his feet as soon as possible."

"What do you mean it's not safe?" I asked.

"Doug wasn't in any fight," Grandpa said. "This was a warning from the Organization."

"What do you mean?"

In the living room Grandpa sat down heavily in the swivel chair.

"Are you dating this Spill fellow?" he asked.

"What? Of course not," I said. I sat down on the couch and looked at him like he was crazy. "Have you noticed me going out on any dates?"

"Well, you could be sneaking out at night."

"I'm way too tired at night," I said.

"Yeah. . . ." He took off his glasses and cleaned them on his shirt, even though they were sparkling already. "That's what I thought. That's why I wasn't too worried about you being friends with him even though he works for the Organization, but this is different."

"What does Spill have to do with Doug?" I asked.

Grandpa sighed. "Hopefully, nothing. But I'm guessing Doug owes on gambling debts and what the Organization did today," he said, "this was just a reminder that they want their money. If they'd been serious, we probably never would've seen him again."

"Are you kidding?" I asked. "You mean he owed money so they beat him up?"

Grandpa nodded.

"What happens if he can't pay?" I asked. "You think they'll do worse?"

"I'm afraid this is just the beginning."

Spill's words about not letting Doug drag us down with him replayed in my mind, and I knew Grandpa was right. We had to get him out of this house. "Do you think the two of us can move him now?" I asked.

Grandpa shook his head. "It would be pretty painful for him and difficult for us, but there is one thing that might work," he said, and I swear he looked a little excited.

"What?"

"Well, a few years ago, a colleague of mine developed a treatment for this kind of injury. It's a double injection," he explained. "One dose causes an acute reaction to soft and bony tissues, which speeds up healing. The other injection shuts down the nervous system temporarily, giving extreme pain relief."

He kind of lost me in the details, but it didn't really matter. "Where can I get it?"

"You can't. It was never approved by the FDA," Grandpa said. "Too risky." He definitely looked excited now. His eyes had a kind of brightness to them. "But if you ride down to the pharmacy and get me the ingredients, I can mix it up."

"Make me a list," I said.

His excitement was suddenly overshadowed by hesitation. "I don't know . . . Molly. It's kind of dangerous."

"What do you mean?"

"Most of the time, it works fine," he said, "but there are risks. You have to administer the injections at precisely the same moment. If the stimulator injection goes in first, the second one can cause paralysis."

"Permanently?" I asked.

"Well, no. But for a good ten or twelve hours."

"That would serve Doug right," I said, only half kidding.

Grandpa took off his glasses and cleaned them on his shirt again. If he wasn't careful, he'd wear a hole through the lenses. "There is the expense too."

I knew exactly where any money to pay for drugs would have to come from. My whiskey money. "Maybe Doug should just tough it out?" I said, even though the most important thing was to get Doug up and on his feet and away from us.

Eventually, Grandpa wrote a prescription for the ingredients and gave me directions to the hospital, which he said was about five miles past the market. Legally, he was still a doctor, but I still had to wait at the pharmacy for almost two hours while they checked out his credentials since he didn't work there anymore. When I finally got home, Doug's face was white as a chicken's egg. It took Grandpa almost another hour to mix up the drugs in the kitchen sink and load the serums into each syringe.

"I taped two syringes together so that I can inject them at exactly the same time," Grandpa said, showing me.

"Will it work?"

He shrugged. "Hope so." Back in the bedroom, he said to Doug, "This is going to hurt a lot, but in less than a minute, you won't even remember it, I promise. Try to relax."

I thought Grandpa would inject it into the ribs, but instead he took off Doug's boot. "We're going to administer it between the toes," he told me. "I need you to hold his foot down. If he jerks, we could have a problem."

"What kind of problem?" Doug asked.

"Put all your weight on his ankle, Molly."

I leaned over Doug's foot, pressing down. Grandpa spread his big toe apart from the next one and lined up the dual plunger. "On three," he said. "One. Two. Three!"

I didn't see what Grandpa did, but Doug screamed so loud I was afraid he'd ruptured my eardrum. His leg jerked violently out of my grasp too. "I'm sorry," I said. "I held him as best I could."

"I think we're okay," Grandpa said.

"Maybe you are!" Doug yelled. "What the hell kind of doctor are you?"

"Do you think it worked?" I asked.

"We'll know in a minute or two," Grandpa said. Sweat dripped down his forehead.

"Hey! What's wrong with my leg?" Doug said. "It's gone all funny and warm."

Grandpa smiled. "That means it's working. The heart is receiving blood and sending it by way of arteries to the rest of the body."

The pain on Doug's face began to ebb away, replaced with a dazed look. "This feels pretty good," he said. "As long as you didn't kill me."

Unfortunately for Doug, it wasn't me and Grandpa that he had to worry about.

27

September 23rd—World Seed Collection &
Distribution Organization established.

AFTER THE WARNING, GRANDPA DECIDED WE BETTER
go to Canada right away. Even though Spill said he was going to
be busy for a while, Grandpa didn't think we should wait for him
to come back, and he sent me out every day to look for him.

I'd seen Randall several times at the market, but I was afraid
to talk to him about Spill in case I got him in trouble with the
Boss. On my eighth cold morning of no luck, I decided I didn't
have a choice.

Randall was making his rounds, talking to each vendor, col-
lecting money, and I followed him around for ten minutes, trying to work up my nerve to speak to him. Finally he stopped,
turned, and smiled.

"Let me guess," he said. "You want to talk to me?"

"Well . . . yeah."

"So talk."

He was still smiling, and my courage surged a little. "I need
to find Spill, er . . . Robert."

"He's away on a job."

"Oh."

"He'll be back soon," he said. "I'll send him around."

"Okay, thanks."

"No problem."

"Oh, and Randall?" I said. "Thanks for, you know . . . the day with the whiskey and everything. Thanks for giving Robert my money too."

"What else would I have done with it?"

"Keep it?"

"Nah. It was yours. Besides, I took my share." He tipped his hat at me. "The house always wins, Molly. Remember that."

"I will. Thanks again."

Two days later, I was standing in the living room playing a classical piece on Jewels that Grandpa had taught me. He and Grandma were sitting in chairs, their eyes closed, smiles across their faces, when someone tapped on the French doors and then Spill stepped into the room.

"I knocked on the front door, but I guess you couldn't hear me, so I came in the back way through the creek," Spill said.

I kept playing, but I smiled at him and nodded.

"That was beautiful," he said when I finished.

"Nice job, Molly," Grandpa said. "There are a couple of spots I'd like to go over with the piano, though."

"Yeah," I agreed. "I messed up a little."

"So, anyway," Spill said. "Sorry to interrupt. I won't stay long. I just wanted to see if tomorrow is good for you to go and sell the whiskey? I have a trailer full of my own stuff, so it would help me out if you come along and haul the whiskey yourself."

"Sure, but I don't have a cart."

"I borrowed one for you. It's in the driveway."

"Great. Thanks."

"I should be able to get you in to use a computer too. So you can email home."

"That would be fantastic," I said.

It had been over two months since I had contacted my family, and I was hoping they'd sent me emails back by now telling me how Mom was doing. Also, tomorrow was Katie's wedding. At least if I couldn't be there, I could send her an email.

28

September 26th—Fear those who do not fear God.
—Iranian proverb

BY THE TIME DAWN PEEKED OVER THE HORIZON, I was already waiting for Spill in the driveway with the trailer hitched to my bike. When he did ride up, he caught me by surprise because he was dressed in a dark suit and a felt hat.

"What are you wearing?" I asked, laughing.

"Hey! I look good."

"Yeah, but a suit? You look like Randall."

"I'm way better looking than Randall. Let's go."

I was still smiling as we maneuvered our way along the dark road. He was right. Randall was short and stocky and probably forty years old. Spill was slender and had a nice smile, and even though I wasn't exactly sure how old he was, he definitely wasn't over twenty-five. Probably younger. Probably closer to my age, in fact.

Still, it unnerved me a little that he was wearing a suit and hat because that meant that this was official business. My stomach turned a little queasy, but what could I do? I had to sell the whiskey or we'd never get home.

The sun climbed over the hills on our right, promising another glorious fall day. Summer had lasted longer here in Oregon than at home, the hot days carrying over well into September, but the mornings had turned crisp, and for the first time, I remembered that I should be in school already.

I'd be home soon, though, and it probably wouldn't be that hard to catch up. This was my last year anyway, but I almost felt too grown up for school. Maybe I wouldn't even go back. I laughed to myself. Wouldn't my highly educated family have something to say about that? No, I'd definitely be back in class soon. Hopefully in less than a week.

We'd ridden north for more than an hour when we came to a wide river. Spill turned east onto a gravel road that soon narrowed into a dirt track. We followed it, twisting through a dense forest. Just as I was about to drop dead from exhaustion, Spill stopped under a fir tree.

"Listen," he said, "when we get there, I want you to do exactly what I say and try not to talk to anyone, okay?"

"What is this place, anyway?"

"This is a trading post. Just try to keep a low profile, all right?"

"Okay."

We pushed our bikes the last twenty yards and walked out into a large open space. My heart was racing. In the center of the clearing stood a metal barn about ten times the size of ours at home. There was a line fifteen deep of men with bikes and carts who were waiting to get inside. Larger wagons hitched to horses stood in the shade of the trees. Two men in suits guarded either side of the entrance, checking IDs. One of them was Randall.

"Follow me," Spill said.

He cut to the front of the line and wheeled his bike up to the enormous double doors, and I hurried behind him. Randall nodded at him and opened the door for us. No one said a word about us cutting, which I knew must mean that Spill was some-one special.

"Okay," he said. "Try to be invisible."

When I stepped through the doors, I was almost blinded. Hanging from the rafters were endless rows of lights, flooding the room with an eerie glow and a lazy buzzing sound, like a swarm of bees. The entire roof must have been covered with solar shingles to power that many lights.

I blinked, waiting for my eyes to adjust. Two men came up to Spill, and he let them lead our bikes and trailers away. On one side of the room were tables loaded with everything you could ever want. Solar phones and computers, bananas, apples, pears, vegetables, clothing, shoes, bikes, wagons, jewelry, canned goods, fresh meat, guns, live rabbits in cages, electric lamps, and a lot of stuff I didn't recognize.

On the other side was obviously where you sold stuff. Men in suits sat behind tables and each one had a guard in mirrored sunglasses standing on either side of them. Behind the tables were crates and cartons of whatever they'd purchased that day. In the back of the room were more double doors like the ones at the front, but this time the two guys were taking a "cash donation" to let you out.

"Don't stare," Spill whispered. "You look suspicious."

I stared down at the ground. "Sorry," I mumbled.

He led me over to a long table with about ten computers on it. Most of them were in use, but halfway down the row was a vacant workstation. "I have to go get your money and take care of my sales," he said. "I'll be about ten or fifteen minutes. You can use that computer over there."

"Thanks."

I sat down and Spill vanished into the crowd. When I got my inbox open, I was excited to see I had fourteen messages. I started reading them instead of sending an email. I knew I didn't have much time, so I skipped over most of the ones asking if I was okay.

What I wanted to know, though, was about Mom. There was good news, and there was bad. James had come back from his summer job at the winery, and he'd been able to talk Mom into going to bed until the baby came. He'd done what none of us could do, so maybe he was right and he was the favorite. Either way, I was glad. The bad news was the midwife, Mrs. Rosetree, was concerned Mom was now showing signs of gestational diabetes. I'd have to ask Grandpa more about it and find out how dangerous it was.

Katie had postponed the wedding until November to give me more time to get back, which made me happy. She'd also done it so Mom wouldn't miss the ceremony by having to stay in bed, which made me worry again. I needed to send an email, but I scrolled down to the bottom quickly, just to make sure I didn't miss anything important. That's when I saw Dad's email about the border.

> Ian McClure CANADA BORDER CLOSING!!! September 21
> Molly,
> Return home ASAP. Epidemic breakout of polio around the Great Lakes has shut down parts of Canadian–U.S. border. Already setting up quarantine tents in Ontario w/ long delays—three weeks or more. Other provinces sure to follow to keep it from spreading. Don't get stuck.
>
> Hurry, Dad

Panic washed over me. We had to get home! Dad had sent the email five days ago and I hoped we weren't already too late. I took ten seconds to send a message saying I had the money and we were on our way and then I signed off. Where was Spill? I had to get back to my grandparents' house and get them packed. I ran up and down the aisles, and just as I was about to burst into tears, Spill grabbed my elbow, jerking me to a halt. He dragged me towards the exit.

"Oh, thank God–"

"Calm down," he hissed. "You're drawing attention to yourself."

"They're closing the Canadian border!"

"I heard," he said. "Let's get out of here."

At the warehouse doors he nodded at one of the giants guarding the exit. The man let us go through with our bikes and Spill's trailer, and we didn't even have to pay him like everyone else had. Outside, I stopped to talk, but Spill kept walking his bike across the clearing, so I hurried after him.

"My dad said in his email that the polio outbreak was only back East," I told him. "Around the Great Lakes."

He got on his bike and so I jumped on mine too. I followed behind him along the narrow trail through the woods and he said over his shoulder, "What I heard from Paul McKenzie, the Organization's transportation director, is that even though all the confirmed cases are in Wisconsin, Illinois, and Michigan, they've canceled all unnecessary travel between the U.S. and Canada."

"But I live there!" I said. "And the island needs a doctor. Do you think they'll let us in?"

"Paul wasn't sure. He said he thought they would eventually, but you might have to be quarantined for three weeks before they let you cross."

"Oh, Spill!" I cried. "Mom can't wait that long for a doctor!"

"Well," he said, "boats might still be getting through."

"How would I find a boat?"

"Shhhh, Molly," he said. "I need to be able to hear. We'll talk in a minute."

Hear what? I wondered. We were riding really slowly through the trees, and Spill checked around us at each turn in the path. Every rustle of leaves seemed to make him more edgy. Were there robbers in the woods? Anything seemed possible today. We went on like that for half an hour before we came out on the gravel road and he stopped.

"Now we can talk," he said.

"So how would I find a boat?" I asked again.

"I'm not really sure," he said, "but before I forget, here's your gold for the whiskey." He gave me a small handful of coins.

"You got gold?"

"It's safer than paper money because you don't have to worry about counterfeit bills."

I examined the shimmering coins. "But isn't this a lot of money?" I asked.

"Well, they're only quarter-ounce pieces," he said, "but it's still about twice as much as I would've gotten yesterday."

"Why?"

"Because most of our whiskey comes from Canada."

That immediately reminded me of the border problem. "Now that I've got the money, I think we should probably leave tonight."

If Spill was right and we could avoid the inspection tents somehow, Grandpa could be taking care of Mom in just a few days.

"Tonight's not good," Spill said. "There's stuff I need to take care of. But we should definitely get going by tomorrow or the next day."

"Wait a minute. Did you say *we*?"

He smiled. "I'm going with you."

"To Canada?"

"Yep. I'm starting over."

I couldn't believe it! And then I got the best idea. "You can come work on our farm!"

Spill shook his head. "Can't. I need to live in a city."

"Why?" I asked.

"Because I'm a cobbler, and I want to find a job in a shoe repair shop."

I looked down at the soft leather boots he'd given me for my birthday. "You're a cobbler?" He nodded. "Did you make these for me?"

"Yeah." His cheeks flushed pink. "I've been an apprentice for the last five years," he said, not looking at me.

We'd been standing there next to our bikes talking, and I leaned mine against a tree and walked over to him. I was so overwhelmed by this amazing thing, that he'd *made* me boots, that I thought I was going to throw my arms around him in a big hug, but at the last second, I just grabbed his hand, feeling kind of shy and embarrassed too.

"These boots are so beautiful, Spill. I love them."

His face turned bright red. I stared at him and he met my gaze and then I sort of leaned in, but instead of kissing me, he spoke. "Do they fit?" he asked.

"Yeah." I nodded. "Perfectly." I didn't move, still hoping. . . .

"They should," he said. His voice was really soft, but now he was staring at the boots instead of into my eyes. "You left lots of footprints in the garden for me to make a pattern."

I laughed, breaking the mood.

"Anyway," he said, removing his hand from mine, "we better get going."

What had just happened? I'd definitely wanted him to kiss me, but in a way, I was kind of glad he hadn't too. Even though he was going to Canada, he would have to be in a city, not my island, and a kiss would've just complicated everything when we had to say good-bye. Still, it might have been worth it.

I grabbed my bike and raced after him, consoling myself with the knowledge that he'd made the boots just for me. Maybe if he was in B.C., he'd come and visit. "How did you end up a cobbler?" I asked.

"It was Aunt Lili's idea. She's my aunt that took me in after my parents died in the flu pandemic." Spill's voice sounded tight. "She apprenticed me to get me away from the Organization."

"She doesn't like your job?" I asked.

He stared straight ahead as we rode. "The Organization wasn't so bad for me when I was a kid and had certain people looking out for me. But I'll be twenty-one pretty soon, and I'd have to join for real, not just be a delivery boy. Neither of us think I have . . . the temperament for that kind of life."

The temperament? What did he mean? And then I remembered Doug's cracked ribs.

"You mean you'd have to . . . to get violent?"

"Something like that." He shut his mouth in a firm line.

Could Spill really get violent if he had to? Had he already done stuff like that? Or did Aunt Lili want to get him out now because he was still innocent? I tried to put my energy into pedaling so I wouldn't have to think. There was only one way to block out worries over Mom's bad health, quarantines, and Spill's ties to the Organization, and that was to play Jewels. Unfortunately, I had a long ride ahead of me before I could get any consolation from her.

29

FINALLY WE CRESTED THE LAST HILL INTO OUR neighborhood. I pointed to two long, low black cars creeping along our street. "I wonder who that is?"

"Oh, no," Spill said. "This is not good."

He stopped his bike and scanned the neighborhood.

"What are you worried about?" I asked. "Who is it?"

"The Boss."

"The Boss? Here?"

"Molly, do you trust me?"

I wanted to. I really did. But even though he'd said he was going to Canada to start over and get away from the Organization, I just wasn't sure. He saw my hesitation.

"You have to," he said. "Please?"

"Yeah, I do." And I did. At least in that moment.

"I might be wrong, but, well . . . you know how things are. You have to do exactly what I say."

"Okay."

"Ride down to the end of this street and cut back around

to the house through the creek. Leave your bike if you have to, just hurry. Get the kids and your grandparents and go down to your basement. Lock all the doors and don't come out under any circumstances until I come for you."

"What about Doug?"

"If he's there, just . . . you can't do anything for him. Just take the kids."

"But, Spill—"

What did he mean we couldn't do anything for Doug? Were they coming to kill him like Grandpa had said they might?

"Now!" Spill said, his voice tight. "There's no time to lose. They'll be there any minute. Hurry!"

"What're you going to do?"

"Slow them down. Now go!"

I started to ask more questions, but Spill took off towards the cars. I raced through the deserted streets, and when I got to the end of Creekside Way, I ditched the bike and plunged into the creek bed. I pushed through where the blackberry brambles had taken over again and came out in our yard. Grandma was holding on to the trunk of the lilac tree, and the kids were running around her, laughing.

Brandy shouted at her, "You can't stay on home base forever! It's not fair!"

"Where's Grandpa?" I yelled.

"Inside," Brandy said. "Taking a nap."

"Come on." I scooped up Michael. "Everyone into the house."

"Why?" Brandy argued. "We're playing tag, and I'm it."

"Now," I said. "Let's go."

Grandma took Brandy by the hand, but she pulled free. "I don't want to go in!" she yelled.

I thrust Michael at Grandma, and she hustled him into the house. I think she must've seen the panic in my eyes. "Now, Brandy. I'm not kidding around."

"I'm gonna tell Uncle!" she screamed as I dragged her inside, slamming the glass doors shut behind us.

"Grandpa! Get up. It's an emergency."

He sat up groggily on the settee. "Why? What's happened?"

Grandma had set Michael down and she ran over to Grandpa and tugged at his arm, pulling him up. If I had ever doubted whether she was following the conversation or not, I didn't anymore.

I nodded towards Doug's house. "The Boss is here."

Grandpa looked around, alarmed. He fumbled with his glasses, trying to get them back on. "What should we do? Should I go out there?"

"No. Spill's handling it. He says to take the kids downstairs and for you to stay there until we come for you."

Brandy was still trying to break free, but I held on tightly. "Stop it, Brandy!" I said, and her crying turned to big, huge sobs. "Take her," I told Grandpa.

"I'll play piano," he said, picking her up. "You can have a lesson."

I watched as the four of them headed for the basement. Spill had told me to hide with them, but I had to know what was happening.

"What about you?" Grandpa asked.

"Spill needs my help," I said.

"Molly, I highly doubt that," he said. "The Organization is nothing to fool with. Remember Doug's warning?" He held out a hand to me. "I want you to come with us."

I ran across the room to the French doors before he could stop me. "Don't worry," I said. "I'll be fine. Spill's there."

Silently, I made my way across the deck and down the stairs into the yard and then edged my way to the gap in the fence. I could hear rumbling voices next door already. I inched closer and closer, step by step, until my body was pressed against the boards of the fence and I could see through the hole we'd made.

Four huge men plus Randall and Spill stood around Doug. He sat in a chair, white and shaking. A slender woman with blond hair twisted up in a knot perched on the edge of the other chair. She wore a dark suit jacket with a slim skirt and the highest stiletto heels I'd ever seen in person.

"I–I can pay, really," Doug stammered.

"So pay," Randall said. His voice was soft, but cold.

"I don't have cash but–"

"All gambling debts are to be paid in cash," growled Randall.

"I can't . . . I don't . . . ," Doug muttered. "Maybe I could work it off?"

"How?" asked the woman.

"I don't know. . . ." The right side of Doug's face was shiny and pink, as if someone had hit him hard already. His hair was loose from his normal ponytail, and his voice sounded shaky, like he was in pain. "I could do what these guys do," he said. "I'm strong."

The woman looked at the sky like she was considering it and then she laughed. "Funny as it seems, I'm not very fond of gamblers. Especially ones who lose and then don't pay me. Besides, I only employ honorable people."

Doug looked like he wanted to run, but the men were grouped around him. "Are you going to kill me?" he asked.

"Now why would *I* do that when I have five employees who would enjoy doing the job more than I would?"

They were going to murder him? They couldn't do that. Spill had to stop them, but he didn't move. His expression was grim and cold. In his suit he looked just like one of them. Or was he simply waiting for the right moment? What if he couldn't help him? Doug had walked away, leaving me to my fate at the market, but how could I face Brandy and Michael knowing I hadn't at least tried to save their only living relative? But what could I do?

"If you're absolutely sure you can't pay," the woman said, "then I guess it's time to take a little ride."

Doug looked around furtively, trying to find an escape route. The only way out was through his own house or through the gaping hole in the fence and into ours. I suddenly knew why Spill had wanted everyone in the basement. Doug started to stand and then he dropped down like he was going to crawl under the table. One of the men flipped it over, and they grabbed him by the hair, dragging him to his feet.

Doug swung his fists wildly and managed to hit one of the

men square in the jaw. The man fell back onto the table as Doug tried to make another run for it, but this time a giant slugged him in the stomach. He doubled over and fell to the ground, writhing, as the men kicked at him. His ribs had gotten better but were not completely healed, and his screams pierced my heart.

"No! No! Please! Stop!" Doug yelled. "I'll pay. I'll pay you somehow. Spill? Help me."

Spill, his face expressionless, didn't move. I felt like he'd poured ice water over me.

"Enough," said the woman. "Let's go."

The men stopped kicking and waited while Doug used the chair to pull himself up. Once he was standing, he grabbed at the chair and tried to swing it, but because of his ribs, he only managed to lift it about an inch off the ground and then he stumbled forward.

"Want some more?" one of the men asked. Instantly they were on him again.

And then I heard Brandy's shrill scream from the deck of my grandparents' house. "Let me go!" she shrieked. "I want Uncle!"

Before I could react, she flew by me and into her yard. "No! Brandy! No!" I ran after her and scooped her up just before she reached the stairs to the deck.

"Uncle!" she screamed, banging at me with her fists and kicking at my shins. I pulled her as tightly to me as I could and ran back towards our yard. Grandpa came hurrying through the gap in the fence, gasping for air, his glasses missing.

"Take her," I said, shoving her into his arms. She wailed one last pitiful howl and then collapsed against him, limp, sobbing. He staggered back to the house, whispering to her.

"Well, well," said the woman, standing and looking across the yard at me. "You must be the famous Handsome Molly."

I nodded, embarrassed that she'd called me that. She seemed to be the one in charge. Maybe she would understand about the kids needing Doug. "Are you . . . are you the Boss?" I asked.

She smiled, but there was nothing behind it. "The one and only."

We stood there staring at each other. Every nerve in my body was tight and twisted. She looked calm and cool. Of course, she was used to this . . . this . . . violence. I looked at Spill for help, but he was watching Doug. Was he was avoiding my eye on purpose?

"What are you going to do to him?" I asked the Boss.

"I think you know," she said. "You were listening the whole time, weren't you?"

I thought about the gold tucked in my pocket and instinctively touched my hand to my jeans. Out of the corner of my eye, I saw Spill shake his head. I looked at him and this time he mouthed something at me. What was he saying? And then I understood.

"He doesn't have any money," I said. "But there's something else."

"What's that?" she asked. Her manner was bored, and she patted her blond hair as if what I had to say was just taking up her precious time.

"Food," I said, my insides sinking into the ground.

"What food? This garden? It's past its heyday, I'm afraid."

"Not the garden. Preserved food," I said. "And potatoes, turnips, carrots . . . other stuff."

What was I doing? What would the kids eat all winter?

"Show me," she said.

I crossed over to the carefully laid cornstalks, kicked them off the root cellar, and yanked open the trapdoor. Randall peered down inside.

"Well?" asked the Boss.

He shrugged. "Hard to see, but it looks like enough to cover the interest."

That was it?

The Boss tapped her fingers on her thigh. "Hmmm . . . the interest. Not good enough."

"What about the house?" I asked.

"What about it?" she said.

"Don't you own this house, Doug? Maybe you could sell it . . . or . . . or give her the house."

"I tried to sell it," Doug said. "No one wants to buy it."

The Boss let her gaze wander over the yard and then back to the house. "Do you really own it? Outright? Your name's on the deed?"

"Yeah," Doug said. "My parents left it to my sister. Now that she's dead, I'm the proud owner of this worthless shack."

"Oh, I don't know about worthless," the Boss said.

She walked over to the French doors and stepped inside. A minute later, she came out. "No furniture," she said. "That's a plus. Nothing to get rid of. I suppose the Organization could always use a big house like this for storage. Especially one that isn't traceable to us by any kind of paperwork and is legitimately owned by someone else. And it's out of the way, but not too far from the market."

She walked over to Doug, who was still lying on the ground. She lifted one foot and placed the heel of her shoe right onto his hand, pinning it to the deck. "I don't like to kill family men," she said, digging her heel into his palm just enough to make him wince. "But I will if I have to. For now, I'll take the food and this house, and we'll call it even. You've got one week to vacate or you're mine. Understand?"

"Yes. Yes, thank you!" Doug said, trying to sit up, but falling back, shuddering with pain.

"Don't thank me," she said. "Thank Molly." She turned to the men. "Load up that food, and let's get out of here."

Spill helped them without ever looking my way.

30

September 28th–Uncle Ralph reminds you,
"A chain is only as strong as its weakest link."

I PERSONALLY WOULD'VE PACKED UP AND LEFT right after the incident with Doug, but unfortunately, he'd disappeared and left us with Brandy and Michael.

"We can't just leave," Grandpa said.

"Forty-eight hours," I told him. "That's all I'm giving him. And then we'll have to figure out something to do about the kids." I didn't know what, but I wanted to get home and now that I had the gold, I wasn't going to wait any longer.

It rained for two days straight, and we were all on edge. The kids snapped at each other, and Grandma couldn't distract them with games or books. Brandy wasn't speaking to either me or Grandpa because even though I don't think she'd seen Doug lying on the ground all bloody, she knew we'd kept her from him for some reason.

Doug's forty-eight hours were almost up, and I wanted to leave, so I went over to his house one more time, just to see if maybe he'd come home in the night. I pounded on his back door, but no one answered so I stuck my head inside and yelled for him. Finally, I went in and spent about ten minutes search-ing the house. He was definitely gone. He'd left the kids and run off.

I hurried back home through the rain, furious that we'd let him out of our sight. What was I going to do now? I couldn't turn Brandy and Michael over to Child Welfare, but I couldn't just take them to Canada, either. I raced up the stairs of our deck, my head down against the wind, and crashed right into Spill.

"Sheesh!" I said. "You scared me to death."

"Sorry." He smiled, but there was worry written all over his face.

"Nice of you to finally show up," I snapped. I brushed my wet hair out of my face. "I thought maybe you might've come around yesterday."

Spill shuffled his feet. "I was kind of busy."

"Doing what? Roughing up some other gambler?"

He looked at me, curious. "Are you mad at me?"

"Maybe," I said. I knew I was pouting like Brandy did when she was being unreasonable.

"Why?" he asked. "What'd I do?"

"More like what you didn't do." He didn't respond. "I *thought* we were friends, Spill."

He smiled like he didn't get what was bugging me. "We are."

"Well, you could've stepped in so we didn't have to give all that food to the Boss."

"That's what you think?" His voice had turned surprisingly cold.

I looked at him, but he wouldn't meet my eye. "Well . . . couldn't you?" I asked.

"For your information, Aunt Lili let him off easy. Yeah, she can use the house, but she could have any place she wants. She knew Doug had Brandy and Michael, so she was being nice."

"That was Aunt Lili? Your aunt Lili is the Boss?"

"Of course. What'd you think?"

I hadn't thought anything. Why would I have made that connection? "You could've mentioned that before!"

He shook his head, frustrated with me for some reason. "I just assumed you knew."

"How would I know?"

He shrugged. "Everyone knows."

Did my grandpa know? And Doug? How come no one had told me? Had they just thought I knew too?

"Look, forget about Aunt Lili," he said. "And forget about Doug. Come inside. I need to talk to you."

I went with him, but not because he asked me to. I went because I was cold and wet and I wanted to get warm. Inside, I wrapped a blanket around myself and sat on the end of the settee, crossing my arms, hoping to look tough.

"Is the money from the whiskey enough to get us home if we have Brandy and Michael too?" I asked.

"You're going to take the kids?"

"I'm not sure, but Doug seems to have disappeared."

"I think it's great that you want to take them, and there's enough gold," he said, "but we have a bigger problem than money."

"What do you mean?"

He sat down on the settee next to me. "Well," he said, "you're not allowed to leave now."

I groaned. "Did they officially close the border?"

"No. I mean, not that I know of," he said.

"So what are you talking about then?"

Spill's face looked pale. He ran his hands through his hair. "Anyone who's involved with the Organization in any way," he said, "even inadvertently, is ranked for the risk they are to its ability to operate without legal interruption."

"Spill, would you speak English?"

"You witnessed the Organization threatening Doug," he said. "Aunt Lili was forced to raise your risk status to Level Four."

"English!" I said again.

He sighed. I had the feeling he was complicating his explanation because he didn't really want me to understand him. "Because we were friends," he said, "you were ranked a Level One Risk. That means the Organization couldn't discount the fact that you might go to the police with information, but you probably wouldn't because you didn't know enough, and because you were my friend. But now that you saw the altercation with Doug, you're a Level Four Risk. That means you can't leave town."

"Who says?"

"Aunt Lili."

I'd been worried for a minute, but if his aunt was in charge, what was the big deal?

"So talk to her," I told him.

"I can't," he said. "Her word is final. And the Organization will enforce it."

"You mean I can't *ever* leave Gresham?"

He nodded.

I stood up and brushed myself off like the matter was settled.

"Too bad for the Organization because I'm a Canadian citizen and I'm going home anyway."

"They'll stop you."

"Will they kill me?"

"Well . . . probably not. You really have to be a Level Eight or higher before they'll do that."

"So what will they do?" I asked.

"They'll watch you closely for a while," he said. "And they'll make all routes out of town pretty much impossible until you give up."

"You mean like stake out the train station?"

He looked uncomfortable. "And the house. You'll have a twenty-four-hour guard for at least a few weeks."

"So I just have to starve here because I can't leave?" I demanded.

"You won't starve. You have the gold to buy food at the market. And Aunt Lili told me you can start playing your fiddle there too. She might even hire you for some private parties." He smiled like he'd given me a gift.

"Oh, well, that *is* good news." I grabbed a book off the end table and threw it across the room, just in case he missed the sarcasm.

"Mol–"

"What about you?" I asked. "If I'm a Level Four, doesn't that make you like a Level Fifty? How can you just leave to go off and be a cobbler?"

He looked down at his handmade boots. "Oh, well . . . maybe I'll stay."

"You can't stay!" I said. "You'll have to join the Organization for real."

"Yeah. . . ."

I grabbed his hand and pulled him up off the couch. Why was he acting so defeated? "You have to get out of here too. We all have to get out of here!"

"It's not that easy for me, either," he said. "Part of the deal is I have to run away too."

"What do you mean?"

"They don't just *let* me go," he explained. "I have to sneak off. If I can make it out of the country, then I'm free."

We were facing each other and I was still holding his hand in mine. "Why did Aunt Lili apprentice you as a cobbler if you can't even leave?"

He laughed, but it sounded bitter. "She's hoping I'll show some initiative and get away."

"I thought she was in charge. Why can't she just say 'See you later—make sure you write' and send you on your way?"

Spill sighed. "The Organization only exists because it has a system of rules that everyone agrees to follow. Even the Boss. If she just lets me go, then she's in violation of the code of ethics and they'll remove her."

I dropped his hand. "You mean, kill her."

"Yeah."

I stared at him hard. "Will they kill you if they catch you?"

He gave me a halfhearted smile. "Not if I leave before I'm twenty-one. Then they'll just bring me back if they catch me."

"I can't believe this!" I said. "What are we going to do?"

He sank back on the settee like he was out of ideas. "We'll think of something."

The chair across the room swiveled around until Grandpa was facing us. "I have an idea," he said with a tiny smile.

31

SPILL SPENT THE ENTIRE DAY WITH US, GOING OVER Grandpa's plan in detail. They'd worked out a bunch of stuff I didn't understand, but in the end, it was me who had been able to provide us with two crucial parts of the escape plan.

First, there was Jane, the old woman I'd met on the train coming down here. She'd told me if we needed a place to stay on the way back, we could visit her. I still had her address in Kelso, Washington, and Spill said he'd get a message to her somehow. I worried a little about involving her, but Grandpa convinced me that the Organization would never know, and that we needed her help.

The other connection I had was Tyler, Poppy's boyfriend, in Seattle. Hopefully he could help us get into Canada.

We'd sorted ourselves out, but there was the little problem of Doug. He seemed to have disappeared for good. We weren't sure what we'd do about Brandy and Michael if he wasn't back by the time we had to leave, because we couldn't take them along. They didn't have passports or birth certificates, and we weren't their legal guardians. All of that would make getting them into Canada impossible, even if we wanted to take them, and I still wasn't sure that was a good idea anyway. How would my parents react to me bringing two more kids to the farm?

The next day, we put our plan into action. Randall had been assigned to make sure I didn't make a break for it, and acting happy was going to be especially difficult with him following me everywhere I went because the whole thing made me angry. But pretending to accept the situation was part of the plan.

I took my fiddle out to the deck, where Randall sat by the fire. He'd added a black overcoat and a red wool scarf to his suit.

"Now that the Boss said it's okay, I'm going to the market to busk," I told him.

He nodded and followed me through the yard. He'd boarded up the front door from the outside, so going through the creek was the only way to get to the street.

"Doesn't someone have to guard my grandparents?" I asked.

Randall didn't answer, and his face remained passive. Spill had told me that guards aren't allowed to speak to their captives, but getting him to talk was also part of the plan, so I didn't give up.

"It's good to have company," I tried.

He smiled like I amused him, but said nothing. Oh, well. I had a few more days to get him to talk. Assuming Grandpa could do his part in time. That was a big if, but it had to work or we really would be stuck here forever. Aunt Lili was giving a formal party in two days and Spill thought that since most of the Organization would be there, that night was our best chance for escape. Our only chance. If we were caught, I'd be upped to a Level Eight Risk and they'd separate me from my grandparents.

At the market, I took out my fiddle and tuned her. It had finally stopped raining, but the air was chilly and I wasn't sure how long I'd be able to play before my fingers were too numb to get the notes right. I hoped I didn't have to stall too long.

I set up near the food vendors, and Randall sauntered over to the doughnut tent to chat with an enormous man and his equally large wife. I noticed Randall kept me in his sight line at all times. I began with "Brianna's Reel" and followed it with two new songs that Grandpa had taught me. I'd just finished when Spill strolled up.

"Hey, Handsome Molly, why don't you play my favorite?"

I glared at him over my fiddle. "Why don't you get lost?" I said, and began a new tune.

He hung around, though, listening.

"Are you still mad at me?" Spill asked when I stopped playing.

I shook my head. "I'm not mad," I said, "I'm just never talking to you again, so could you please just leave?"

"It's a free country," he said.

"Fine. I'll go somewhere else."

I guess because I'd stopped playing, Randall thought he'd better come over, which was perfect because the whole point of our fight was for him to see it. Before I could get my case,

Spill picked it up off the ground. I grabbed at it with my free hand, but he held on.

"Don't touch my fiddle!" I said.

"I'm not." He laughed. "This is your case. You've got your fiddle."

I pulled harder. "You know what I mean! Let go!"

He yanked it out of my hands and held it behind his back. "Come on," he said. "Let's talk about it." He made a face like he was really sorry, and I almost laughed at how bad of an actor he was.

"There's nothing to talk about." I reached around him, trying to get the case.

"Look, it's not my fault," he said. He smiled like there was nothing wrong, which was a lot better than his fake-concern face.

"It's all your fault!" I yelled. I was a pretty good actress, I thought.

By now people were lingering to hear what we were arguing about.

"Molly—"

"You can't explain it away," I said, planting one hand on my hip. "I'm stuck here because of you."

"You know I was trying to help," Spill said. Now he actually looked sorry, and I knew that even though we were pretending, he meant that part. "I didn't mean for things to get all messed up."

"Fine," I said, tucking Jewels under my arm. "You can keep the stupid case. I'm going home."

"Wait," Spill said. "Take it. I'm sorry."

He held it out, open, so I could set Jewels inside. I snapped it shut and tore it out of his hands. I stormed across the market, practically running, and didn't slow down until I was going up the hill towards home. Randall came huffing behind me.

"You okay?" he asked. His face was red.

"What do you care?"

"It's not his fault you can't leave," Randall said. His breath was still coming out in gasps. "You spied through the fence."

I scowled at him, not answering. We were coming up to the turnoff to Creekside, and while I was breathing pretty easily, poor Randall was really fighting for air.

"It won't be so bad once you get used to the idea," he said, puffing. "Living here."

"Well, it's not like I have a choice."

I guess that's when Randall remembered he wasn't supposed to talk to me, because he clamped his mouth shut. Or maybe he was just so breathless he couldn't speak. I left him on the deck and hurried inside and into the garage, where Grandpa was working.

"Did you get it?" he asked.

"I think so!" I set Jewels down on the workbench and opened the case. Under the piece of silk I always kept to wrap her in were four sheets of paper that Spill had slipped inside during our tug-of-war.

"And do you think Randall fell for the fight?" Grandpa asked.

"Hook, line, and sinker," I said, grinning.

32

September 30th–I am not an adventurer by choice but by fate.
–Vincent van Gogh

BY THE TIME BREAKFAST WAS READY, GRANDPA WAS already huddled over his workbench. I had to force him to come out for lunch so Randall wouldn't get suspicious, but he refused to stop for dinner.

"If we're going to be ready by tomorrow night, I need to keep working," he told me.

I'd made a huge pot of potato and leek soup, one that would last us a week, just to throw Randall off a little. I didn't know if he'd noticed or not, but the soup smelled delicious, and in the end, I talked him into having some, which was also part of the plan. I needed to make sure he trusted me not to poison his food. Which, of course, I hadn't. And I didn't even plan to, either. But I did need his trust.

Brandy had shown a stubborn streak I hadn't anticipated by not talking to either me or Grandpa for almost two full days, but on the third morning, she woke up cheerful and herself, which was a big relief to all of us as we needed her happiness to buoy our spirits.

The house was really getting cold at night. I'd gone upstairs to get my blankets because Brandy and Michael had begged me to sleep with them on the foldout couch in my grandparents' bedroom and I'd finally agreed. I'd shared a bed with my sister ever since I was three, and I kind of missed having someone to cuddle with on cold nights.

My grandparents were getting ready to turn in, and I'd left the kids in the living room to choose a story from a pile of really old picture books Grandma had given them. I'd just come out onto the landing when I heard Doug's voice downstairs. I hurried over to the balcony that looked down onto them below.

"But you want to live with Molly, don't you, Brandy?" he asked.

"I guess. But I miss you."

"I miss you too, but it's better this way."

So Doug had come back and it looked like he planned to hand the kids over to me permanently.

"Molly said you were gone," Michael piped up.

"I wouldn't leave without saying good-bye," he told them. "I want to hug you both, but you have to be careful. I'm still sore from my fall."

When the Organization had given Doug the first warning, he'd told the kids he'd cracked a rib falling off a horse, and of course, they'd believed him. Doug tried to squat down, but his face went ashen and he visibly clenched his jaw, a little moan escaping.

"Maybe you'll just have to hug my legs," he said, straightening up. "It's kind of hard to bend over."

The kids flung themselves at him, practically knocking him over, and wrapped their skinny little arms around his thighs. He blanched in pain, and for a second I thought he might pass out.

"Easy now," he said. "Not too tight."

"We're only hugging your legs, silly," Brandy said, giggling.

"I know, sweet pea, but I'm sore all over." He ruffled their hair with his big hands, and laughter floated up to me as I watched.

"Okay," he said after a while. "I gotta go. You two be good for Molly, and do what she says, all right?"

"We will," they said together.

He motioned to a large envelope on the end table. "And don't forget to give her the papers I left."

"We won't," they said.

His voice got so soft I almost couldn't hear him. "Tell her I'm sorry too," he added.

"Okay."

"Hey, Doug?" I called over the balcony. "Where are you going?"

He looked up at me, and flinched from the sudden movement.

"Mexico," he said.

"You're leaving Brandy and Michael with me for good?" I asked.

"Is that okay?"

I couldn't believe he was asking me that now when he'd obviously planned to just sneak away without them.

"The Organization's keeping me here now," I said. "But if

they ever let me go, I'll have to take them back to Canada with me." I wanted to make sure he understood he'd probably never see them again.

"Yeah." He nodded. "I know."

I did not want to be nice to him, but he looked so pathetic standing there. He'd chopped off all his long hair, probably so people would stop grabbing it in fights, and he was obviously in a lot of pain. "Do you need some money?" I asked.

"Nah, I'm good."

"Well . . . be careful."

"You too, Molly," he said. "Their birth certificates and stuff are in the envelope."

"Okay."

He rubbed the tops of their heads. "Take care of my kids."

"I will."

"I know." He waved and was gone.

If he was going to Mexico, he wouldn't be back, so it didn't really matter if we took them away from here or not. He'd entrusted them to me, and they belonged on our island farm now. Assuming we could ever get back.

Brandy was curled up against me in the foldout bed and Michael had one leg over mine. I shifted trying to get more comfortable, but someone was standing over me with a candle, shaking my shoulder. "Wake up, Molly," Grandpa said.

"What?"

"I did it!"

"What's going on?" Brandy mumbled.

"Jack?" I heard Grandma's voice say from across the dark room where she was tucked into her own bed.

"It's okay," he told her. "I just wanted to tell Molly that I did it. The module works!"

I disentangled myself from the kids and hunted for my jeans. "I want to see it," I said.

"There's not much to it," Grandpa said.

"Can I come?" Michael asked. Brandy had already fallen back asleep.

"No, you stay here."

He started to whimper and so I picked him up and put him into bed with Grandma.

In the garage Grandpa had lit two whole boxes of candles in order to see what he was doing. Gleaming in the middle of the floor was the Studebaker, its hood propped open and a slight hum coming from it.

I leaned in and inspected Grandpa's handiwork. The Super Seven Solar Battery had been replaced by a red metal box with a curved top. The lid was hanging open, and I could see a mess of wires he'd pulled out of the wall, a hose made from one of Spill's spare inner tubes, what looked like two circular saw blades, some string, and duct tape. Obviously whatever was really powering it was hidden from view. Even I knew you couldn't build a power source from duct tape.

"How fast do you think it will go?" I asked.

Grandpa examined the pages that Spill had given us. "It says it will go seventy miles an hour, but I doubt the Studebaker will go more than about twenty because she's made of steel."

"It's amazing that you could build this out of scrap pieces."

"But that's the whole point. Anyone who can follow directions can build it."

When Grandma had been in the hospital, Grandpa had found an old *Today's Mechanics* in the waiting room. In it was an article about how to build a self-generating power source that was capable of running any car. He'd wanted to try it on the Studebaker, but later discovered he was missing several pages. That's where Spill had come in. He'd downloaded the rest of it from the internet.

"We can't risk taking the car out," Grandpa said, "but I can back her up a little, just so you can see it works."

"Okay."

I climbed in and he backed up about two feet. It was sort of anticlimactic unless you thought about the fact that he'd made it run himself.

"You did it!" I said, and scooted across the bench seat to give him a hug. Unfortunately, because electric cars are almost silent, I hadn't realized that he hadn't turned the module off. His foot slipped on the pedal, sending us backward with a bang right into the garage door. He put it in park, switched it off, and we jumped out. Randall was off duty and our night guard was out in the backyard by the fire, but he would've heard the thump for sure. I started pinching out the candles with my thumb and forefinger.

"Leave them," Grandpa said. "He'll check the bedroom first, and if we're there, hopefully he won't come in here. Let's go!"

I wasn't sure it was a good idea, but I followed Grandpa anyway, racing through the house. I dove into the bed next to Brandy and heard heavy footsteps in the living room. I'd just pulled the covers up over us when someone shone a Crank Light in my face.

"What's going on?" I mumbled, faking grogginess.

The beam danced around the room, settling onto my grandparents' bed.

"Nothing," the guy said. "Just my nightly head count. Sleep tight."

The light preceded him out of the room, and I heard the French doors to the deck click shut behind him. I waited five minutes, climbed out of bed, snuck back to the garage, and put the candles out. The car worked! Now we just had to get away.

33

October 1st–An apple a day keeps the doctor away.

IT WAS REALLY HARD TO ACT NORMAL THE NEXT DAY, but we tried our best. I spent the morning stripping the garden of anything that was left, which wasn't much. I had no idea if we'd be able to cook along the way, and I wasn't counting on fresh water, so I had Grandma wash and prep everything we had left for the journey with the idea that we'd just eat it raw if we had to.

When Randall came on duty, I went out and sat by the fire with him. I did a double take because over his lip was the very faint start of a thin moustache. With his felt hat and short stocky body, and now this, he was looking more and more like an old-time movie gangster.

"How exactly do I spend a piece of gold?" I asked him.

At first he didn't answer, and I thought he was back to the silent treatment.

"I guess I could change it for you at the market," he finally said. "Why?"

"I want to stock up on food," I said.

He nodded. "You ready?"

"Sure. I want to busk too, though. Let me get my fiddle."

I ran inside and got Jewels and a couple of cloth bags, and then Randall and I walked down to the market one last time. Of course, *he* had no idea it was the last time. According to the plans we'd made, today Spill was supposed to send us the go-ahead message hidden inside an apple. My heart was racing, and I was glad for Randall's silence because I wasn't sure I could keep the nervousness out of my voice.

He led me into the scary bit of the market, but everyone moved swiftly out of our way and no one looked directly at either of us. He went into a tent to change the gold and I stood outside. After a few minutes, he came out with my money and then he led me around to buy dried goods, bread, and cheese. When I asked a vendor how much something cost, they gave me a price right away. Not one person asked me "how much do you have?" like usual. And, after a glare from Randall, the bread vendor lowered his price considerably.

"You ready to busk now?" Randall asked.

The bags were overflowing, and it was so cold I knew I'd be fumbling around, sounding horrible, but I needed the all-important message from Spill, and I knew busking was how he'd get it to me.

"Yeah, I'll play for a while. Do you mind?"

"It's your life."

Ha! That was a joke. I took out Jewels, and once she was tuned and I was playing, Randall slipped away to talk to his pals. "I'll be back as soon as you stop, so don't get any ideas," he said before he went. I made a sweet-and-innocent face, and he laughed.

I played for almost forty-five minutes without anyone dropping any kind of fruit into my case. My fingers were freezing, and I sounded terrible. I had stopped playing to blow on my hands when a little boy came over and handed me an apple.

This was it! Before I could even look at it, though, Randall was standing over me. "I'll take that," he said. "If you don't mind, Molly."

"Uh, sure."

What could I say?

"You ready to go?" he asked.

"Yeah."

I packed up Jewels, watching him out of the corner of my eye. I thought he'd somehow figured out that Spill and I were up to something. Was he going to inspect the apple? No, instead he bit into it. We walked back through the market and up the hill, Randall chomping on the apple the whole time. Spill had told me he was going to remove the core and place a note inside, and then slide it back in so the apple would look whole. I was sure that any second Randall was going to bite into something that shouldn't be inside it.

"Can I have the core when you're finished?" I asked as casually as I could. "I'm saving the seeds."

"Gonna plant an orchard?" he asked, laughing.

"Well . . . not really . . . but Grandpa and I are going to start homeschooling the kids," I improvised. "I thought this would be a fun project, just to keep them busy, you know? We can try and sprout them."

Randall took one last bite and then handed me the core. I tossed it in the bag with the food and kept walking like nothing had happened. As soon as I got home, I ripped the core to bits. The piece of paper inside was so small I was surprised Randall hadn't eaten it. In tiny handwriting was one word:

Tonight.

Grandma seemed to understand the entire plan and the two of us made a big show of cooking dinner over the fire. I even played my fiddle until my fingers were so cold I had to quit. Randall sat in one of the chairs, bundled in his coat, laughing and singing along with us. Instead of relaxing me, his trust made me feel worse about what I was planning to do. After a while, we all went inside, leaving him there to stay warm by the fire. He was on duty until midnight, and by then it would all be over.

I took Jewels to the garage, where Grandpa was making last-minute adjustments to the load. Brandy and Michael were perched on top of an enormous suitcase in the backseat, rolling the windows up and down. Grandma sat next to them, smiling like she was going out for a Sunday drive.

We'd packed the trunk with food, several liters of water, and ancient camping gear from Grandpa's attic. My bike was strapped to a makeshift bike rack attached to the rear bumper just in case we needed it.

"Don't you think we could just drive away?" I asked him. "Randall might not even hear us."

"Spill said not to take any chances."

"I just feel kind of bad about it. He's so nice."

"Molly, you're sympathizing with your captor. It's a weird psychological phenomenon that happens to the best people, though, so don't worry about it."

I didn't really know what he was talking about. Or maybe I just wasn't paying attention. "Okay," I said. "If you're ready, then here goes nothing."

"We're ready."

He grabbed a roll of duct tape and followed me back into the living room, where he picked up a book and sat on the settee, pretending to read. I stepped out into the cool October night with a pan of water in one hand and my other hand deep in my pocket.

"I thought I'd make some tea," I told Randall.

He nodded. I came down the deck stairs onto the sunporch, where the fire was burning brightly in the fountain. Just as I got to the bottom step, I stumbled forward, the pan of water sloshing. Randall jumped from his chair and reached out to steady me so I wouldn't fall into the flames. As soon as he had hold of my arm, I dropped the pan and plunged a syringe into his thigh. He leapt back in surprise, pulled it out of his leg, and rubbed the spot.

"What was that?" He started shaking his leg. "What'd you do? My thigh feels funny." He staggered a little and sat down hard in his chair. "Did you poison me?"

"No! I wouldn't do that," I said. How awful did he think I was? I'd stabbed him with some of the leftover painkiller we'd given Doug when he'd been hurt. According to Grandpa, with-

out the other dose to counteract it, Randall should be para-
lyzed almost immediately. "It's just a serum that numbs the
central nervous system. Your body's going to stiffen up and
you won't be able to move, but that's all. It'll wear off in ten
to twelve hours."

"Oh." He looked relieved that I hadn't killed him, but there
was still fear in his eyes.

I could see his body going rigid in the chair. It was working!
I couldn't believe how easy it had been. I really hated to do the
next part, but Spill had made me promise. As soon as I could
see that Randall couldn't move, I reached inside his coat and
pulled out his gun.

"Molly, you don't want that," he said, through gritted
teeth.

Even his jaw was seizing up. That was good. Then he
wouldn't be able to yell for help at midnight when his replace-
ment showed up. Spill had told us to bind him up and drag him
into the house where he wouldn't be found for a while. I called
Grandpa, who came running with the duct tape.

"Can you do it yourself?" I asked him. "I'm shaking."

I'd been anxious before we started the whole thing, but
now it was like every nerve in my body was pulsing with
adrenaline. Had I really done this to Randall?

"No problem," Grandpa said. "I can handle him."

"You know, Molly," Randall said as Grandpa struggled to
unroll the sticky tape, "when you do something to someone,
poison them, or inject them with paralyzing potion or whatever, never tell them what's supposed to happen."

I wished Grandpa would just hurry with the tape. Why didn't he find the end of it when he was inside?

"Do you know why?" Randall continued through gritted teeth.

"No, why?"

"Because," he said, just as Grandpa leaned in to tape his ankles together, "it's easy to pretend it's working, when it's not." Moving jerkily, like a robot, but still with more dexterity than I was expecting, Randall forced his stiffening arms to act and he had Grandpa in a choke hold before I could even move.

34

GRANDPA'S FACE WAS ALREADY TURNING PURPLE IN Randall's grasp, and his glasses had clattered onto the patio. What was I going to do? Randall could snap Grandpa's neck in a tenth of a second and then come after me and Grandma.

"Let him go!" I screamed.

"Here's what happens next," Randall said stiffly. His jaw was definitely tight, but we could still understand him. "You give me my gun, and I let him go. Then we all sit here quietly until my relief arrives. After that, we'll decide what to do next."

When he mentioned his gun, I realized I was still holding it. I didn't even hesitate. Instead of handing it over, I pointed it at him. "Let him go," I said as calmly as I could.

"Molly," Randall said, "you can't shoot me."

"I can, and I will."

"I don't think so."

"You forget that I'm a farm girl, Randall. My dad's had me shooting target practice since I was seven years old. And I always hit my mark."

"Shooting targets isn't like shooting a person," he said.

Grandpa struggled, and Randall tightened his grip.

"I've shot two mad dogs," I said. "And I put the deer they were terrorizing out of its misery."

"It's not the same."

"And when my mother tells me to go out and get a chicken for supper, she isn't sending me to any market, but to the hen-house." I tried to sound cold and tough. "You're nothing more than an animal to me, and if you don't let him go, I'm going to shoot you."

Randall stared hard at me, the firelight flickering in his eyes. I was pretty sure I *could* shoot him if I had to. I mean, I would just maim him or something, not kill him. But I felt like I could do it, and I guess he must've seen it in my eyes because with a jerky movement of his arm, Randall released Grandpa. He stood up, choking and spluttering, the color slowly returning to his face.

I was afraid Randall would go for the gun, but he sat there motionless.

"You cover him, Molly, while I tape him up," Grandpa said, acting like he'd somehow gotten out of the jam all by himself. "Shoot if you have to, but warn me so I can get out of the way."

"I will." My voice was shaking, but my hand was surprisingly steady.

It looked like the serum was finally starting to work, because Randall's fingers were clenched and only his eyes were moving. I stood close enough to him so I had a clear shot, but not close enough for him to wrestle the gun from me if he was still faking it. He stayed in his chair, though, not moving a muscle, while Grandpa wrapped the tape around and around his ankles.

We stood him up, and he swayed stiffly on his feet. Grandpa bound his wrists together behind his back like Spill had told us to do, and I tried not to think about why Spill knew the best way to tape someone up. I put the gun in my inside coat pocket, and we half carried, half dragged Randall into my grandparents' bedroom, leaving him on a soft fluffy rug.

"Let's get out of here," Grandpa said, heading for the garage.

"Hey, Handsome Molly?" Randall called to me. His jaw was so stiff now I could barely understand him. "Nice knowing you," he said.

"You too, Randall."

"I'm sure we'll meet again." Even though he could barely talk, the amusement he obviously felt by telling me this showed in his voice.

"I hope not," I said.

"Oh, we will," he assured me. "And Molly?"

I was antsy to get out of there, but I stood still, wanting to hear what he had to say.

"Don't wait too long for Robert," he said. "He's not going to show up to meet you."

"How do you know?" I demanded, but worry flared up inside me.

"Because right now," Randall said through gritted teeth, "the Boss is hosting a big party."

"I know," I said. "That's why we're leaving tonight."

"I guess Robert didn't tell you the party is for him. For his twenty-first birthday. It's also his induction ceremony into the Organization."

I stared at Randall. It couldn't be Spill's twenty-first birthday! He knew he had to leave before then! "I don't believe you," I said.

"The house always wins, Molly. You should know that."

I ran out after Grandpa, slamming the bedroom door on Randall's words.

35

ON THE WAY TO THE GARAGE, I LITERALLY RAN INTO Grandpa, who was stumbling through the living room. "You're going to have to drive," he said.

"What? Why?"

He held up his mangled glasses. "Can't see a thing at night without them."

"But I don't know how to drive!"

"I gave you a lesson."

"It was a fake lesson!"

"You'll be fine. Come on."

"Just go easy," Grandpa said once I'd backed out of the drive-way and onto the road.

I went so easy he told me that maybe I should speed up a little if we ever planned to get out of Gresham tonight. "I'm trying," I said. "But I can't see anything."

The kids were jumping up and down on the suitcase with excitement, but I was concentrating so hard on not driving into a ditch that I hardly noticed them. Most of the market was already closed, but the scary bit glowed with activity, so I kept the headlights off until we'd slid noiselessly past. Once we'd crossed the main road and were on Highway 26, I turned them on.

"Won't she go any faster?" Grandpa asked.

"Faster! Faster! Faster!" Brandy and Michael chanted from the backseat.

I put the pedal to the floor, shooting us down the road.

"Wooohooo!" Grandpa yelled. "That's my girl!"

But after the initial burst of power, the car slowed. "She's straining now," I said. "I think we're too loaded down."

Grandpa leaned over me and studied the dials on the dashboard. "Hmmm . . . nineteen miles per hour. Even going this slowly we should make it to Jane's house before dawn."

I really hoped that when Jane had given me her address and said we could stay over on our way back, she meant it. Grandpa and Spill had worked out a back-roads route for us because I-5, the most direct way to Seattle, was too dangerous. In the old days, there would've been so many cars that even the Studebaker might not have drawn much attention, but now the interstate was practically empty. The only people who used it were the ones we wanted to avoid the most. The police, Transporters, and the Organization.

I'd had to ask what Transporters were.

"They're the trucks you see on the road," Spill explained. "They're government owned and operated, and they deliver anything that's rationed by the Feds. Like certain kinds of food—sugar, coffee, chicken, and pork—and any kind of fuel. Shoes and clothing and stuff too."

As far as we knew, no one had any idea we had a car, but we had to play it safe because most people would probably give us away for a price.

We'd been going for a while and the kids had fallen asleep in the back. I had just started to feel somewhat confident about driving when Grandpa said, "We're coming up on the Ross Island Bridge."

"A bridge?" Panic flooded through me. "I hate bridges."

"Don't worry. A bridge wouldn't dare collapse with a car as cool as a Studebaker on it," he said.

I sucked my teeth. "Go ahead and joke," I said, "but how many bridges have come down in the last thirty years?"

I had him there, and he knew it. Why wouldn't tonight be this bridge's turn to crumble under us?

"There won't be any traffic, so I'm sure our little car won't bring it down," Grandpa reassured me. "Besides, there is no way out of Portland without crossing at least one bridge, and as far as I know, this is a stable one."

All I could do was keep driving. I followed the road, anticipating it, my heart thumping, my breath coming fast. We rolled on and on until I couldn't stand it any longer. "Where is this stupid bridge?"

"Uh . . . Molly, you're halfway across it already."

I slammed on the brakes. "What? Why didn't you tell me?"

"You were doing fine," he said in his bedside manner. "Now just put your foot back on the accelerator and keep going."

"I can't."

"Sure you can," he said.

Blackness was all around us, but I just knew that below me was the Willamette River, and like a monster, it was waiting for the weight of the Studebaker to crack the aging concrete and send us plunging into its swirling waters.

"Go on," he said. "You can do it."

I sat there frozen. And then Grandma reached over the back of the seat and stroked my hair just like my mother always did when I was scared of something. I pressed tentatively on the pedal, and the car began to roll forward again.

"See where the road curves ahead?" Grandpa asked. "When you get there, you're over the bridge."

I followed it to the right and let out my breath. I'd done it. We'd made it across. I wiped at silent tears, glad for the dark. Grandpa directed me through a deserted downtown Portland, and eventually we found Highway 30. The road here was five lanes wide, and we were the only people on it. I knew the river was somewhere to my right and so I drove down the middle just in case.

Around midnight, Michael woke up because he had to go to the bathroom. I was stiff from driving, so I just stopped the car in the middle of the road and we all got out. Grandpa took Michael off into the dark, and Grandma and I stretched while Brandy kept sleeping. The cold night air helped me shake the sleepies, and I had a sandwich because I hadn't eaten much dinner.

"How're you doing, Molly?" Grandpa asked when they came back.

"Fine."

"If you need a longer break, we can take one. We've probably only got three more hours of driving."

"I'd rather keep going," I said.

"Okay, but don't let yourself doze off."

"It's not like we're going a hundred miles an hour," I said, laughing. "If I did fall asleep, you'd probably have plenty of time to wake me up."

All the way up to Scappoose and through the town of St. Helens, the road had been pretty good, but just north of there it became a mess. It was like someone had chewed up the pavement and spit it back out again. Big clumps of asphalt appeared out of nowhere, sending us bouncing in one direction and then the other.

"Lots of landslides in here over the winters," Grandpa explained. "And no one to do repairs. We might have to wait for daylight."

"I want to be at Jane's house and have the car hidden before then."

"Single-minded, just like your mother," he mumbled.

I didn't answer. My butt was hurting from the stiff seat, and my foot ached from trying to press the accelerator enough to keep us going but not so much that we smashed into every piece of debris in the road. It took us twice as long to get through the stretch leading up to the town of Rainier than we'd planned, and the sun was already coming up when we saw the turnoff.

"Turn right here," Grandpa said.

I eased the car onto the exit, and suddenly, looming in front of us, was another bridge. This one arched to the sky and disappeared into the fog. I slammed on the brakes. "My God!"

In the dim light we stared at the relics of what had once been some sort of historical landmark sign.

The Lewis and Clark Bridge
Built 1930, 8,192 feet long

Across the top, someone had nailed a hand-lettered sign that said: *BRIDGE MAY BE UNSTABLE. CROSS AT OWN RISK.*

36

I LOOKED THROUGH THE FOG AND SAW A DARK SHAPE moving across the bridge towards us. "Someone's coming."

It took the man almost fifteen minutes to reach the car, and Grandpa and I were standing next to it, waiting to talk to him when he got to us. We'd made Grandma and the kids hide inside on the floorboards, and then we placed ourselves in front of the windows, trying to block them from view. The dark shape turned out to be a small cart being pulled by a single pony and a grizzled man hobbling along beside it.

"Morning," Grandpa said.

The man stared at the car and didn't say anything.

"We were wondering about the bridge," Grandpa said. "Is it safe enough to cross in our car?"

"That's a Studebaker!" the man said.

"Yes, sir."

"We had one of those when I was a kid."

"Really? Did you get it new?" Grandpa asked.

"Right off the assembly line."

"What year was it?"

I cleared my throat.

"Let's see . . . ," the man said. "Musta been sixty-one or maybe sixty-two. I was only about four or five."

"What model?"

"Lark. Just like this one. Only a two-door."

"This color?" Grandpa asked. I nudged him in the ribs. "Uh, right. So, about the bridge. Is it safe enough to cross?"

The man rubbed his whiskers. "Well, how heavy do you think your Studie is?"

"I'm not really sure," Grandpa said.

"It's all steel," the man mused. "Pretty heavy . . . Maybe unload it and take your stuff across separately. Then drive the car real slow."

"Is it that dangerous?" I asked. "I mean, are there holes?"

"Not really. They just put that sign up there to keep the Transporters off it with their trucks."

That was good enough for Grandpa. "Well, thanks. We're off, then."

The man walked up to the car and ran his hand over the hood. "Nice to see one of these again." And then he moved away and led the pony down the road.

"So what do you think?" I asked Grandpa. "Unload it or not?"

"Well, I'm sure he thought it still had its motor. That would make it a lot heavier, so we're probably okay to drive it loaded."

The fog had begun to lift, but I couldn't really see very far across the bridge because of its slope. Two lanes ran in a straight line and just sort of disappeared into the distance. A low railing ran along either side, and you could see right through the gaps to the water below. Overhead, an intricate pattern of steel beams crisscrossed one another, reaching high into the sky.

"It's not that far," Grandpa said. "Here's what we'll do. I'll walk across with your grandma and the kids. And I'll take your bicycle with me. If I see anything that looks too dangerous for the car, I'll ride back and we'll figure out what to do then."

"Okay."

"And if I don't ride back in, say"–he thought about it–"an hour, then you can just assume it's safe and come across in the Studie."

"And hopefully, the reason you didn't come back isn't because you all fell into the river," I said.

Grandpa laughed. "Well, at least we'd all die together."

I really didn't see how he could joke at a time like this.

After the four of them headed off across the bridge, Grandma holding the kids' hands and Grandpa pushing the bike, I took an apple out of our food box and made myself eat it, even though my stomach was churning.

There still wasn't any sign of Grandpa after what I was sure had been an hour, so I decided it was okay to go. Grandpa moved slowly, but even he could've walked over and ridden back by then. I slid into my seat and turned the key. It hummed reassuringly, and I gripped the green plastic and chrome steering wheel. Slowly I began to ease the car up onto the bridge.

Look straight ahead. Stay away from the edge. Focus on going forward. Follow the road. You can do it.

I stared at the pavement, not daring to look around me. Grandpa had told me the bridge was just over a mile long. That would take me about ten or fifteen minutes to get across. I was probably halfway there, still creeping slowly, when a red-tailed hawk swooped across in front of me. I took my eye off the road to watch it, and that's when I saw the wide expanse of blue water below me, framed by mist-covered hills in the distance.

I slammed on the brakes, too stunned by the sheer beauty of it all to keep driving. Bands of green ran along the water's edges like shining ribbons. I'd never been this high up before, or seen anything from such a distance, and I couldn't take my eyes off the water, the fields, the mountains, the sky.

I put the car in park, turned off the engine to be extra safe, and climbed out. As soon as I was standing on the bridge, the wind whipped at my hair. My heart sped up. What was I doing? This was crazy. All I had to do was get back inside and drive. Instead, I gripped the car, edging my way around it to the passenger side. Against all reason, I took tiny, daring steps all the way over to the railing. Well, maybe not all the way, but I got pretty close.

When a crow drifted by on a current of air, I snapped out of my daze. Remarkably, my stomach had settled. I took deep, gulping breaths of the fresh air, and it invigorated me. I floated back to the car filled with a new sense of energy. And urgency. We were on our way back to the island, and once I conquered this bridge, I knew I could get us there no matter what!

I turned the key, imagining the engine roaring to life. And then I stepped on the accelerator so hard the tires squealed. I hardly had to steer at all because the bridge was so straight.

I kept glancing at the speedometer. *Ten . . . fifteen . . . twenty. . . .* Without the other people in the car weighing it down, it flew along just like the bird it was named for. *Twenty-five . . . thirty . . . thirty-five!*

As I reached the end of the bridge, Washington lay spread out before me. I was still flying, almost up to forty-five miles per hour, and as the exit road from the bridge widened, I hurtled past my family. I heard them screaming, and I imagined they were cheering for me! I slammed on the brakes, and that's when it occurred to me that they might have been yelling because they were frightened.

One second I was speeding happily along and the next, the car was careening to the right and all time seemed to slow down. My vision narrowed and I tugged on the steering wheel, but when I did, the car slid out from under my control and spun around in a circle. My hands were jerked off the wheel. And then, in what still seemed like slow motion, the car plowed forward about fifty meters and banged head-on into something solid.

Everything went black.

37

WHEN I CAME TO, MY GRANDPA WAS STANDING over me asking me questions like my name and date of birth and what year it was.

"Is the car okay?" I asked. My head was throbbing, but I was able to climb out on my own.

"I'm more worried about you right now," he said.

The kids were huddled next to Grandma, and Michael was crying.

"I'm fine. We've got to get to Jane's before we attract attention."

"You hit your head," Brandy said. "It's got a bump."

I touched my forehead. "Yeah. . . ." I grimaced. "Don't cry, Michael. I'm okay." I gave him a quick hug and then I walked around to the front of the car. Both the headlights were broken and the front grill had been pushed in. "The car looks like it will still drive," I said.

"Of course it will," Grandpa said. "It's a Studebaker. They're battleships."

I ignored how dizzy I felt. "Great, let's go." Grandpa was still poking at me, trying to see into my eyes. "You can examine me at Jane's, okay?"

"Well . . . all right. But I'm driving."

"You were going really, really fast!" Brandy said, leaning over the seat once we were back inside.

"Yeah, I remember." Was her voice always that shrill?

"Why?" Grandma asked.

I laughed. "I couldn't help myself. It was fun."

"Teenagers and cars," grumbled Grandpa.

I rolled my eyes and instantly regretted it because it made my head swim with dizziness.

"You give me directions," Grandpa said.

He owned a detailed map for every state in the country, and we had been able to find approximately where Jane lived before we'd even left Gresham. I navigated while Grandpa drove five miles per hour.

Jane was outside in her front yard mulching the flower beds when we pulled up. Her long, white braid swung over her shoulder like a rope when she bent down.

She dropped her rake and hurried over to the car. "You made it!" she said.

I jumped out and gave her a hug. She was even tinier than I remembered.

"Oh, your face!" she said. "Are you all right?"

"Yeah, I think so." I tried to smile, but it hurt.

She fussed over my forehead while Grandpa parked the car,

hiding it from view. In less than ten minutes, I'd been put to bed with a cold compress and a cup of tea.

"Don't get too comfortable, girlie," Grandpa said. "I'll be waking you every two hours to make sure you're not dead."

"I knew I could count on you," I said.

He tousled my hair, and it seemed like every follicle hurt. He went off to have breakfast, leaving me to rest. We'd made it to Kelso in one piece, and now all we had to do was wait for Spill. Assuming he could get away from the Organization. Assuming he really wanted to. After all, he'd stayed until he was twenty-one when he should've left. Had he done that for a reason, or had he changed his mind?

Except for a stunning green and purple bruise on my forehead, I was fine. I'd been resting in the back room since we'd arrived the day before, but I couldn't really sleep because my nerves were practically raw with worry. The Organization had to know we were gone by now. Plus, I was uneasy about connecting with Spill.

We'd stayed overnight at Jane's to give him a chance to catch up with us, but because we had no way of knowing when he'd be able to leave Gresham for sure, we also had designated a meeting spot just outside of Seattle two days from now. We were both hoping to meet up on the road somewhere along the way, though.

At lunchtime, Grandma brought me a bowl of steaming vegetable soup.

"Are we ready to leave tonight?" I asked her.

"No," she said, shaking her head. "Tomorrow."

"We promised Spill we'd drive at night," I said.

"No light," Grandma said.

"Right. Okay. After dark. I get it."

She shook her head, frustrated, and let fly some choice swearwords that made me laugh. Then she made a motion like she was driving the car and then crashing into something. We both giggled. "No light!" she said again.

"Oh! The headlights? I smashed the headlights, didn't I?"

She nodded. "Dawn," she said. "Eat."

I accepted the food, but my appetite was gone. This was bad. It was dangerous to drive during the day because we might be spotted, but without lights, the condition of the road was probably too risky in the dark. This was all my fault. If I hadn't been messing around, the headlights wouldn't be smashed.

I stirred my soup, letting it get cold while I sat there feeling sorry for myself because I'd been such an idiot. I could hear everyone laughing and joking while they ate, and it made me kind of lonely. There was only one thing to do. Play Jewels. Someone had brought in my stuff from the trunk, and when I moved my coat, it felt extra heavy. I reached inside the pocket and pulled out Randall's gun.

38

I'D FORGOTTEN I EVEN HAD THE GUN. SPILL WAS
going to kill me when he found out. He must've told me about
five times to make sure that I left it near Randall once we got
him tied up. I guess he didn't want me carrying it, but I wasn't
a child. Of course, that's probably what he was worried about,
that Michael or Brandy would find it.

Back at the house, when I'd been pointing it at Randall, I
hadn't even looked at it, but now I examined it closely in the
golden afternoon light. I'd only ever handled a rifle before, and
I didn't know much about handguns. This one was big. The barrel was at least twenty-five centimeters long, and the handle was
probably twenty. Plus it was computerized. There were different
settings depending on how you twisted the barrel. I tried turning
it, and as it clicked into place, a different word would light up
along the top. There were settings for *Stun, Burn, Tranquilize,
Fireball,* and *Shoot to Kill.*

The trigger was like any gun's, but the handle had a sort of touchpad on the left side. And there was a section that slid away and revealed a tiny keyboard! I heard the kids coming down the hall and had only a second to shove the gun back in my coat before Brandy and Michael burst into the room.

"Wait till you see the car!" Michael shouted.

"You weren't supposed to tell her." Brandy whacked him on the arm.

"Don't hit your brother," I said automatically. "You mean where I bashed it in?"

"Not that," Michael said.

Brandy clamped her hand over his mouth. "Come see!"

I pulled on Grandma's old sweater, and the three of us went out through Jane's kitchen door. Behind the house was a single-car garage, and in front of it stood Jane and my grandparents next to what had once been Grandpa's beautiful car.

"What happened?" I asked.

"We painted it," Jane said, when Grandpa didn't answer.

I stared at it in disbelief. They had used something black, and possibly sticky, to cover the entire car, including all the beautiful chrome trim! Grandpa wore a glum expression.

"Hawaiian Green attracts attention," he said.

He'd just realized that now? He looked like he was about to cry so I didn't say anything. We were still standing there staring at it when someone rode by on a bicycle. My heart leapt and I ran to the front yard with everyone following me, but whoever it was kept going.

"Oh, that's just a missionary," Jane said.

"You've got those around here too?" Grandpa asked.

She nodded. We went back inside and settled in for the night. I suppose everyone else slept, but I sat propped against the headboard in my bed and stared out into the dark, praying for Spill.

We'd meant to leave at dawn, but what with sleepy kids, breakfast, and teary good-byes, it was almost ten o'clock before we'd pulled out of Jane's. We followed the twisty roads out of town, and green marshes bordered the edges, so I drove down the middle again, just in case I lost control. We passed a few people, but not Spill. At one point, we came around a curve and there was a missionary, one of those guys wearing black and white, standing next to his bike, waving at us.

"Do you think he needs help?" I asked as we got closer.

"Keep going," Grandpa said. "He just wants to tell us about God, and if we stop, we'll be here all day."

I stared straight ahead and sped past him. By one o'clock Michael and Brandy were already bickering and tormenting each other, making my head throb. We were all hungry too, so I pulled the car off into a thicket and we sat by the side of the road in the weak October sunshine to have a picnic. I forced myself to join in with the chatter so I wouldn't worry about Spill.

"Oh, no," Grandpa said, sighing deeply. "Here comes that missionary. Let's hit the road."

He began to scoop up the remains of our lunch, and I called the kids to come back from where they were digging in the dirt. The lenses in Grandpa's glasses hadn't been broken in the scuffle with Randall, just scratched, and Grandma and Jane had mended the frames with glue, so he was going to drive for a while to give me a break.

Grandma had packed three huge suitcases, but I'd talked her into paring down to one. She hadn't brought hardly any clothing, but instead stuffed it with mementoes of my mother's childhood that she'd apparently been keeping all these years. I'd promised the kids they could ride in the front seat, but I had to lug the suitcase up there with them so there would be room for my legs in the back.

Before we were situated, the missionary guy was close enough to call out to us. "Hi, there!" he yelled. "Can I talk to you folks about the Lord?"

I knew that voice! I dropped the suitcase and ran out into the road waving at Spill. I was jumping up and down, pretty much like an idiot, but I didn't care. I was so relieved to see him. By the time he braked the bike, we were all trying to hug him.

"Now, that's a welcome I could get used to," he said. He looked at me and did a double take. "My God, Molly! Did Randall do that to your face?"

"Of course not. And I don't think someone posing as a missionary should be using the Lord's name in vain," I joked.

Ten minutes later, the two of us sat on our bikes and watched my grandparents and the kids drive off along the dusty road. I wasn't completely sold on the idea of splitting up from them, but Spill was worried that someone might remember seeing our little group if anyone from the Organization asked the right questions. Grandpa was only going to drive twenty-five more miles and then we would all camp together for the night, so I'd agreed.

Spill had given me my very own missionary outfit to wear, complete with white shirt, helmet, black pants, and a necktie. "Very nice," he'd said when I'd come out from behind the tree after changing my clothes. "Between that bruise and what you stand for, no one's going to want to talk to us."

"I do what I can," I said, laughing.

The ride was really easy for us because I wasn't hauling anything, and Spill had put all his camping gear in the Studebaker so he was pulling an empty trailer. The day was cool but sunny, and we took the ride at a nice pace.

"How did you get away from the Organization?" I asked him.

"Well," he said, very seriously, "I was at my induction ceremony, and at the end they gave me my gun."

"Yeah?" I glanced at him. Was he carrying it now?

"And . . . ," he said slowly, building up to something. "I just shot my way out of the room. I didn't really have a choice."

"Spill! Did you kill anyone? Oh, my God! I can't believe it!"

And then he cracked up laughing. "I'm kidding, Molly."

I felt myself blush, but then I laughed too.

"It was so easy to get away," he said, "it was almost boring. I just took the MAX downtown like I had some business to do. Then I bought a new bike, trailer, and camping gear from a Transporter I trust and rode out of town. They probably didn't even miss me until this morning."

"What about your stuff?" I asked.

"What do you mean?"

"Your things . . ." I'd never seen where Spill lived, but he must've had personal items he'd wanted to bring. "Your clothes and . . . I don't know. . . ."

He shrugged. "I had to leave it all behind," he said. "It would've looked suspicious."

I didn't have a lot of possessions, but if I were leaving home forever, there were some things I'd want. Like the doll Mom had made me, and photos . . . Spill had left everything behind. And not just things, either. The Organization might not be good for him, but they were the people he was close to, all the people who loved him. We were going to have to be his new family.

Around dusk we'd caught up with my grandparents just north of Chehalis. We'd decided to stop there because we were going to have to cross the interstate in order to stay on the back roads, and we'd wanted to try and get some sleep and do it early in the morning, just before dawn.

After a cold dinner of bread, apples, cheese, and salad, Grandma stretched out on the backseat of the Studebaker with the kids sharing the front. I laid out the sleeping bags for us, intending to take the one next to Spill, but Grandpa jumped into it before I could. It wasn't like I was looking for romance with Spill or anything, especially with my grandpa right there, but I did think it would be nice to lie next to him and look at the stars. And I was so relieved he'd escaped that I almost didn't want to let him out of my sight.

I lay there staring up at the sky and hoped that someone in

my family was looking up at the same time, seeing the Little Dipper too. I must've drifted off because a strange humming noise broke the silence and made me sit up.

"No!" I shouted, startling Spill and Grandpa. "Wake up! Wake up, you two! Someone's stealing the car!"

39

October 4th–Hard times, hard times, come again no more.
—Stephen Foster

WE STRUGGLED OUT OF OUR SLEEPING BAGS, BUT we lost precious time because we kept bumping into each other. Grandpa elbowed me on my bruise, making me see shooting lights too.

"Quick, Molly, help me get this camping stuff together," Spill said. "Jack, you climb in and I'll pull you."

We threw the gear and Spill's backpack into the trailer. Grandpa sat precariously on top of the load and I hoped we didn't hit any bumps or he might fall out. We jumped on our bikes and rode after the fading red taillights.

"At least they're going north," Spill said.

My front tire hit a rock and I almost lost control of my bike. "Should we turn on our lights?"

"I guess we better," Spill said. "I doubt they'll worry about being chased by bicycles."

We flipped on our bike lamps, but in the pitch black they barely illuminated anything. The taillights were getting further away and then the car disappeared around a bend. Spill and I were riding neck and neck despite his load, and I would've been impressed if I'd had time to think about it, but all I could do was worry about Grandma and the kids.

"I have an idea," I said. "I'll ride on ahead and I'll shoot out a tire."

"*What?*" Grandpa and Spill both yelled together.

"With Randall's gun."

"I thought I told you to leave it next to him after you taped him up," Spill said.

"I forgot. I stuck it in my pocket and I just found it when we were at Jane's."

Spill let out a long groan. "You have no idea what you've done, Molly."

"What's the big deal?"

"The big deal is that Randall can get thrown out of the Organization for letting someone take his gun off him. He's not going to rest until he gets it back."

"Really?"

"Really."

Crap.

"Don't let her fire it, Spill," Grandpa yelled from the trailer. "I don't want her shooting up my car!"

"Your car's ruined anyway," I said.

"Well, what about your grandmother?" he yelled. "And the kids!"

My fiddle was in the trunk too, which gave me second thoughts.

"Relax, Jack. No one's shooting that gun."

"Why not? I'm an excellent marksman, and if I ride faster, I can get close enough to shoot out a tire."

I actually wasn't sure I could ride faster. I was starting to lose my breath already, and I found it really annoying that Spill seemed perfectly fine. Of course, I'd just been in a car accident. That was probably why I felt so light-headed.

"Did you figure out Randall's password?" Spill asked in his infuriatingly calm way.

"What do you mean?"

"His gun has a thumbprint screen," he explained. "If your thumbprint doesn't match his, then you can't fire his gun without typing the password into the micro-computer first. It's so no one can use it against him."

"You mean I can't shoot Randall's gun?" I asked. "At all?"

"Exactly."

"But I held him at gunpoint, and he let us go," I said.

"He did?"

"Yeah," I said. "He did."

"Huh," Spill said.

I could hear the smile in his voice. And that's when I knew. *Randall had let us escape.* I had pointed his gun at him, and he had released Grandpa so we could get away. What exactly did that mean? Would he let Spill go too if he met up with us? And how hard would they look? Would Aunt Lili send Randall? Were we safer than we thought?

"That was the interstate," Spill said. "We're across it now. I guess that's one good thing."

"If we catch them, it is."

After almost twenty minutes of riding, we came around a bend and saw the taillights of the Studebaker stopped in the road. Except they were at a weird angle—sort of lifted in the air higher than they should've been.

"Oh, my God! They've crashed!" I said.

I put everything I had into that last stretch, and when we pulled up next to the car, our bike lamps showed Grandma, Brandy, and Michael standing there chattering like birds.

"What happened?" we all yelled. "Are you guys all right?"

"Okay," Grandma said.

"A bad man stole the car!" Michael said.

"And Grandma hit him on the head with a statue!" Brandy added.

"And he ran away!" Michael said.

"Bam!" Grandma held up a black trophy with a silver cheerleader on the top. I took it from Grandma and examined the little plaque in my bike lamp.

Spirit Award
Brianna Buckley
Barlow High School
2017

I wasn't sure what was harder to believe, that they'd all survived unhurt, or that my mother had been a cheerleader.

It was clear, even in the dark, that there was no way we were ever going to get the car out of the ditch. Plus, the right fender was crushed against the tire. We put the kids in the back of the trailer to sleep, and the four of us sat around a campfire arguing about what to do next.

"We're still around eighty miles from Seattle, but only twenty or so from Olympia," Spill said. "I think we should put Jack and Katharine and the kids on a train and meet them at Union Station."

"I don't like it," I said.

"It makes the most sense," he argued. "Seattle is too far for them to walk."

When Grandpa agreed, and Grandma added, "Yes–train," I gave in.

At first light, we unloaded the Studebaker while Grandpa removed his module from under the hood because he wanted to take it back to the farm. We packed as much of our gear onto my bike rack and into Spill's trailer as we could, but the suitcase was a real problem because even though Grandma had reluctantly left behind a pile of mementoes she'd been carrying for my mother, Grandpa had added his module to the suitcase and now it was even heavier. He insisted on pulling it along behind him, though, so I didn't argue. I figured his arms would get tired eventually and we could get rid of more stuff then.

We were all set to go when I noticed Grandpa staring at his car. The front end was bashed in from my joyride, black goop hid the brilliant chrome and once-sparkling paint, and tears glittered in Grandpa's eyes.

I put my arm around his shoulder. "Grandpa, I–"

He shrugged me off. "It's just a car. Let's go."

He turned and went after the others, but I knew he wasn't leaving just his car behind. The Studebaker stood for everything he'd worked for. He was walking away from his home, his career, his life as an American, everything he knew. I looked for some kind of souvenir to take from the car. There wasn't anything inside worth keeping, and just when I was about to give up, I spotted the lark hood ornament. It had come loose in the accident and I wrenched the statue off and stuffed it in my pack.

We had to walk our bikes in order for my family to keep up with us, which is actually a lot more tiring than riding them, but even so, twenty miles wasn't much to me or Spill. It was difficult for my grandparents, and horrible for the kids, though. After two hours, Brandy and Michael were begging to be carried. Spill put them in the back of the trailer and rode on ahead.

By two o'clock we'd been on the road for five hours, and I was willing to bet we hadn't walked more than halfway to Olympia. My grandparents and I finally caught up to Spill and the kids. He was chasing them around a grassy meadow.

"We're not going to get there today," I told him.

"I know. We'll camp here. Your grandma looks worn out."

I'd noticed this too and made her sit down while Grandpa and I put together lunch. By the time we'd finished eating, I felt like I could nap, but the kids had to explore every inch of the little field and the creek, so instead, I rested on the bank, watching them make mud pies. "You'll be sorry," I said, "when

I give you a bath later." They laughed then, but I had to listen to them scream and cry while I washed them with icy water before dinner.

After we ate, we gathered around a small campfire, trying to stay warm. "Play us a tune," Grandpa suggested.

Spill added a log to the fire. My arms were tired from walking the bike and I knew it was too cold to play, but we could all use a boost, so I got Jewels out. "Sing along," I said. My bow slipped sadly across the strings, and music filled the glade, drowning out the sound of the creek.

> Let us pause in life's pleasures and count its
>   many tears,
> While we all sup sorrow with the poor;
> There's a song that will linger forever in our
>   ears;
> Oh, hard times, come again no more.

I sang softly, but Grandpa's deep voice rang out loud and clear. Grandma hummed, every once in a while joining us in a phrase. Spill sat silently with Michael on his lap and Brandy leaning against him for warmth.

> 'Tis the song, the sigh of the weary,
> Hard times, hard times, come again no more.
> Many days you have lingered around my cabin
>   door;
> Oh, hard times, come again no more.

The song was almost two hundred years old, and everyone I knew had at least one reason to sing it. Hopefully, our hard times would be over soon. In the morning, against my better judgment, we would put my grandparents and the kids on a train, and all I could do was hope that we'd meet up in Seattle. If I lost them now, I might as well forget about ever going back to the farm.

40

October 6th—As you sow, so shall you reap.

I STOOD OUTSIDE THE OLYMPIA STATION WITH THE bikes while Spill went in to inquire about trains. It was early afternoon on the second day of walking, and we'd finally made it. My grandparents had taken the kids inside an hour before while we'd waited down the road. I was scanning the crowd for men who looked scary enough to be in the Organization when two guys in white shirts and black pants rode up to me and stopped their bikes next to ours.

"Hello, Brother," the first one said to me.

"Uh, hello."

"I'm Brother Paul," he said. "And this is Brother Samuel."

I'd tucked my hair up inside my helmet, but it seemed unlikely I could pass for a boy. Still, I tried to make my voice deeper. "I'm . . . uhh . . . Brother James," I said, using my older brother's name.

The guy was definitely scrutinizing me, but all he said was, "Nice to meet you."

"You too."

"Are you getting on the train?" Brother Samuel asked.

"No. Uh, I'm waiting for Brother . . . Brother Quinn. He's just using their washroom."

"Washroom?"

"Bathroom," I said, correcting myself.

"Oh."

Spill came out of the doors then, and I waved, "Hi, Brother Quinn!" I called. He didn't show even the tiniest flicker of surprise. Instead he walked right up to the boys and shook their hands warmly. Fifteen minutes later, the four of us were riding up the Portland-Seattle bike path that ran along I-5, Brothers Paul and Samuel leading the way.

"You were amazing," I whispered to Spill.

"This is a great cover," he whispered back.

He'd assessed the situation in about ten seconds flat, immediately getting the picture when they referred to me as Brother James. He listened to their story and told them that we'd also come to the train station to spread the Word and were on our way north.

The Brothers told us the news was that as of that morning, there'd been six confirmed cases of polio as far west as Idaho. Even if the border officials thought a person had a legitimate reason to travel, he still had to have a physical exam to get into Canada.

They were short of doctors too, so the waits were long, and they'd set up campgrounds for people who had to wait for an exam. If even one person came down with polio in Washington, they were going to set up three-week quarantines for all the travelers. Brothers Paul and Samuel were going up there to save the souls at the camp.

Spill and I rode side by side, and I asked if he'd seen my family inside the station.

"Yep," he said. "There's a train around midnight, and they should be there by tomorrow morning,"

"Did you talk to them?"

Spill laughed. "No, but I definitely saw them. Subtlety isn't your grandpa's strong suit."

"What do you mean?"

"Well, apparently"–he smiled–"he wanted to make sure I knew he got the train tickets because he waved them around so much everyone in the station could see them."

I was glad they were safe, but there was one more thing I had to know. Spill had decided that it looked kind of obvious for me to have Jewels on my bike rack so my grandparents had taken her with them. I did not like this one bit. "Was my fiddle okay?"

"Michael was holding it on his lap," Spill said.

"Well, I guess Jewels will be safe enough with him," I said. "He loves that fiddle almost as much as I do." As soon as we got home, I was going to give Michael my quarter-size fiddle from when I was his age and start teaching him to play.

The four of us had been riding about two hours when we decided to take a break at an interstate rest stop. It was a big one, full of Transporters and lots of people on foot or traveling by bike. As soon as we stopped, we'd met up with two other missionaries also heading north. Spill's eyes never stopped moving, even though he sat on the grass with us, drinking water and looking relaxed.

The sun was weak, but warm, and made me sleepy. I forgot I was supposed to be a boy and was half leaning against Spill when a low, black car pulled in not ten feet from us. Out of my peripheral vision, I saw Randall and another man in a suit climb out and I felt Spill stiffen next to me, even though his expression never changed.

"Oh, my God!" I said.

The brothers looked up at me in surprise. The only thing that kept me from bolting was Spill's grasp on my arm.

"Let us pray," Spill said. "For a safe journey."

"Good idea," Brother Samuel agreed.

The six of us stood and gathered together in a little knot, bowing our heads. Because the Brothers never took their helmets off, it was hard to tell them apart. They all had very tan arms and faces from being outside so much, and even their body types were similar, fit and muscular. Brother Paul began to murmur a prayer. All I was aware of was Spill's hand on my arm and the sound of Randall's voice as he talked to the other man. Cigarette smoke wafted from their direction, stinging my eyes. It would've been great if they had been rattling off their plans, where they were going next, and all that, but they were just talking about the weather.

"Don't get used to this sunshine," the man said. "Always rains in Seattle."

"Don't I know it," Randall agreed.

"Brother James?" one of the missionaries asked.

I snapped my attention back to our group. "Yeah? What?"

"The prayer's over. We're going."

I realized I still had my head bowed even though I'd been faintly aware of them saying *amen*. They were all getting on their bikes, and I hurried to jump on mine and go with them. Spill and I blended into the middle of the group and we got away without Randall seeing us, but my heart was still beating furiously when the black car zipped by on the interstate.

That night, we stayed with the Brothers about fifteen miles outside of Seattle. This was a permanent campsite with Elders, and maybe sixty or seventy members, a canvas mess tent, and a wooden building for meetings. After dinner and evening prayers, we all broke off into little groups around small camp-fires and laid out our sleeping bags. It was cold, but clear, so hardly anyone bothered with tents. I could see the Elders mov-ing from group to group and saying good night. The one called Elder Mathew was nearest to us.

Everyone called him Elder, but I don't think he could've been more than thirty. Of course, most of the Brothers looked to be about my age, so he'd probably been around for a while. He had thick blond hair, almost white, and a meaty look to him, but not really muscular. Soft, I guess was the word I was look-ing for. When he reached us, he asked if we minded if he sat with our group for a while.

"Please," Brother Samuel said.

We all sat there, waiting for someone to speak. Finally Elder Mathew did. "Sometimes," he said, "as with our Catholic brothers, there is a time for confession. I was wondering if anyone has something to confess."

No one said anything, but my heart raced right up into my throat because he was looking directly at me.

"No one?" he asked, turning to Spill. "What about you, Brother Quinn?"

"Nope," Spill said easily.

"Brother James?"

"Uh . . . no?"

"Well, then," he continued, "I have a confession to make. I confess that we know you two are not members of our brotherhood."

"Sure we are," Spill said.

No one around the fire seemed to be breathing.

"No," he said. "And shall I tell you how I know this?"

"Okay," Spill said, his expression totally blank.

Elder Mathew looked straight at me. "Because we do not have women in the brotherhood."

I folded my arms across my pounding chest and stared at the fire. What did they do to imposters? I had no idea how to get us out of this, so I hoped Spill had a plan.

"Do you believe in redemption?" Spill asked Elder Mathew.

He looked surprised. "Of course. That's what we're about."

"But I mean here on Earth," Spill said.

"Absolutely."

Spill gazed steadily at Elder Mathew. "Would you say that it is your role to help people who want redemption?"

"Most definitely."

Where was he going with this?

"So, if I were to tell you a story about two people," Spill said, "one doing a good deed and the other trying to redeem his wicked ways, would you promise to help them?"

Elder Mathew considered this for a minute.

"If it did not hurt others, or put my mortal soul in peril, then yes, I would help them."

"Oh, it wouldn't," Spill said. "In fact, assisting them would be helping more people than you'll ever know."

"Tell me your story, then."

I thought Spill was going to lie. I thought he'd been quickly coming up with fake names, stories, places, and people, but he hadn't at all. The only thing he said that wasn't a hundred percent true was he called himself Spill instead of Robert.

I sat, my heart pounding, and listened to him tell our entire story from the arrival of Grandpa's letter about Grandma having a stroke and my family thinking she was dead to us sitting there now. He included how sick Mom was, how Dr. Robinson had been kicked in the head and died, how Poppy had snuck me into the United States, our meeting on the MAX, my starving grandparents, the long, hard summer in the garden, Doug, the gambling, the kids, Spill's years as a delivery boy, the Organization keeping us in Gresham, the escape, leaving my grandparents and the kids at the train station in Olympia, and finally meeting Brothers Paul and Samuel.

He explained about Randall being at the rest stop and probably on his way to the train station in Seattle and how we had to rescue my grandparents and the kids somehow. And he told them how he planned to be a cobbler once we reached Canada and leave his past far behind him. It took over an hour to tell our story, and when he finished, Elder Mathew had a few questions that Spill answered. Then he asked him to swear on the Book that our story was true.

"Your book is not *my* book," Spill said. "But I'll swear on it and keep my word."

"There's always hope that you will embrace our teachings," Elder Mathew said. He held up a copy of the Book, and Spill laid his hand upon it and took the oath.

And then, without another word to us, Elder Mathew stood up and called to the brotherhood. "Come! Gather around!" he shouted. "Rise out of your beds and hear what I have to say. We, my dear, dear brothers, have been given a mission from God!"

41

October 7th–Compassion is the basis of all morality.
  –Arthur Schopenhauer

THE "MISSION FROM GOD" BIT HAD BEEN PRETTY DRA-
matic, but it was nothing compared to what happened at dawn.
Sixty-five of us, dressed in the uniform of the Brothers, mounted
our bicycles and rode in a streaming line, three bikes abreast,
along the bike path right into downtown Seattle.

The streets were mostly empty, but the few people on the
sidewalks gazed at us, surprised and even a little frightened.
Maybe they thought we were taking over the city. It certainly
looked that way as we fanned out, filling the empty road. I
doubt if anyone noticed six Brothers pulling away from the
crowd, riding towards Elliott Bay while the rest of us headed
for Union Station.

We'd decided that it was too dangerous to involve Poppy's
boyfriend in our escape. On the advice of Elder Mathew, Spill
had gone directly to the marina to try and secure us passage to
Victoria on a boat with a captain who only cared about money
and could be bribed.

Elder Mathew had shaken his head and said, "There are plenty of those men these days."

I, for one, was glad to hear it.

"I want you to understand," he told me. "Generally, I believe that laws are laid out to serve the public and should be followed. But sometimes, like in the case of these children that you're trying to help by giving them a stable home with your family, you have to bend the rules."

"We are trying to do the right thing," I said.

"And I'm not too worried about you all having polio," he said, "since there aren't any confirmed cases in Washington."

His words made me consider what we were doing more seriously than I had so far. We weren't only trying to avoid possible quarantine by crossing illegally, but we were sneaking the kids and Spill into Canada too. There was a time when I would've thought that was wrong, but like Elder Mathew said, sometimes you have to bend the rules.

"Remember," Elder Mathew told a little group of Brothers when we got to the station, "stay on all sides of Molly. Don't let her out of your sight."

"She's safe with us," they all answered.

And oddly enough, I did feel safe with them. The waiting room was crowded with people wanting to board the train when it came in, and we immediately went to work, trying to spread the Word. I had a solid wall of boys around me, though, so I never had to talk to anyone directly. I just carried the Book, still wearing my helmet and keeping my head down.

Spill was positive that Randall and his partner didn't know about the Studebaker and would be checking all the trains into Seattle just in case, and it turned out he was right.

When it finally pulled in, there was mass confusion as the people in the waiting room pushed to get out onto the platform and the debarking passengers swam upstream to get inside. Four of us jumped up onto a bench, the other three surrounding me, blocking me from view. I had two jobs. The first was to find my grandparents and the kids, and the second was to watch out for anyone I recognized from the Organization. I saw them all at once.

"They're right behind them!" I whispered to Brother Samuel.

"What? Who?"

"Randall and his partner. They've spotted my grandparents, and they're following them!"

I pointed them out and a message passed from Brother to Brother. I watched in amazement as first one Brother and then another wormed his way in between Randall and my grandparents. In less than thirty seconds, the gap between them had widened to twenty people. I saw Randall's partner push Brother Paul out of his way, and I ducked my head and turned my back, just as Randall shoved past our bench, trying to catch up with my grandparents and the kids.

More Brothers worked their way between them, stopping other passengers and asking to talk about the Lord. By the time my grandparents got to the big front doors, the Brothers had encircled them, and Randall and his partner were being swept away, back towards the train, with the last of the passengers who wanted to board.

We jumped down off the bench and ran through the crowd after my family. By the time we got outside, I could just see the tops of my grandparents' heads as they were being pulled away by the Brothers in trailers. I couldn't see Brandy or Michael, but I knew they must be with them, and I said a little prayer of thanks.

The mission was a massive Victorian house on the outskirts of the downtown area. All the houses around it looked like they might collapse with the next breath of wind, but the mission stood proudly, painted white with blue trim, in a perfectly manicured front yard surrounded by a welcoming picket fence with an open gate.

It was run entirely by women, and they ushered us inside. Before I'd had time to do more than hug my grandparents and the kids, the women had us sitting down at the table to steaming bowls of oatmeal.

"Wait," I told Brandy and Michael, reaching out and stopping them from digging in. My grandparents never said the blessing, but we always did at home, and I had a feeling that's why the Matron was standing at the head of the table.

"Please bow your heads," she said.

Everyone at the table did, including my grandparents, and I nodded to Michael and Brandy to follow along.

"Amen," we said, when she had finished saying grace.

"Now you can eat," I told the kids.

Spoons clinked against bowls all up and down the long narrow tables. About two dozen people shoveled the food into their mouths without a word. They looked rough and dirty against the spotless floors and shining windows.

I brought my grandparents up to speed in hurried whispers while we ate. "Spill told the Brothers our whole story," I explained to my grandparents. "And they decided to help us."

"We sure were surprised," Grandpa said, "to get swept up by them at the train station. We were already in the trailers before we even knew what was going on."

"I was standing on a bench," I said. "You should've seen it from there. It was almost like a dance."

Before we finished, Michael had laid his head down on the table and fallen asleep. A girl about my age, in a long black skirt and white blouse, took our bowls away. "The dormitories are usually closed during the day for cleaning," she said, "but Elder Mathew requested that we let you all sleep. I'll show you the way if you're ready."

"I want to wait for Spill," I said.

There was a common room, also closed until the evening, but I offered to clean it in exchange for being allowed to stay in there, and the girl said I could. I took the bucket she gave me, glad to have something to do, and got to work. I had dusted the worn furniture, emptied the ashes out of the fireplace, swept and scrubbed the floor, and cleaned the mirror, and Spill still hadn't shown up. After that, I alternated between pacing up and down the small room and staring out the front window. Finally, I saw four Brothers riding up on their bikes. I ran out to meet them.

Spill and Paul weren't with them, though.

"Where are they?" I asked.

One of the boys handed me a note and then they all rode away.

It said:

> The Brothers will take you to Elliott Bay
> tonight at 10:45. We sail at 11 pm on the
> Marybelle, moored about halfway down dock
> J on the left side. Meet you there. S

Why hadn't he come back to wait here? I went to the common room half mad, half worried. I was still there, pacing, when Grandpa came down later in the afternoon.

"Sit down," he said. "Try to relax. Have a sandwich with me."

"I can't relax," I said, still pacing. "I'm just so worried we're going to end up in quarantine somewhere. We have got to get you home to take care of Mom."

Grandpa got up and led me over to the couch. "You're doing the best you can, Molly. You have to stop being so hard on yourself. We'll get there. And your mom will be okay."

"But what about the diabetes?" I demanded.

"If your dad has to," Grandpa said, "he'll get her to the hospital."

"It's a ferry ride," I said. "And then twenty-two kilometers away! She can't travel that far."

"Molly . . . all you can do is have faith. That's how I got through your grandmother's illness."

I hadn't really considered how hard Grandma's stroke must've been on Grandpa. "Yeah, okay." I sighed. I knew he was right. "I'm just feeling blue."

He put his arm around my shoulder. "We're almost there."

"I'm also worried about Spill. I just keep thinking that because he's twenty-one they're not going to give up now. The Organization wants him back, and as Randall says, 'The house always wins.'"

"Ah . . . Soriano."

"What?"

"*The House Always Wins*. It's a famous book."

Grandpa took a bite of his sandwich.

"It is?"

"Sure. It came out in twenty-nine or thirty. This guy, Soriano, wrote a book predicting that while the Collapse was inevitable, it wouldn't really affect the rich because *the house always wins*, or the rich are always rich. The people who run the world, just like the people who run the casinos, always come out on top. Get it?"

"Yeah . . . ," I said. "And he was right too, wasn't he?"

"Well, he was right about one thing."

"What's that?"

"If you want to make a lot of money fast so that you're one of the rich ones, write a book telling them how to hold on to their money. The ebook was a huge success. It was on the *New York Times* Best-Seller list for over a year."

Something clicked into place in my brain. "And the author's name was Soriano?"

"Yeah. I can't remember his first name. Alfonso? Maybe . . . no, Alfonso Soriano was a baseball player. . . . Hmmm."

Grandpa flipped through the pages of his memory, but I wasn't listening anymore. If my hunch was right, I had all the information I needed. Soriano's first name didn't matter because passwords were usually just one word.

42

A GROUP OF ABOUT TEN BROTHERS TOOK US TO Elliott Bay, and I gave them my bike as a thank-you for their help. "God be with you," Elder Mathew said, shaking my hand.

"And also with you," I answered, feeling a little silly, but that was how the other boys always answered him.

The five of us made our way down the long dock towards the *Marybelle*. About half the berths were filled, and even though most of the boats had at least one lighted lamp hanging on them, all the decks were deserted. The *Marybelle*'s single lantern illuminated the peeling letters spelling out her name. The smell of saltwater sent a wave of homesickness over me.

Because of the polio threat, boats from the U.S. were banned from going into Canadian waters. The captain of the *Marybelle* told us as we boarded that the plan was for him to let us out on a deserted beach near Victoria.

He wore black pants and a heavy wool coat with the collar turned up. His hat was pulled down low, and he had a bushy mustache that flopped around when he spoke. "That guy earlier never mentioned a suitcase," he said.

I shrugged and heaved it onto the deck anyway.

"Cost you extra, that will. It'll slow us down."

"How much?" Grandpa asked.

"What's in it?"

"Why?" I asked.

"Weight."

"No gold bars," I said, "if that's what you're thinking. Just personal stuff."

"Well, we'll discuss it when we get there."

If we got there. The boat's paint was peeling and cracked, the sails looked like they were made of scrap paper, and the ladder leading to down below was rickety and shaky. In the hull, Grandpa had to hunch over to keep from hitting his head. There were two tiny seats, kind of like the ones on the airplane, except they had some sort of harness that strapped over your whole front.

"I'm going to wait for Spill," I said. I hurried up the ladder before Grandpa could stop me. The boat was barely rocking, but even the tiny bit of motion had sent my stomach reeling.

I wasn't sure what kind of a deal Spill had made with the captain, but if it cost more than one piece of gold per person, he was going to make up the difference and my father would pay him back. Before we'd split up, I had given Spill all my gold except one piece, which we'd placed in a tiny secret compartment that Spill had built into the heel of my boot.

"I'll be back," I told the captain.

"We sail at eleven, with or without you."

I jumped onto the dock and ran about halfway towards land. There was a big wooden crate with heavy ropes spilling out the top, and I crouched behind it to wait. I wanted to make double sure no one was following Spill. If someone was, I had Randall's gun, and this time I could use it if I had to.

Less than five minutes later, I heard voices, and I could just make out two figures moving down the dock towards me. I watched, and as they got closer, I realized that one of them was Spill, walking on his own, but the other figure was actually two people. Randall had hold of Brother Paul, his arms twisted behind his back and a knife to his throat. I waited until they were about ten yards away and stepped out of the shadows.

"What's going on?" My fingers clenched Randall's gun in my pocket.

They all jumped. "Jeez, Molly! You scared me!" Spill said. His hair was a mess, and even in the dim light from the closest boat lantern, I could see he'd been hit in the face and a bruise was already coming up.

"Just the person we wanted to see," Randall said. He smiled like we were old friends.

"Why are you holding Paul like that?" I demanded.

"Because I'm here to make a deal," Randall said.

I waited.

"Robert's already agreed to come back with me. If you come quietly, I'll let your grandparents go, and this guy too."

"I can't do that," I said. Slowly I took the gun out of my pocket and aimed it at Randall. Spill moved towards me like he was going to try to stop me, but I waved the gun at him and said, "Nobody move. Where's the other guy? Randall's partner?"

"I hit him with a piece of metal piping," Spill said. "He's in the alley, out cold."

Randall laughed. "You shoulda seen Robert. He was like an action hero in the movies."

"Are you all right?" I asked Spill, and he nodded.

"You gonna shoot me, Handsome Molly?" Randall asked. Paul shuddered and let out a little moan. "You didn't do it last time you had the chance."

"I would've if I'd had to," I said, breathing slowly to keep my voice steady. "Or I would've tried anyway. I know you let us go. Spill explained about the password."

"I can't let you get away twice, though," Randall said.

I stood up straighter. "It's not up to you this time."

Randall laughed. "Am I supposed to be worried that you've guessed my password?"

"I didn't take you for the book type, Randall," I said. "*Soriano* had it all wrong, though. The house doesn't always win."

I saw him blanch, but he kept grinning, and the lamplight reflected off his white teeth.

"I'll make *you* a deal," I said. "You let Paul go, and I'll give you your gun back so you don't get kicked out of the Organization."

"And what's to stop me from shooting you and Robert?"

"Oh, I'm going to stun you first and then we're going to escape."

"That could work. Or I could kill this guy," Randall said, "and then take you both down anyway."

"I guess you could try, but right now I have the gun set on *Shoot to Kill* and I really want to get home."

Paul whimpered again, and I felt kind of sorry for him because he didn't know what an excellent marksman I was.

"So let me get this right," Randall said. "I let the kid go. You stun me. You leave my gun, and you and Robert ride off into the sunset?"

"Something like that, yeah."

"Deal." In one swift motion he flipped the knife closed and pushed Brother Paul away. "Get outta here!" he said.

Paul stood there in shock for about a tenth of a second and then he ran, disappearing into the night. I'd had the gun set on *Stun* the whole time, and I didn't hesitate. I laid my thumb on the thumbprint pad and fired. A red laser shot out and hit Randall in the chest. He fell to the ground, writhing, and then he lay still.

"Quick," Spill said. "Let's get out of here."

I laid the gun down on the dock, and we started running for the boat. I heard Randall scramble to his feet.

"I told you once, Molly," he yelled after us, "never tell your enemy what you plan to do or they can pretend it worked."

"Keep running!" I told Spill.

"Go! Go! Go!" Spill yelled at the captain as we threw ourselves onto the deck of the little boat.

The captain had already untied the thick rope, and he flipped a switch, sending a hum through the air, but Randall had caught up to us. Luckily the boat had pulled just far enough away to make it a long jump, and instead of trying it, he stopped and aimed his gun at us. "My suit's got a lining of HyperFoil," Randall told me. "Completely stun proof."

Spill flattened himself onto the wooden deck and tried to

pull me down too, but I just stood there, smiling. "I figured," I said. "That's why I had a backup plan."

As the tiny boat pulled away from the dock, Randall tried to fire the gun, but nothing happened. We were thirty yards away by the time he realized what I'd done.

"That's right," I called to him. "I didn't just override your thumbprint, I reprogrammed it to mine. You have to figure out *my* password now!"

Randall lowered the gun, and I swore he even laughed, but I couldn't be sure.

"Have a good life, Robert!" he yelled. "I'll miss ya!"

Spill stood up. "You too, Randall. Thanks for everything."

"Here's a clue," I yelled. "Eat your veggies!"

If he answered, we couldn't hear him.

"You chose a vegetable?" Spill asked. "That won't take him long."

"Oh, I don't know," I said, laughing. "I chose *zucchini,* and I can never remember how to spell it."

43

WE SCRAMBLED DOWN THE LADDER, AND GRANDPA grabbed me in a bear hug before I was all the way into the hull. "Oh, thank God!" he said. "I was afraid he was leaving without you."

I clutched his arm. "I don't have a good feeling about this boat."

"Shush," he said, glancing at the kids.

"You don't think we're going to sink, do you?" I whispered to Spill.

He laughed. "It's all appearances, Mol. Relax."

But how could I relax? Worrying about ending up in quarantine or worse had wound my nerves up tighter than my curls on a wet day. Now that we were aboard, all my fears of trying to sneak the kids into Canada came rushing back like a tidal wave too.

"Strap yourselves in!" the captain yelled through the open hatch above us. "Better hold the kids." And then he slammed it shut, taking every extra scrap of fresh air with him.

"Seems a bit excessive for a sailboat," I said.

"This boat's a runner," Spill explained.

"What's a runner?" I asked.

"You'll see," Spill said, smiling.

Grandpa's eyes lit up. "Really? A runner? I thought those were only for the military."

"That's why it's disguised as a decrepit fishing boat," Spill said. He helped Grandpa get into one of the tiny seats with Brandy in his lap and hooked the harness over both of them. Then he strapped Grandma and Michael into the other seat and put my fiddle, our packs, and Grandma's suitcase in a storage bin and latched the lid.

"I guess we're on the bunk," Spill told me.

I sat on the edge. "I don't think I'll last for two days in here."

"Who said anything about two days?" he said. "It's more like three or four hours."

"Yeah, right," I said. "I did study geography in school. Sailboats are really slow, you know?"

Spill scooted onto the bunk until he was near the wall. "I told you, this is a runner."

The volume of the humming increased, and I watched in amazement as everyone's hair slowly rose in the air and stood on end. Brandy and Michael burst out laughing and then we all joined in. "What's happening?" I asked.

"Static electricity," Spill explained. "It's a by-product of the Magno Waterborne Ocean Module."

Whatever that meant. It was pretty funny to see everyone's hair sticking up, though.

"Hold on, Molly," Spill said.

All the slow rolling as we wove our way out of the marina made my stomach turn over. I swallowed hard. Once we were in the open water, there was a loud whine from the engine and then we suddenly picked up speed. It felt more like flying than being on a boat. We could hear the water shooting out behind us, and it gave me this really powerful rush of adrenaline, which actually was kind of exhilarating.

"It seems like we're airborne!" I yelled over the noise.

"Almost," Spill yelled back.

I was just thinking that it wasn't so bad when the boat lurched to one side, tossing us to the end of the bunk, then flinging us the other way before we could regain our balance. On the third lurch, we lost our grip and were thrown onto the floor right at my grandparents' feet.

"What's going on?" I yelled over the noise.

"It's the zigzag effect," Spill explained, also shouting. "That's why everyone else is strapped in and we wish we were."

I struggled towards the bed, and Spill gave me a shove onto the mattress.

"What does that mean?"

"The boat goes in a zig–" His words got lost as we slammed together. I'd never had Spill's body pressed up so close to mine, and I think I would've liked it a lot if I hadn't been about to lose my dinner.

"The boat goes in a zigzag," he tried again, breathlessly. "But I don't really know how it works."

"I do!" Grandpa said, glowing with pride under the green pallor of his waxy skin. "There's a computerized module that's in sync with the magnetic float sensors, and it's programmed to avoid hitting the swells of the ocean straight on. It sort of zips in between them, allowing for greater speed and less friction."

"Less friction for who?" I yelled.

The boat lurched again, sending me towards the floor, but Spill grabbed hold of my leg before I was tossed all the way out.

"You two all right?" Grandpa yelled.

"Is it like this all the way?" I asked.

"Probably," Spill said as we slid off the bed onto the floor again. We got back on the mattress, and Spill managed to get a grip, but this time we were crushed together.

"Molleee?" Grandma called.

"I'm okay," I gasped.

Brandy and Michael began to cry.

"I feel like the chicken pieces Mom puts in a bag with flour and shakes up before she fries them," I said.

Spill gave me a wan smile, but he looked like he wished I hadn't mentioned food. Eventually I got the idea of lying on the bunk and weighing myself down with Spill. Or maybe it was his idea. Either way, it wasn't the romantic scenario I'd imagined. I clung to him around the waist, and he crushed me into the mattress. Still . . . having his body pressed against me like that made me kind of flustered. When I caught his eye, he actually blushed and turned his head away.

After what might have been days, but was probably only hours, the boat slowed to an easy glide and finally rested, bob-bing on the water.

"Everyone okay?" Grandpa asked.

His face was a lovely shade of green. Brandy had been sick and looked like she might be again. It was stifling hot in the hull, and the stench was enough to make me heave too. When the hatch opened and a rush of salty sea air poured over us, we all gulped in deep breaths.

The captain's face poked through the hole. "Canadian Coast Guard's out in full force. We're gonna have to go up north to Parksville or thereabouts."

"That's great news!" I said. "That's a lot closer to home."

Finally something was going our way!

Spill and I lay on the bed next to each other not moving, letting our organs settle back into place. His warm body pressed against my side and relaxed me. I lost track of how long we floated with the hatch open. I might have even dozed a little.

"I think we should try to stick together," Spill said after a while. "But with the Coast Guard out there, we might have to split up."

"If we do, we should meet at the north end of town on the highway. It'll be pretty easy for you to find it because there are signs that say Canada 1 everywhere," I said.

"Sounds good," Spill agreed.

The captain stuck his head through the hatch again and told us it was time to climb up on deck, but we had to lie low and follow instructions or he'd throw us overboard.

Spill went first, and Grandpa lifted the weakened kids one at a time up to him on deck. Then we passed the luggage and Jewels up. Grandma and I followed. Grandpa brought up the rear. We all lay down on the deck, the ocean wind tearing at our hair and clothes, damp air filling our lungs.

"Scoot on over closer to the railing and wait," the captain said. "I've lowered the extra magno-floats so I'm getting enough lift to run this baby almost onto the sand and still get away fast if I need to, but you'll have to wade in."

"When we're all out safe," Spill told him, "you'll get the second half of your fee." He slipped me the gold. We didn't want the captain to know exactly who had the money.

"And I want extra for the suitcase," the captain said.

"How much?" I asked.

"Another piece of gold."

I started to argue, but Spill said, "Fine. I'll cover it."

"It's too much money," I protested.

"We're not really in a position to negotiate now," Spill told me. "I'm going first. Jack, you're next. Molly, you hand down the kids and then help Katharine."

The captain scoured the shore with night-vision goggles. "Go now!"

Spill was over the edge in a flash, and Grandpa flung himself out of the boat so fast he sent up a splash, drenching the rest of us. We handed down Michael and Brandy, and then I helped Grandma over the railing. She had a lot of trouble raising her right leg, but she got over in the end, and Spill steadied her as she landed in the water. I handed down the backpacks next.

"Give me the suitcase," Spill said.

As I reached for it, so did the captain. "I'll be keeping that," he said. "If you think it's worth a whole piece of gold, there must be something really valuable in there."

"There's not! At least not to you!" I said. I grabbed the handle and pulled as hard as I could, but the boat was swaying on the shallow waves and my feet slipped on the smooth planks. In the distance, dogs began to bark.

"Let it go, Molly," Spill ordered me. "Hurry. Someone's coming!"

I yanked on it, bracing my foot against an old wood box. This was all my grandmother had left of her life, and I was not leaving without my half-sewn maid-of-honor dress, either.

"Here's your pay," I said. I tossed the coins across the deck with a clatter. The captain let go and scurried after the rolling gold. I heaved the suitcase to Spill, grabbed Jewels, and had one leg over the railing when I froze. All I could see was black below me and it seemed reckless and crazy to just jump into it.

"It's only a few inches deep," Spill said. "Come on!"

The barking dogs got closer, and I could see a light onshore bobbing up and down. A flat hand smacked me square on the small of my back. "Get off my boat!"

I toppled over the edge and landed on my butt in the icy water, holding Jewels over my head.

44

THE WATER WAS BARELY ANKLE-DEEP, AND I STAGgered to my feet as the boat sped away. We all stood breathless in a little knot.

"Molly, you're going to have to create a diversion," Spill said. "Go towards the shore and start screaming for help. We'll stand here as long as we can and then we'll hide somewhere."

"North end of town," I said. "Tomorrow."

"Who's out there?" yelled a man onshore. The dogs barked and whined, plunging into the water.

I took a deep breath. "Help! I've been thrown overboard!" I yelled. "Help me!" I took a few steps towards the shore, but then Michael began to cry. He screamed and yelled like someone was beating him. Grandma thrust him into my arms. I splashed forward, clutching him to me.

A man with a lantern was waiting for us onshore. He whistled to the dogs, and four energetic Labs came running and sat at his feet. "Are you all right?" he asked.

I wanted to yell for joy. Of course I was all right. I was back in Canada! But I knew that I wasn't home free yet. "I think we're okay," I said. "Just wet. And my brother's scared of the dogs."

The man tried to help me by taking either Michael or the fiddle, but I held on to both. "Thanks, but I've got them." Michael clung to me so tightly I couldn't have set him down if I'd wanted to anyway.

"What're you doing out here?" the man asked.

"I was visiting my grand–er, *our* grandparents in the States, and I paid a man to bring us home, but he dumped us here."

"You're Canadians?"

"Yes, sir."

"Got your passports?"

"In my fiddle case."

"Come along."

I walked with the man up a rocky beach to a path leading through the woods, the dogs snuffling around at my wet feet. The man wasn't more than a large dark shadow, and I couldn't tell from his demeanor so far if he'd be nice or a rule follower.

"Don't you know that there's a moratorium on all boat crossings into Canada?" he asked.

"I'm not sure what you mean," I said.

"Because of the polio epidemic in the States," he explained. "You have to be examined by a doctor at a land crossing before you're allowed into the country. No boats allowed until further notice."

"Oh. I didn't know." I was glad I didn't have to look him in the eye when I told that lie or he'd probably be able to tell I was scared. "The captain never said. He just told me we couldn't land in Victoria for some reason, and the next thing I knew he was tossing us overboard."

The man led us into a tidy log cabin with a roaring fire in the stove. That's when I noticed he was wearing a RCMP uniform. He was a police officer? Crap.

"Am I in trouble?"

"Depends," he answered. "How are you feeling?"

"Ummm . . . fine." I could see him now, and he was huge and hairy. He towered over me and Michael, his wild beard and furry eyebrows practically covering his face.

"Been exposed to polio?" he asked, but he didn't sound as if he really cared.

I shook my head and Michael pressed his face into my shoulder. "No," I said. "Not that I know of, anyway."

"That's what they all say." The officer sighed. "But it doesn't really matter to me because they'll never stop it. You'd think they'd know after all the flu pandemics that having everyone camping together is a great way to spread disease. If not polio, then something else."

That was exactly what Grandpa had told me too. And another good reason to avoid the camps, as far as I was concerned.

"Wait here," he said. He slipped into a back room and came out with a couple of blankets. I took Michael into the washroom with me, but I didn't have anything to change him into, so I stripped off his wet clothes and wrapped him in the blanket. I was hoping one of my grandparents had my pack, because I didn't have it anymore. I took off my soaked jeans and made a skirt out of the other blanket for myself. When I came out, there was a plate with a piece of smoked salmon and a chunk of bread on the table by the stove.

"Eat," he said.

I dug my passport out of the inside of my fiddle case instead, and handed it to him.

"Nice violin," he said, eyeing Jewels.

"Thanks."

He studied my passport by the light of the fire. "Looks all right, eh? But what about your brother?"

"I . . . I . . . lost his. In the water."

He studied me. "Uh-huh."

"Really."

"Get some sleep. We'll discuss it in the morning. I'm supposed to lock you up overnight, but I've got a bunch of men in the jail already who were tossed overboard earlier. You two can sleep on that couch."

"Thank you," I said. "And thanks for the food."

"You're welcome. Don't even think about sneaking off in the middle of the night. The guard dogs are outside, and I keep them just a little bit hungry."

In the morning, the RCMP officer made us a pot of oatmeal on the woodstove. He said I could play Jewels, but I stopped after the first song.

"You really don't mind?" I asked. "She's awfully loud in such a small place."

"I like it," he said.

When the food was ready, I packed Jewels into her case and managed to talk Michael into eating a few spoonfuls.

"Where's Brandy?" he whined. "I want Grandma and Grandpa."

"Shhh," I said. That was the first time I'd heard him call my grandparents that, and even though it surprised me, I liked it. "We'll be home soon."

I washed our dishes in a tiny sink and then I sat down on the couch with Michael, ready to find out what our fate was going to be. The only plan I had was to beg for mercy if I had to.

"The way I see it," the officer said, sitting in a blue chair across from us, "your *brother* doesn't have a passport, and you want me to look the other way."

Michael buried his head against my shoulder.

"And there's the whole polio thing too," he continued. "But we've already established I don't care much about that. However, you do have something I want, so we trade."

He looked right at me, and I squirmed in my seat. There was only one thing I had that he could possibly want. I'm sorry, but there was no way I was going to have sex with that big furry man. Even for Michael!

"I'm a minor," I said with as much dignity as I could muster.

"And I'm married," he said. "I was talking about your violin."

"What?" I jumped up, dislodging Michael. "My dad gave me this fiddle. I can't."

He shrugged. "Your choice. Let's go." He stood and opened the door.

"Where?"

"Down to the jailhouse. I have to scan your passport, and

you'll both need a physical. We'll probably have to take your brother into foster care until we can verify his identity too."

Foster care? That might not be such a bad option. Mom and Dad could come back and adopt him. Or Spill could break him out. Yeah, that was a good plan. I'd let this man take him and then we'd follow Michael and get him back. I shook my head, trying to clear it. Was I crazy? I couldn't let him take Michael.

"They're shipping most foster kids back to the mainland," the man said casually. "Would make it harder to get him back, if he really is your brother. Ferries are pretty expensive these days."

I knew he was lying. Wasn't he? He had to be. There was no reason to do that. Still . . . I glanced at Jewels' case.

The man smiled at me, knowing he'd won. Before I could change my mind or Michael figured out what was going on, I took him by the hand and we walked out the open door, leaving Jewels behind on the couch.

45

October 8th–Everybody wants a good life. Everybody wants a family and some friends. It's just a simple truth. That's what it all comes down to in the end.
— Victor Mecyssne

MICHAEL AND I SAW OUR GROUP SITTING UNDER A tree before they noticed us, but by the time we got to the little grove of firs, everyone was standing.

"Do you want a rest, or can we get going?" Grandpa asked.

"We're fine," I said. "But what about you guys? Did you get any sleep?"

"Under the stars, on the beach." He sighed happily.

"Nice," Grandma said, smiling.

"We had a fire," Brandy added.

"Sounds good."

"Before you go," Spill said, "I need to talk to Molly in private, for a minute."

Grandpa gave him a stern look that almost made me laugh. "Don't be too long," he said. "We need to get moving."

Spill led me away from the road into the woods. The earth smelled like it should: damp, scented with pine. The needles padded my steps, welcoming me home.

"Weren't you guys freezing without the sleeping bags and stuff?" I asked. We'd left the camping gear with the Brothers.

"I had a bunch of HyperFoil blankets," he said. "And the fire helped. We weren't exactly comfortable, but we did okay." He stopped walking in a little clearing surrounded by a grove of towering fir trees. "So . . ."

"So?" I smiled and brushed a stray curl away from my face.

"I guess this is it," he said. His blue eyes sparkled, and he held my gaze.

"It?" I asked.

"Time to go our separate ways."

This was stupid. We didn't have to go separate ways. I grabbed both his hands. "Come back with us."

"Nah . . . I can't, Molly."

"Just for a little while?" I asked. "Why not?"

"Because," he said, smiling, "I want your dad to take me seriously when he meets me for the first time."

"After all you've done for us, how could he—"

"Seriously," he repeated. "You know why."

My stomach gave a little flutter. He wanted Dad to like him.

"Will you visit?" I asked.

He took my hand and held it. "I'll keep in touch," he said. "I promise not to just disappear."

I couldn't really imagine my life without Spill. I'd gotten so used to having him around. Even when I went weeks without seeing him, he was always on my mind. I threw my arms around him and hugged him tightly.

His hold on me was softer, more gentle, and I tipped my

head back to look at his face, and he did the same. And then he leaned in, pressing his mouth to mine, his lips so soft I couldn't believe it. He'd lived such a tough-guy life, but his mouth felt like warm velvet. After not long enough, he pulled away.

"Time to go," he said.

I tried to hold on, knowing that as soon as I released him, he'd leave, but he untangled himself anyway and took one of my hands in his. We walked back, fingers entwined, my feet dragging.

"Where's your fiddle?" he asked.

"Oh, you know . . . ," I said as casually as I could, "the RCMP officer who put us up last night . . . he wanted a fiddle."

He simply nodded, but there was a glint of fire in his eyes. "Why didn't you give him your gold?" he asked.

"My gold?"

"In your boot."

"Oh, my God!" I said, stopping. "I forgot all about it. Let's go and see if he'll take it."

Spill held firmly to my hand to keep me from running back the way I'd just come with Michael. "It's too late, Molly," he said. "It's done."

"But, Spill!"

"Trust me. I know about these things."

I slumped against him, and he put his arm around my shoulder. "You did the right thing," he said.

"Yeah . . . I know." But doing the right thing didn't bring Jewels back to me.

We were in view of everyone else by then, and I could feel them all staring at us.

"Time to say good-bye," Spill said.

I nodded, resigned. We all took turns hugging him, and then he gave me the briefest kiss, his lips just brushing mine, before he walked back the way I had just come. When I looked at my grandparents to see if they'd noticed, I swear Grandpa's eyes were twinkling. Grandma grinned big at me, and I knew I was blushing. Michael didn't care, but the kiss gave Brandy something to tease me about for at least two kilometers. I didn't really mind, though. In fact, I couldn't help smiling every time she mentioned it.

We'd only been on the road for half an hour, and the kids and Grandma were already dragging. "How far is it to the island?" Grandpa asked.

"Well . . ." I did the math from kilometers to miles. "Around thirty miles, I think."

"Too bad we left all the camping equipment behind," he said. "We might need it."

"Actually," I said, "today's the day the ferry crosses, and if we can catch some rides with farmers, we should make it." I hoped that was true.

The day wore on, cold and breezy, but we were all warm from the exertion of the walk. We'd stopped for a lunch of hard cheese and even harder bread, and as we were getting up to go, a woman with an empty wagon pulled by two horses rattled up to us.

"Need a lift?" she asked. "I could do with the company."

"Yes, please!" we all said.

Grandpa hoisted Grandma up onto the seat next to the

woman, and the rest of us scrambled into the back. She wasn't going as far north as we needed to go, but when she let us out, we were only about an hour's walk from my island. The kids were tired, but also excited to be on the ground again, and they ran ahead, forward and back, like puppies.

"Wagon," Grandma said, pointing behind us.

I turned and looked. Even from the distance we could see that it was completely full of hay. There wouldn't be another ride for us in it. I hustled the kids to the side of the road as the horse's clip-clops got louder.

"Afternoon," the farmer said as he passed.

I was digging out a water bottle from the pack for Brandy, not paying any attention to the wagon, when I heard my name.

"Molly! Is that you?"

I looked up. Sitting on a hay bale in the back of the wagon was Katie's fiancé, Nick. His red hair glinted in the weak sunshine, and his smile was wide. I shoved the backpack into Grandma's arms and ran after the wagon.

"Nick!"

"You made it back!" he said.

"Yeah. Almost! What are you doing on that wagon?"

"Hitching a ride," he called. He was getting further away, even though I was running as fast as I could. "I went to the city to get my wedding clothes!" He held up a brown package. "I'd walk with you, but I have to catch the ferry so I can do the milking. Boy, will your family be glad you're finally home!"

"Me too!" I yelled. I had to stop jogging then, but both of us kept waving until he was out of sight. It was while I was bent over double trying to catch my breath that I realized we pretty much had no chance of making the last ferry. I hoped Nick was smart enough to figure that out and would send someone in a fishing boat to get us, but it was hard to say for sure.

As my brother James often said about Nick (not when Katie was around), he was a nice guy, but he was sometimes a sandwich short of a picnic. Which reminded me, all we had left to eat was dry bread. It was going to be a long night if he didn't send a boat.

46

WE GOT TO THE EMPTY FERRY LANDING JUST
before sunset. I tried not to think about how we'd missed the
last one by about half an hour. The ferry only ran two days a
week these days too, so I'd have to flag down a fishing boat
in the morning. For now there was nothing to do but camp on
the bank and hope for the best. At least Spill had given us the
Hyper-Foil blankets. I was about to tell Grandpa that we'd
have to build a fire when Merter Jones stalked up the path
from the shore, his boots crunching on dry twigs.

"'Bout time you got here," he said.

My heart leapt! *Thank you, Nick!* I'd never let James say
another bad word about him. "Hi, Merter," I said. "Were you
waiting for us?"

"Nick Spartan told me you needed passage. He wasn't lyin',
was he?"

"Yes. I mean, no. I mean, yes, we want to go home and, no,
he wasn't lying."

Merter's fishing vest was missing a button, and the rest

were straining against his potbelly. "Suppose you want to cross over on credit?" he demanded.

"My dad will pay you," I said.

"Well, let's go, then." We followed him down to the dock and climbed aboard the rickety boat. I hoped we wouldn't drown now when we were so close to home. In the old days, the ferry made the crossing in ten minutes. His little boat ran on ethanol that Merter made from corn, but the motor was tiny and it took forever to get anywhere. Especially loaded down with all of us.

I gripped the edge of my bench seat, and spun stories for Brandy and Michael about Mom's pancakes, my kitchen garden, Katie's piano playing, my brothers and their tepee by the creek, Dad's golden fields and his fiddle.

I told them about Black Bart herding chickens into the coop during thunderstorms, and the woodstove in winter, and kittens—anything to keep me distracted from thinking about the fact that I was about to find out how Mom was doing. I couldn't bring myself to ask Merter, but I consoled myself with the fact he probably would've passed on bad news.

Michael pushed his wavy brown tangles out of his face, and I wished I'd thought of cutting his hair for him. "Do you have worms on the farm, Molly?" he asked.

"Oh, yes. Lots and lots of worms."

He smiled. After what seemed like forever, the little boat bumped into the shore, and we all stumbled out onto my island. I scrambled up the rocky path that twisted through scrub and saplings, helping each person behind me. "There they are!" someone shouted as we reached the top.

I looked up, and in the gathering twilight, there was my whole family. Dad rushed to meet us, squeezing my shoulder as he hurried past to help Grandpa with the giant suitcase. Jackie, James, Katie, and Nick swarmed us, but I sidestepped their hugs and ran to Mom, who was leaning on the back of the wagon and holding a tiny bundle in her arms.

"Oh, Molly!" she cried. She leaned into me, hugging me with one arm and showing me the baby.

"Mom! Are you all right?"

"I'm fine . . . fine. Meet your sister," she said. "Chelsea."

I lifted the blanket away from her face and saw her rosy cheeks. "She's so tiny."

"Well, you would be too if you were a month early," Mom said, smiling.

Then Jackie flung himself around my waist and Katie grabbed me in a hug too. "Hi, Katie." I squeezed her hard, surprised by how much I'd missed her. "Hey, Jackie." I ruffled his dark curls.

Just then a breeze came up off the water blowing my hair away from my face, exposing my forehead.

"Molly! Molly!" Jackie yelled. "What happened to your face?"

I touched the bump. "It's just a bruise. I'm fine."

"My friend Rich had a black eye—"

"Later," Katie said, pulling him off me.

"Who are those kids?" Jackie demanded.

"Oh, that's Brandy and Michael," I told him. I met Mom's eye. "They're going to stay with us for a while." She raised her eyebrows, and I mouthed the word *orphans* at her.

"Let's go say hi," Katie said, dragging Jackie away to give me a minute with Mom.

"It's a long story," I said. "We'll tell you and Dad the whole thing later, okay?"

"I can hardly wait," she said, shaking her head, but smiling.

The wind came up off the ocean, and I filled my lungs with the salty scent of home. "I'm so glad to be back," I said.

"Oh, Molly," Mom said, "we've missed you . . . and we were so worried. When Nick came with the news . . ." She couldn't even get the words out.

"And you're both okay?" I asked her.

"Pretty much," she said. Mom looked over my shoulder at my grandparents. "We'll see what the doctor says."

She handed Chelsea to me, and I nestled her tiny body into my arms. I peeled the blanket away from her head, just to check. Sure enough, she had a shock of brown, curly hair.

I leaned against the tailgate, watching Mom walk over to my grandparents. They stood apart for just a second, drinking each other in, and then Mom opened her arms and they stepped into her embrace. The three of them huddled together, soft voices, mixed with crying and exclamations of joy, floating on the sea breeze around us.

Dad and Katie were trying to get Michael to talk, but he was just staring at them with big eyes, and for the first time, it struck me how well he and Brandy both fit into our family with their dark hair. Little Jackie had already dragged Brandy away from the group and was showing her something on the ground. Probably a petroglyph.

Standing there, holding Chelsea and watching my family

together, finally made the whole trip worth it. My tears dripped down leaving dark spots on the baby blanket, but for the first time in months, they were tears of happiness.

"Let's go to the house," Dad said. "Everyone in the wagon."

When Mom was settled on a bench in the back, I handed Chelsea up to her.

"Hey, Dad," I said. I unzipped my backpack and pulled out the almanac. "Safe and sound."

He hugged me hard. "That's my girl," he said. "I always knew you'd bring it back."

Brandy sat chattering to Katie, already part of my family, but Michael crawled into my lap and hid his face in my shoulder. Dad raised his eyebrows at me, but didn't say anything. He just took the reins in his big hand, clucked at the horse, and then led us towards home. As we bumped along, a few stars popped out above us.

I had tried not to think too much about what everyone would say about Brandy and Michael, but soon we'd have to figure something out. I was pretty sure my parents would welcome them, but adding two more kids to the mix wasn't going to be easy. Especially two children who were here illegally. Mom and Dad would want to make it right if they could, and that probably wouldn't come cheap.

"I hope your trip wasn't too hard," Mom said to my grandparents.

The three of us looked at each other and cracked up laughing.

"What?" Mom asked, smiling, but not seeing the joke.

"We made it," Grandpa said. "That's all that really matters."

On the ride, Grandpa asked Mom a lot of questions about her health. She tried to brush him off, but he was persistent. Luckily for her, we didn't have far to go to get to the farm. I swear my heart swelled in my chest when we turned down our lane.

The drive curved slightly to the right, and the house was still out of view for the first stretch. Overhead the fir branches swayed, and the twisty arbutus trees bent down to greet us. As we made the turn, I breathed in the scent of home. Cedar, wood smoke, and soil. The overgrown log cabin sat sprawled out in all its glory. Black Bart raced towards us, barking wildly.

"Look, Michael," I said. "There's your new house."

He lifted his head for a moment and then snuggled back into my shoulder. I squeezed his tiny body closer to mine. There'd be plenty of time for him to see everything. He was going to grow up here, just like I had. He would never want for food or love or attention again. He'd be clean and educated and a farmer's son. He'd be surrounded by brothers and sisters, grandparents, animals, and hard work. Michael was home because I was home. We were all home.

47

December 24th–Other things may change us, but we start and end with family.
–Anthony Brandt

I PUT ANOTHER LOG IN THE WOODSTOVE, PICKED up Chelsea, and sat back in the rocking chair, cuddling her close and inhaling that soft, milky-baby smell. High voices drifted in from the kitchen, where Mom had put Jackie, Brandy, and Michael around the table with paper and crayons to make last-minute cards for Santa. She and Grandma had snuck upstairs to take naps.

Chelsea gurgled in her sleep, and I looked down at her tiny face. She'd grown so much in the two months I'd been back, I could hardly believe it. Before we knew it, she'd be writing letters to Santa too. I was running the chores for Christmas Eve through my head when Brandy burst into the living room, fat tears dripping down her cheeks.

"Molly!" she sobbed. "Jackie said–"

"Santa doesn't like a tattletale," I reminded her. "Go back and finish your card and ignore Jackie."

She swallowed her tears. I felt kind of mean because I really wanted to set Chelsea down and take Brandy onto my lap, but we'd both be going back to school in the new year, so I was trying to wean her off leaning on me. She wiped her eyes with her sleeve and, dragging her feet, went back into the kitchen.

Chelsea was so sweet and warm that when I first heard the fiddle music, I thought I'd drifted off to sleep and was dreaming, but then I realized someone really was playing on the porch. Dad must've been a whole verse into the song before I recognized it as "Handsome Molly."

It sounded so squeaky and shrill. What was wrong with him? Maybe his hands were half frozen from the cold. I knew he loved the great outdoors, but this was ridiculous. When he hit a note as flat as a pancake, I laid Chelsea down in the bassinet and flung open the front door.

"Are you trying to murder that fiddle?" I asked.

The music stopped. And for a second, so did my heart!

"I've only been playing a couple of months," Spill said. "I'm doing the best I can."

I flung myself into his arms, a dangerous thing to do since he was holding a fiddle in one hand and a bow in the other. He looked the same, only his hair had darkened a bit now that it was winter. And the sprinkle of freckles across his nose had faded too. After I'd finished jumping up and down and trampling his handmade boots with mine, I remembered I was mad at him.

I pushed him away. "Spill! Where have you been? I thought you said you were going to stay in touch! I've been worried sick!"

"Nice to see you too, Molly," he said, laughing. He balanced the fiddle precariously on the porch railing.

"For all I knew, you were dead!" I snapped. I turned away from him.

He put his arms around my waist and pulled me close, my back pressing into his chest, his breath warm on my cheek. "Did you really think so?"

"Well, not really."

He turned me around, drew me close, and kissed me. The flannel of his shirt pressed softly against my neck, and we stood there kissing for I don't know how long. We might have gone on all day, but then my mother cleared her throat from the doorway.

"Mom," I said, pulling myself away from him, "this is Spill!"

"Well, I should hope so," she said. "Come inside, you two. You're letting in the cold."

She ducked back in, half closing the door behind her, leaving us on the porch to gather up Spill's things. I reached for his fiddle because I wanted to see if it was any good. I certainly couldn't tell from his playing! Before I could even examine it, there was this strange moment where the neck of the instrument just nestled itself into the palm of my hand like an old friend.

"*Oh, my God!* Spill? It's Jewels! You've found Jewels!"

I lifted her to my face and breathed in her musty, sweet scent. Without even stopping to tune her (and she needed it!), I launched into "Handsome Molly," the bow flying across her strings. I danced myself the length of the long porch while the notes floated around me, then down the front steps and into the yard. Tears streamed down my cheeks, and I'm sure my smile could've lit up the darkest corner of the world.

"Spill? How?" I asked breathlessly, afraid to stop playing, in case Jewels vanished into thin air.

"Oh, you know," he said all casually, "an RCMP officer sold her to me a couple of months ago."

"But why didn't you write and tell me?"

"I wanted to see your face when you got her back," he said, grinning. "Besides, I had to learn to play your song. I think I might need a few more lessons, though."

"No! You were good!" Then we both broke out laughing. "Well, you're reasonably good. For a beginner, anyway. Dad and I'll whip you into shape."

"I'm counting on it," he said. "Come on, let's go inside."

"Yeah. It's way too cold out here for my baby!"

We went into the living room, the heat from the wood-stove hitting us like that July day so many months ago when we'd first met. I ran my fingers lightly over Jewels' curves.

"Will you trade me?" I asked. "I've got another fiddle that Dad swapped an old banjo for. It's not as nice as Jewels, but it's perfect for a beginner."

"Molly," he said, laughing and shaking his head, "do you really think I got Jewels for me? She's *your* fiddle."

"You're the best!"

He smiled. "So I've been told."

All I could do was hug Jewels and stare happily at him. Like the fiddle, I was afraid Spill would somehow disappear if I took my eyes off him. We sat knee to knee in front of the fire, and I began to talk a mile a minute about Christmas and traditions and how happy I was to see him.

"Breathe," he said, laughing. "You talk as fast as you play!"

"I can't help it," I said. I'd set the bow down and was holding Jewels like a ukulele. I plucked a Christmas carol while we talked. "I've missed you!"

"Yeah." He nodded. "Me too. I mean, I've missed you too."

Spill told me that he'd gotten a job in Victoria, working in a shoe repair shop, and that he made custom boots at night.

"And you don't . . . well . . . work for anyone else?" I asked. "Like you did in Oregon?"

He shook his head. "Nope. All finished with that line of work." I'd never seen Spill smile so brightly before.

"Oh, good," I said. "So how long can you stay?"

"Until the first of January. Assuming your parents don't mind putting me up," he said. "I brought your dad the new almanac . . . just to get off on the right foot."

I laughed. I couldn't believe it! Spill was nervous to meet my dad!

"My family will be happy you're here," I said. "Plus now Katie can stop teasing me, saying I must've made you up because you sound too good to be true."

He laughed.

"Oh, and I can give you lots of fiddle lessons while you're here too!" I said.

He nodded seriously. "Great. I'd love that."

"And you'll come back again to visit, right?" I demanded.

"Of course."

"And you'll write to me in the meantime?" I insisted.

"Every day," he said, smirking.

"Oh, yeah." I punched him lightly on the arm. "Like you have for the last two months?"

He laughed, and I set Jewels down and pulled him up out of his chair. I hugged him tightly, and he squeezed me. He'd be back to see me. I just knew it. And once he saw the island in the summer, he'd want to live here because it is the most beautiful place on Earth. And by the time I was done giving him fiddle lessons, the man would be able to play with the best of them. We were going to make a long and lasting duo, too, because I knew lots of tunes with two-part harmony.

ACKNOWLEDGMENTS

My list of people to thank is long, but I'll try to keep to the minimum. Still, if you need to get a snack, maybe now is the time because anyone who says that writing is a solitary business doesn't write the way I do. I need all the help I can get!

A big, huge thank-you and hug to Stacey Barney, editor extraordinaire! Thank you for finding the story in all my many, many words and helping me to shape it into a book. You're the best.

Michel Bourret, *vous êtes tout simplement le meilleur agent littéraire quune fille pourrait espéré avoir. Merci!*

Without my critique group, this book would not exist. Thank you to Linda Anthony, Wanda Collins Johnson, Eileen Cook, Victor Anthony, and Alexa Barry. Everything I write is richer for your input. Much gratitude to my fact checkers and advisers, Frank Anthony, Coe Booth, Nicole & Kelly Berthelot, Louis Freeman, Nancy Rowan, Tim Tommerup, Sarah Tradewell, and Sara Zarr. Also, thank you to Penny Mason of Penguin Canada, and special thanks to John Rowe Townsend & Jill Paton Walsh—mentors, friends, and wonderful writers.

I am eternally indebted to these women who have taken the time to blog so that aspiring writers can learn about the business side of publishing. Thank you so much, Dia, Rachel, Jennifer, Kristin, Janet, and the Divine Miss Snark.

If this were a televised awards show, the music would be swelling to a crescendo to let me know I've gone on far too long, but there is one more person who I can never thank enough. My wonderful husband has given me time, financial support, musical expertise, encouragement, a great author photo, and most of all, love. And to top it off, he lets me steal every funny thing he's ever done and run with it. Without him there would be no book at all. I love you, Pea.